Paddington's
Adventures

MICHAEL BOND began writing the stories about a bear called Paddington in 1958 while working as a cameraman for BBC television. They are loved the world over and have been translated into more than 30 languages. The 50th anniversary novel *Paddington Here and Now* was shortlisted for the Roald Dahl Funny Prize.

In 1997 Michael was awarded the OBE for services to children's literature, and in 2007 he received the honorary degree of Doctor of Letters from Reading University. He lives in London with his wife Sue, and two guinea pigs named Olga da Polga and Vladimir.

Michael Bond

Paddington's
Adventures

Illustrated by
Peggy Fortnum

HarperCollins *Children's Books*

This edition first published in paperback in Great Britain by
HarperCollins Children's Books in 2014

Paddington Goes to Town first published in Great Britain by HarperCollins*Publishers* Ltd in 1968
Revised edition published by Collins in 1997
New edition published by HarperCollins Children's Books in 2008

Paddington Takes the Air first published in Great Britain by HarperCollins*Publishers* Ltd in 1970
Revised edition published by Collins in 1999
New edition published by HarperCollins Children's Books in 2008

Paddington on Top first published in Great Britain by HarperCollins*Publishers* Ltd in 1974
Revised edition published by Collins in 1999
New edition published by HarperCollins Children's Books in 2008

1 3 5 7 9 10 8 6 4 2

Collins is an imprint of HarperCollins Children's Books Ltd.
HarperCollins Children's Books is a division of HarperCollins*Publishers* Ltd,
77-85 Fulham Palace Road, Hammersmith, London W6 8JB.

Visit our website at:
www.harpercollins.co.uk

Text copyright © Michael Bond 1968, 1970, 1974
Illustrations copyright © Peggy Fortnum and HarperCollins*Publishers* Ltd
1958, 1968, 1970, 1974, 2008

Cover illustrations adapted and coloured by Mark Burgess
from the originals by Peggy Fortnum

ISBN: 978-0-00-756096-7

Originated by Dot Gradations Ltd, UK
Printed in Great Britain by
Clays Ltd, St Ives plc

MIX
Paper from
responsible sources
FSC **FSC C007454**
www.fsc.org

FSC™ is a non-profit international organisation established to promote
the responsible management of the world's forests. Products carrying the
FSC label are independently certified to assure consumers that they come
from forests that are managed to meet the social, economic and
ecological needs of present and future generations,
and other controlled sources.

Find out more about HarperCollins and the environment at
www.harpercollins.co.uk/green

CONTENTS

Paddington
Goes to Town

CONTENTS

Chapter One

A Day to Remember

Mrs Brown stared at Paddington in amazement. "Harold Price wants you to be an usher at his wedding?" she repeated. "Are you sure?"

Paddington nodded. "I've just met him in the market, Mrs Brown," he explained. "He said he was going to give you a ring as well."

Mrs Brown exchanged glances with the rest of the

family as they gathered round to hear Paddington's news.

Harold Price was a young man who served on the preserves counter at a large grocery store in the Portobello Road, and the events leading up to his forthcoming marriage to Miss Deirdre Flint, who worked on the adjacent bacon and eggs counter, had been watched with interest by the Browns, particularly as it was largely through Paddington that they had become engaged in the first place.

It had all come about some months previously when Paddington had lent a paw at a local drama festival in which Miss Flint had played the lead in one of Mr Price's plays.

A great many things had gone wrong that evening, but Mr Price always maintained afterwards that far from Paddington causing a parting of the ways, he and Miss Flint had been brought even closer together. At any event, shortly afterwards they had announced their engagement.

It was largely because of Paddington's part in the affair, and the numerous large orders for marmalade he'd placed with Mr Price over the years, that all the

Browns had been invited to the wedding that day; but never in their wildest dreams had it occurred to any of them that Paddington might be one of the officials.

During the silence which followed while everyone considered the matter, he held up a small, bright metal object. "Mr Price has given me the key to his flat," he announced importantly. "He wants me to pick up the list of guests on the way to the church."

"Well, I must say it's rather a nice idea," said Mrs Brown, trying to sound more enthusiastic than she actually felt. "It's really a case of history repeating itself."

"Remembering what happened last time," murmured Mr Brown, "I only hope it doesn't repeat itself too faithfully."

"Everything turned out all right in the end," Mrs Brown broke in hastily, as Paddington gave one of his hard stares. "Harold's play *did* win first prize and he was very glad of Paddington's help when the sound effects man let him down."

"I think he's been let down again, Mrs Brown," said Paddington earnestly. "He's got no one to keep quiet during the ceremony."

"No one to keep quiet?" echoed Jonathan. Paddington's thought processes were sometimes rather difficult to follow, and his present one was no exception.

"I've no doubt that bear will do as well as anyone if he sets his mind to it," said Mrs Bird, the Browns' housekeeper, as Paddington, having startled everybody by announcing that he was going to have a special bath in honour of the occasion, disappeared upstairs in order to carry out his threat. "No doubt at all. After all, it's only a matter of lending a paw and showing people to their right places in the church."

"Knowing the usual state of Paddington's paws," replied Mr Brown, "I think I'd sooner find my own way."

"He *is* having a bath, Daddy," reminded Judy. "He's just said so."

"He may be having a bath," retorted Mr Brown grimly. "But he's still got to get to the church. All sorts of things can happen before then."

"'Ush!" cried Jonathan suddenly. "I bet he thinks being an usher means he has to keep 'ush during the service."

"Oh dear," said Mrs Brown, as Jonathan's words sank in. "I do hope he doesn't tell Deirdre to be quiet when she's making her responses. You know what a quick temper she's got and I expect she'll be all on edge as it is."

Mrs Brown began to look somewhat less happy about the whole affair as she turned the matter over in her mind, but at that moment the shrill sound of the telephone bell broke into her thoughts.

"It's Harold Price," she hissed, putting her hand over the receiver. "He wants to know if it's all right. What *shall* I say?"

Mr Brown looked up at the ceiling as the sound

17

of running water came from somewhere overhead. "Whatever we say it had better not be 'no'," he replied. "Not at this stage. We shall never hear the last of it if Paddington's had a bath for nothing. Especially one he's volunteered for.

"All the same," he continued, giving his suit a passing flick with the clothes-brush, "I can't help feeling it isn't the best of ways to start married life. I don't think I should have been very keen on having a bear as an usher at my wedding – even if I had been let down."

Mr Brown wasn't over enthusiastic about weddings at the best of times, and the thought of attending one at which Paddington was lending a paw filled him with foreboding.

Nevertheless, even Mr Brown's fears were gradually set at rest as the day wore on, for Paddington's behaviour seemed beyond reproach.

When they arrived at the church he was busily engaged with a long and important-looking list of names which enabled him to check the invitations and sort out the friends of the bride from those of the groom, and as he led them down the aisle towards their allotted places they couldn't help noticing how spick and span he looked. His fur had a newly brushed, glistening appearance, and his whiskers were so shiny they made the large white carnation which he wore tied round his neck look almost dowdy by comparison.

If the Browns had any criticism at all it was that he was taking his job a little too seriously. Jonathan's earlier theory proved all too correct and as soon as anyone so much as parted their lips he hurried up to them with his paw raised and gave them a hard stare. Some of his stares, which had been handed down to him by his Aunt Lucy in Peru, were very powerful indeed and in no time at all it would have been possible to have heard the proverbial pin drop.

Even the vicar looked most impressed when he came into the church and saw the attentive state of his congregation.

"I don't see how we *can* explain now," hissed Mr Brown. "It's a bit difficult when you're not allowed to say anything."

The others contented themselves with a nod of agreement, for at that moment Paddington, having carefully checked the list of guests for the last time to make certain everyone was present, settled himself down in a nearby pew in order to consult his programme and enjoy the forthcoming ceremony in comfort.

In any case, they soon had other matters to occupy their minds, for a moment or so later Mr Price and his best man arrived and took up their places near the front.

They both looked unusually agitated, even for such a nerve-racking occasion as a wedding, and Mr Price in particular kept jumping up and down like a jack-in-the-box. He seemed to want to speak to Paddington, but each time he turned round and opened his mouth Paddington put a paw firmly to his lips.

"I don't remember Harold having that nervous twitch before," whispered Mrs Brown, uneasily.

"I think it's got something to do with the ring," whispered Judy, passing on what little bit of information she'd been able to glean from those in front. "They're having to make do with a brass one off Mr Price's bedroom curtains. Apparently the real one's disappeared."

"Disappeared!" echoed Mrs Brown. For a moment she quite forgot Paddington's presence in the nearby pew, but as it happened she needn't have worried, for Paddington seemed even more affected than anyone by this latest piece of news. His whiskers sagged, his face took on a sudden woebegone expression, and even the carnation round his neck seemed to wilt in sympathy.

"Deirdre's not going to be very pleased when she hears," murmured Mr Brown. "I shouldn't like to be the person who's got it!"

"Ssh!" hissed Mrs Brown. "Here she comes!"

The Browns fell silent as there was a rustle of silk behind them and Deirdre, resplendent in a snow-white wedding gown, sailed past on the arm of Mr Flint.

Only Paddington failed to join in the general gasps of admiration which greeted her entrance. For some reason best known to himself he appeared to be engaged in a kind of life and death struggle on the floor of the church. Several times he was lost to view completely and each time he rose again he was breathing more and more heavily and his expression looked, if possible, unhappier than before.

However, unhappy though it was, it seemed almost joyful by comparison with the grim one which came over Miss Flint's face a moment or so later when she took in the whispered aside from her husband-to-be.

For one brief moment indeed, it looked as if for two pins Miss Flint would have called the whole thing off, and when it came to the time for her to say "I do", there was quite a nasty pause before she managed to get the words out.

When the ceremony finally came to an end both she and Harold hurried towards the vestry in order to sign the register rather as if they had a bus to catch, and not a bit like two people who had just agreed to spend the rest of their lives together.

"I'm glad I'm not in Harold's shoes," said Mr Brown, as the door closed behind them. "Deirdre looked as black as thunder."

"Ssh!" began Mrs Brown. "We don't want Pad..."

She was about to say that one upset was enough and they didn't want to add to the confusion by having Paddington take up his 'ushing duties again, but as she looked round the church it was only to discover that Paddington was nowhere in sight.

"There he is!" cried Judy suddenly, as she looked back over her shoulder.

Turning round to follow her gaze the rest of the Browns were just in time to catch a glimpse of a familiar figure hurrying up the aisle in the direction of the entrance doors.

"Perhaps he wants to be in the front of the photograph," said Mrs Brown hopefully, as Paddington, after casting an anxious glance over his shoulder, picked up his suitcase and hat from behind a nearby pillar and disappeared from view.

"He's always very keen on anything like that for his scrapbook, and he looks as if he's got something on his mind."

"Hmm," said Mrs Bird. "That's as may be. But if you ask me that young bear's mind is not the only thing he's got something on."

Mrs Bird's sharp eyes had noticed a momentary gleam from one of Paddington's paws as he'd gone out into the sunshine. It was the second time within the space of a few minutes she'd spotted the strange phenomenon. The first occasion had been during the service itself, when the vicar had asked the assembly if anyone present knew of any good reason why Deirdre and Harold shouldn't get married. Paddington had half raised his paw and then, much to her relief, he'd changed his mind at the last moment.

Mrs Bird was good at adding two and two together as far as Paddington was concerned, but wisely she kept the result of her calculations to herself for the time being.

In any case, before the others had time to question her on the subject a rather worried-looking churchwarden hurried up the aisle and stopped at their pew in order to whisper something in Mr Brown's ear.

Mr Brown rose to his feet. "I think we're wanted in the vestry," he announced ominously. "It sounds rather urgent."

Mr Brown was tempted to add that the churchwarden had also asked if Paddington could accompany them, but in the event he decided not to add to their worries.

All the same, as he led the way into the vestry he began to look more and more worried, and if he'd been able to see through the stone walls into the churchyard outside, the chances are that he would have felt even more so.

For Paddington was in trouble. Quite serious trouble. One way and another he was used to life having its ups and downs, but as he held his paw up to the light in order to examine it more closely even he had to admit he couldn't remember a time when his fortunes had taken quite such a downward plunge.

Sucking it had made no difference at all; jamming

it in the rails which surrounded the churchyard only seemed to have made matters worse; and even the application of a liberal smear of marmalade from an emergency jar which he kept in his suitcase had been to no avail.

As far as paws went, his own was looking unusually smart and well cared for. Apart from the remains of the marmalade it wouldn't have disgraced an advertisement for fur coats in one of Mrs Brown's glossy magazines. Even the pad had an unusual glow about it, not unlike that of a newly polished shoe.

However, it wasn't the pad or its surroundings which caused Paddington's look of dismay, but the sight of a small gold wedding ring poking out from beneath his fur; and the longer he looked at it the more unhappy he became.

He'd found the ring lying on the dressing table when he'd gone to Harold Price's room in order to pick up the wedding list, and at the time it had gone on one of his claws easily enough. But now it was well and truly stuck, and nothing he could do would make it budge one way or the other.

In the past he had always kept on very good

terms with Mr Price. Even so, he couldn't begin to imagine what his friend would have to say about the matter. Nor, when he considered it, could he picture Deirdre exactly laughing her head off when she heard the news that her wedding ring was stuck round a bend on a bear's paw. From past experience he knew that Deirdre had a very sharp tongue indeed when even quite minor things went wrong with her bacon slicer, and he shuddered to think what she would have to say about the present situation.

As if to prove how right he was, his thoughts were broken into at that very moment, as the sound of Deirdre's voice raised in anger floated out through the open window above his head.

By climbing on top of his suitcase and standing on tiptoe, Paddington was just able to see inside the vestry and when he did so he nearly fell over backwards again in alarm, for not only was Deirdre there, laying down the law to a most unhappy-looking Mr Price; but the best man, sundry relatives, the Browns and quite a number of other important-looking people were there as well.

Indeed, so great was the crowd and so loud the argument, it gave the impression that more people were attending the signing of the register than had been present at the actual ceremony.

Paddington was a hopeful bear at heart but the more he listened to Deirdre, the more his spirits dropped and the more he realised the only thing they had in common was a wish that he'd never been invited to the wedding in the first place, let alone act as an usher.

After a moment or two he clambered back down again, took a deep breath, picked up his suitcase and headed towards a large red box just outside the churchyard.

It wasn't often that Paddington made a telephone call – for one thing he always found it a bit difficult with paws – but he did remember once reading a

poster in a phone box about what to do in times of an emergency and how it was possible to obtain help without paying.

It had seemed very good value at the time and

as far as he could make out it would be difficult to think of a situation which was more of an emergency than his present one.

His brief appearance at the window didn't go entirely unnoticed, but fortunately the only person who saw him was Judy, and by the time she'd passed the message on to Jonathan he'd disappeared again.

"Perhaps it was a mirage," said Jonathan hopefully.

"It wasn't," said Judy. "It was Paddington's hat."

"Paddington!" echoed Deirdre, catching the end of Judy's reply. "Don't mention that name to me."

"Look!" she announced dramatically, holding up her wedding finger for what seemed to her audience like the hundredth time. "A curtain ring! A brass curtain ring!"

"I thought it would be better than nothing," said the best man, hastily cupping his hands under Deirdre's in case the object of her wrath fell off. "I was hoping you might have big fingers."

Deirdre gave the best man a withering glare and then turned her attention back to the unfortunate Harold. "Don't just stand there," she exclaimed. "*Do* something!"

"Look here," broke in Mr Brown. "I still don't see why you're blaming Paddington."

"My room's on the fifth floor," said Mr Price, briefly. "And there are only two keys. Paddington had the other one."

"Fancy asking a bear to be an usher," said Deirdre, scornfully. "You might have known *something* would happen. I shall never be able to show my face in the shop again. Practically all our best customers are here."

The new Mrs Price broke off as quite clearly above her words there came the sound of a siren, at first in the distance, and then gradually getting closer and closer.

The vicar glanced nervously out of his vestry window. Quite a crowd seemed to have collected outside the church and even as he watched, a large, red fire engine, its siren sounding furiously, screamed to a halt and several men in blue uniform jumped off, their hatchets at the ready.

"That's all I need," said Deirdre bitterly, as the vicar excused himself and hurried off to investigate the matter. "A fire! That'll round off the day nicely!"

A Day to Remember

The room fell silent as Mr Price's bride, having exhausted the topic of the things she would like to do, embarked on a long list of the things she *wasn't* going to do under any circumstances until she got her wedding ring back; including signing the register, having her photograph taken and going on her honeymoon.

It was just as she reached the last item, and Mr Price's face had fallen to its longest ever, that the door burst open and the vicar hurried back into the room closely followed by a man in a fireman's uniform, and behind him, Paddington himself.

"*There* you are, Paddington," said Mrs Brown thankfully. "*Where* have you been?"

"Having a bit of a sticky time of it, if you ask me, ma'am," began the fireman, "what with one thing and another."

"My ring!" broke in Deirdre, catching sight of a shiny object in Paddington's outstretched paw.

"I'm afraid it got stuck round a bend, Mrs Price," explained Paddington.

"Stuck round a *bend*?" repeated Deirdre disbelievingly. "How on earth did that happen?"

Paddington took hold of the ring in his other paw in order to demonstrate exactly what had gone wrong. "I'm not sure," he admitted truthfully. "I just slipped it on for safety and when I tried to take it off again…"

The fireman gave a groan. "Don't say you've done it again!" he exclaimed. "I only just got it off."

"Bears!" groaned Deirdre. "I'm not meant to get married."

"What I can't understand," said Mr Price, "is why you put it on your paw in the first place, Mr Brown."

"You said you were going to give Mrs Brown a ring," said Paddington unhappily. "I thought I'd save you the bother."

"I said I was going to give Mrs Brown a ring?" repeated Harold, hardly able to believe his ears.

"I think you did," said Mrs Brown. "Paddington probably didn't realise you meant a ring on the telephone."

"Quite a natural mistake," said Mrs Bird in the silence which followed. "Anyone might have made it in the circumstances."

"Never mind," said the fireman. "What goes on must come off – especially the second time.

"I tell you what," he continued, sizing up the situation as he got to work on Paddington's paw with a pair of pliers, "if the happy couple would like to sign the register while I do this, I'll get my crew to form a guard of honour outside the church."

"A guard of honour!" exclaimed Deirdre.

"With axes," said the fireman.

The new Mrs Price began to look slightly better pleased. "Well, I don't know really…" she simpered, patting her hair.

"It's a bit irregular," whispered the fireman in Paddington's ear, "and we don't normally do it for people outside the service, but we've a big recruiting drive on at the moment and it'll be good publicity. Besides, it'll help calm things down a bit."

"Thank you very much," said Paddington gratefully. "I shall ask for you if ever I have a real fire."

"It'll make a lovely photograph," said Harold persuasively, taking Deirdre's hand and leading her across the room. "And it'll be something to show the girls back in the shop."

"If the ring won't come off, perhaps I could come on the honeymoon with you, Mrs Price," said Paddington hopefully. "I've never been on one of those before."

Deirdre's back stiffened as she bent down to sign the register.

"I don't think that'll be necessary," said the fireman hastily, as he removed the ring at long last and handed it to Mr Price for safe keeping.

"Tell you what, though," he added, seeing a look of disappointment cross Paddington's face. "As you can't go on the honeymoon perhaps we'll give you a lift to the wedding breakfast on our way back to the station instead.

"After all," he continu d, looking meaningly at Mrs Price, "if this young bear hadn't had the good sense to call us when he did he might still be wearing the ring and then where would you be?"

And to that remark not even Deirdre could find an answer.

"Gosh!" said Jonathan, as the Browns made their way back up the aisle. "Fancy riding on the back of a fire engine!"

"I don't suppose there are many bears who can say they've done that," agreed Judy.

Paddington nodded. A lot of things seemed about to happen all at once, and he wasn't quite sure which he was looking forward to most. Apart from the promised ride he'd never heard of anyone having their breakfast in the afternoon before, let alone a wedding one, but it sounded a very good way of rounding things off.

"If you and Mrs Price ever want to get married again," he announced, as Harold led Deirdre out of the church and paused for the photographers beneath an archway of raised fire axes, "I'll do some more 'ushing for you if you like."

Deirdre shuddered. "Never again," she said, taking a firm grip on Harold's arm. "Once is quite enough."

Mr Price nodded his agreement. "It's as I said in the beginning," he remarked, from beneath a shower of confetti, "young Mr Brown has a habit of bringing people closer together in the end, and this time it's for good!"

Chapter Two

PADDINGTON HITS OUT

"I KNOW IT'S none of my business," said Mrs Bird, pausing for a moment as she cleared the breakfast table, "but do you think Mr Curry's suddenly come into some money?" She nodded towards the next-door garden. "He's out there practising with his golf clubs again this morning. That's the third time this week."

"I must say it's very strange," agreed Mrs Brown, as the clear sound of a ball being hit by a club greeted her housekeeper's remarks. "He seemed to be turning his lawn into a putting green yesterday and he's got some plus-fours hanging on the line."

Paddington, who until that moment had been busily engaged in finishing up the last of the toast and marmalade before Mrs Bird removed it from the table, suddenly gave vent to a loud choking noise. "Mr Curry's plus-fours are hanging on the line!" he exclaimed when he had recovered himself.

He peered through the window with interest, but Mr Curry's clothes line seemed very little different from any other day of the week. In fact, apart from a tea towel and jerseys the only unusual item was a pair of very odd-looking trousers which hung limp and bedraggled in the still morning air.

"Those *are* plus-fours," explained Mrs Brown. "They're special trousers people used to wear when they played golf. You don't often see them nowadays."

Mrs Brown looked just as puzzled as her housekeeper as she considered Mr Curry's strange behaviour. Apart from having a reputation for meanness, the Browns' neighbour was also noted for his bad temper and unsportsmanlike attitude generally. The idea of his taking up any sort of game was hard to picture and when it was an expensive one like golf then it became doubly so.

"That reminds me," she continued, turning away from the window. "Henry asked me to get *his* golfing things out for him. There's an 'open day' at the golf club on Saturday and he wants to go. They're expecting quite a crowd. Arnold Parker's putting in a special appearance and he's judging one or two competitions. I don't know whether Henry's going in for any of them but apparently there are some quite big prizes. There's a special one for the person whose ball travels the farthest and…"

"Hmm," said Mrs Bird as Mrs Brown's voice trailed away. "There's no need to say any more. That's one mystery solved!"

Although she wasn't in the habit of interesting herself in other people's affairs Mrs Bird liked to get to the bottom of things. "Trust Mr Curry to be around when there's a chance of getting something for nothing," she snorted as she disappeared towards the kitchen with her tray.

As Mrs Brown picked up the remains of the crockery and followed her housekeeper out of the room Paddington climbed up on to his chair and looked hopefully out of the window. But Mr Curry was nowhere in sight and even the sound of shots being practised seemed to have died away, so he climbed back down again and a few minutes later hurried out into the garden in order to investigate the matter more closely.

In the past he'd several times come across Mr Brown's golf clubs in the cupboard under the stairs, but he'd never watched the game being played before and the possibility of seeing Mr Curry practising on his lawn and being able to take a closer look at his plus-fours into the bargain seemed an opportunity too good to be missed.

Crouching down to the ground behind Mr Brown's shed he put his eye to a special knothole in the fence which usually gave a very good view of the next-door garden, but to his surprise there was nothing to be seen but a wall of blackness.

Looking most disappointed Paddington picked up one of Mr Brown's old bean sticks and poked it hopefully through the hole in an attempt to unblock it. As he did so a loud cry of pain suddenly rang out and he nearly fell over backwards with surprise as the familiar figure of the Browns' neighbour suddenly rose into view on the other side of the fence.

"Bear!" roared Mr Curry as he danced up and down clutching his right eye. "Did you do that on purpose, bear?"

Hastily letting go of the stick, Paddington jumped back in alarm. "Oh, no, Mr Curry," he exclaimed. "I was only trying to unblock the hole. If I'd known you were there I'd have done it much more gently. I mean…"

"What's that?" bellowed Mr Curry. "What did you say?"

Paddington gave up trying to explain what he meant as the face on the other side of the fence turned a deep purple.

"I wanted to see your sum trousers, Mr Curry," he said unhappily.

"My *what* trousers?" repeated Mr Curry.

"Your sum trousers, Mr Curry," said Paddington. "The ones you play golf in."

Mr Curry gave Paddington a searching look with his good eye. "If you mean my plus-fours, why don't you say so, bear," he growled. Removing his hand from the other eye he glared suspiciously across the fence. "I was looking for my golf ball. It went over into your garden."

Anxious to make amends, Paddington looked around Mr Brown's garden and almost immediately spied a small white object nestling among the tomato plants. "Here it is, Mr Curry," he called. "I think it's broken one of Mr Brown's stems."

"If people don't take the trouble to build their fences high enough they must expect these things," said Mr Curry nastily as he took the ball.

He examined it carefully to make sure it wasn't damaged and then looked thoughtfully at Paddington. "I didn't realise you were interested in golf, bear," he remarked casually.

Paddington returned his gaze doubtfully. "I'm not sure if I am yet, Mr Curry," he said carefully.

On more than one occasion in the past he'd been

caught napping by a casual remark from the Browns' neighbour and had no wish to find himself agreeing by mistake to build a golf course for ten pence.

Mr Curry looked over his shoulder in order to make sure no one else was around and then he signalled Paddington to come closer. "I'm looking for someone to act as caddie for me in the golf competition tomorrow," he said, lowering his voice. "I have some very expensive equipment and I need someone reliable to take charge of it all.

"If I find the right person," he continued meaningly, "I might not report whoever it is for nearly poking my eye out with a stick."

"Thank you very much, Mr Curry," began Paddington even more doubtfully.

Almost before the words were out of his mouth Mr Curry rubbed his hands together. "Good! That's settled then," he said briskly. "I'll see you on the links at two o'clock sharp.

"Mind you," he added sternly as he turned to go. "If I let you do it I shall hold you responsible for *everything*. If any of my balls get lost you'll have to buy me some new ones."

Paddington stared unhappily after the retreating figure in the next-door garden. He wasn't at all sure what duties a caddie had on a golf course but from the tone of Mr Curry's last remarks he had a nasty feeling that not for the first time he was getting the worst of the bargain.

In the event his worst fears were realised and any ideas he might have entertained of actually having a go himself were quickly dashed the following day when he met Mr Curry at the entrance to the golf course.

The Browns' neighbour wasn't in a very good mood, and as the afternoon wore on and Paddington laboured wearily up hill and down dale, struggling with the bag of clubs, his hopes grew fainter still.

Mr Curry seemed to spend most of his time climbing in and out of one or other of the many bunkers scattered about the eighteen holes on the golf course, his temper getting shorter and shorter, and Paddington was thankful when at long last the spot where the big competition of the day was being held came into view and they stood awaiting their turn to start.

"You'll have to keep your eyes skinned here,

bear," growled Mr Curry, surveying the fairway. "I shall be hitting the ball very hard and you mustn't lose sight of it. I don't want it getting mixed up with anyone else's."

"It's all right, Mr Curry," said Paddington eagerly. "I've put a special mark on the side with some marmalade peel."

"Marmalade peel?" echoed Mr Curry. "Are you sure it won't come off?"

"I don't think so, Mr Curry," replied Paddington confidently. "It's some of my special marmalade from the cut-price grocers in the market. Mrs Bird always says their chunks *never* come off anything."

Paddington glanced around while he was explaining what he'd done. Quite a large crowd had assembled to watch the event and he felt most important as he leaned nonchalantly on Mr Curry's club in the way that he'd seen Arnold Parker do in some of the many posters advertising the event.

Even Mr Curry himself began to look slightly better pleased with things in general as he took in the scene around them.

"Of course, bear," he announced in a loud voice for the benefit of some nearby spectators, "I've only been practising so far. Getting my hand in, so to speak. It's a long time since I played golf so I've been saving myself for this event. Now, when I go up to get my prize I'd like you to..."

Mr Curry's voice broke off and whatever else he'd been about to say was lost for posterity as a loud crack rent the air and Paddington suddenly rolled over on to the grass clutching a short length of stick in his paw.

"Bear!" bellowed Mr Curry. For once words deserted him as he pointed a trembling finger at the broken end of his golf club.

Paddington sat up and peered unhappily at the two jagged pieces. "Perhaps you could tie them together, Mr Curry," he said hopefully.

"Tie them together!" spluttered Mr Curry. "Tie them together! My best driver! I'll... I'll..."

"Look here." A voice at Mr Curry's elbow broke

into the argument. "If anyone is owed an apology it's this young bear. From the way you were playing earlier on I'm not surprised that club snapped. It's a wonder there wasn't a nasty accident. And if this is your best one I must say I wouldn't care to see your worst. It's all rusty!"

The owner of the voice looked distastefully at the remains of Mr Curry's club and then bent down to give Paddington a hand. "My name's Parker," he announced. "Arnold Parker. I'm acting as judge here this afternoon."

"Thank you very much, Mr Parker," said Paddington, looking most impressed at having such a famous person help him to his feet. "My name's Brown. Paddington Brown."

"Arnold Parker?" repeated Mr Curry. The cross expression on his face disappeared as if by magic. "I was only joking," he said, creasing his face into a smile as he reached into his golf bag. "These things happen. I *do* have another driver. It's a much heavier one, of course… I really only keep it for when I'm playing in important matches… but still…

"Remind me to give you ten pence when we

get home, bear," he added in a loud voice for the benefit of Arnold Parker.

Paddington blinked at the Browns' neighbour in amazement. It was most unlike him to want to pay out ten pence at the end of a hard day's work let alone offer one without so much as being asked.

"Do you happen to have my tee handy, bear?" asked Mr Curry, as he took up his position at the start.

"Your *tea*, Mr Curry?" repeated Paddington. Taken even more by surprise at this sudden request, he reached hastily under his hat in an effort to make amends for his accident, and withdrew a marmalade sandwich.

Mr Curry took the sandwich, looked at it for a moment as if he could hardly believe his eyes, and then threw it on the ground. "I don't mean *that* sort of tea, bear," he growled, his smile becoming even more fixed than before. "I mean the kind you place the ball on."

Taking a deep breath he reached into his pocket and withdrew a small object made of yellow plastic which he pushed into the ground in front of him.

Balancing Paddington's specially marked ball on top of the tee, Mr Curry stood back, took careful aim along the fairway, swung the new club over his shoulder, and then to everyone's surprise gave a loud yell as in one continuous movement he turned head over heels like a Catherine wheel.

"Oh dear," said Arnold Parker. He bent down and examined something on the ground. "I think you must have accidentally trodden on Mr Brown's marmalade sandwich!"

The golf club was situated close to a railway line and fortunately for the ears of the onlookers in general, and Paddington in particular, Mr Curry's remarks for the next few minutes as he sat digesting this piece of information were drowned by the noise of a passing train.

"Marmalade!" he exclaimed. "All over my best plus-fours!" He sat up rubbing his leg. "*And* I've hurt myself," he groaned. "Now I shan't be able to play."

Arnold Parker began to look rather concerned as Mr Curry screwed up his face. "If I were you I'd go along to the First Aid tent," he said. "It may be serious."

"Bear!" roared Mr Curry. "It's all your fault, bear. Leaving marmalade sandwiches lying around like that."

"Nonsense!" said Arnold Parker, coming to Paddington's rescue again. "If you hadn't thrown it down in the first place it would never have happened. It's a judgement."

"Perhaps *I* could have a go for you, Mr Curry," said Paddington eagerly.

Arnold Parker looked at him thoughtfully. "There's no reason why not," he said, turning to Mr Curry. "It doesn't say anything in the rules about bears being barred and it'll save you losing your entrance money."

Mr Curry pricked up his ears at this last piece of information. He glared at Paddington and then, swallowing hard, handed over his club. "All right, bear," he said ungraciously. "I suppose it's better than nothing. But mind you make a good job of it.

"And make sure you address the ball properly," he barked, as Paddington took up his position.

"Make sure I address the ball properly, Mr Curry?" exclaimed Paddington, looking most surprised. "I don't even know where it's going!"

"I think he's worried about your stance, Mr Brown," said Arnold Parker soothingly.

"My *stamps!*" echoed Paddington, growing more and more confused. Looking at Mr Curry's ball there didn't seem much room for even a short address let alone a stamp as well and he was most relieved when Arnold Parker explained that addressing the ball was only another way of saying you were getting ready to hit it and that 'stance' simply described the way you stood.

Paddington looked around at the crowd. It seemed to him that golfers used a lot of very long and complicated words to describe the simple act of hitting a small white ball with a club.

Taking hold of Mr Curry's club he closed his eyes, and to the accompaniment of a gasp of alarm from some of the nearby spectators, swung the club with all his might.

"Er... perhaps you could try standing a little nearer," said Arnold Parker, after a few minutes and quite a number of goes had passed by without anything happening. He looked at his watch and then at the queue of waiting competitors. "It must be a bit difficult with paws," he added encouragingly.

Paddington mopped his brow and stared at the ball in disgust. He felt there were several improvements he could make to the game of golf, not the least of which would be to have a bigger ball. All the same he was a determined bear and after deciding to have one last try he closed his eyes again, gripped the club as hard as he could, and took a final swing.

This time there was a satisfying crack as the end of the club made contact with the ball.

"Fore!" shouted someone in the crowd behind him.

"Five!" exclaimed Paddington, falling over in his excitement.

"Congratulations!" said Arnold Parker, as he picked himself up off the ground. "Did anyone see where it went?"

"I did," shouted Mr Curry above the noise of a passing goods train. "Over there!" He pointed towards a large patch of scrubland between the tee and the railway line and then turned back to Paddington.

"Bear," he said slowly and carefully, "I'm going to the First Aid tent now to get my leg seen to. If you haven't found my ball by the time I get back... I'll... I'll..." The Browns' neighbour left his sentence unfinished as he hobbled away, but the expression on his face more than made up for any lack of words and Paddington's heart sank as he bade goodbye to Arnold Parker and made his way slowly in the direction of the railway line.

From a distance the piece of land had looked bad enough, full of long grass and brambles, but now that he was close to it Paddington decided he wouldn't fancy his chances of finding a football let alone anything as small as a golf ball, and even the friendly sight of the train driver waving in his direction as the engine disappeared round a bend failed to cheer him up as he settled down to his unwelcome task.

Mr Curry sat up in bed in the Casualty Ward of the hospital and stared in amazement at the shiny new bag of golf clubs. "Do you mean to say *I* won these?" he said.

"*Paddington* won them," replied Mrs Bird firmly. "And now he's very kindly giving them to you."

"And I've brought you a 'get well' present too, Mr Curry," said Paddington, handing over a small white plastic object with holes in the side. "It's a special practice ball which doesn't go very far so it won't get lost."

"Thank you very much, bear," said Mr Curry gruffly. He stared first at Paddington and then at his presents. "It's very kind of you. I was going to give you a good talking to but I shan't now."

"I should think not indeed!" exclaimed Mrs Bird fiercely.

"Fancy you hitting a ball farther than anyone

else," said Mr Curry, still hardly able to believe his eyes or his ears.

"He didn't exactly hit it farther," said Jonathan, nudging his sister. "It only travelled farther. But Arnold Parker said it was probably a world record all the same."

"Especially for a bear," added Judy, squeezing Paddington's paw.

"A *world record*!" Mr Curry began to look even more impressed as he listened to the others. "Very good, bear. Very good indeed!" He fingered his new clubs and then looked thoughtfully at the new practice ball. "It makes me want to have a go."

"I shouldn't if I were you," said Mrs Brown anxiously, reading Mr Curry's thoughts. "You don't want another accident."

"Nonsense!" exclaimed Mr Curry, sticking his legs out of the bed. "They're letting me out soon. I feel better already." He bent down, placed the ball in the middle of the polished floor, and then, before anyone could stop him, took careful aim with one of his new clubs. "One go won't do any…"

Mr Curry's voice broke off and for a second he

seemed to disappear in a flurry of arms and legs. Then a loud crash shook the ward.

"Crikey!" exclaimed Jonathan. "Not again!"

"Oh dear," said Mrs Brown. "We did warn you…"

"Nurse!" bellowed Mr Curry, as he sat up rubbing his injured leg. "Nurse! Where are you? Who left all this polish on the floor?"

The Browns exchanged glances as the doors burst open and a crowd of figures in white led by a lady in a Sister's uniform rushed into the ward.

"I think we'd better beat a hasty retreat," said Mr Brown, voicing the thoughts of them all.

"It certainly wasn't Paddington's fault that time," said Mrs Bird firmly.

"You know what Mr Curry's like," said Mrs Brown.

"Can't we tell him the rest of the story?" asked Jonathan.

Mr Brown shook his head. "I think it'll have to wait," he said, trying to make himself heard above the hubbub. "Anyway, I don't suppose he'll believe us."

Mrs Brown took one last look at the crowd round Mr Curry's bed as she led the way up the ward. "Nine miles does sound a long way for a golf ball to go," she agreed. "What a good job the rules didn't say anything about *how* it travelled."

"Fancy landing in the cab of a railway engine," said Jonathan. "No wonder the driver was waving at you."

"It was jolly good of him to have sent it back," added Judy. "What do you think, Paddington?"

Paddington considered the matter for a moment. He gave a final wave of his paw in the direction of Mr Curry's bed and then, as the familiar voice of the Browns' neighbour rang out, he hastily followed the others through the door. "I think," he said, amid general agreement, "it's a good job I put a marmalade chunk on the side of the ball to mark it. Otherwise *no one* would have known it was mine!"

Chapter Three

A Visit to the Hospital

Mrs Brown gave a sigh as she searched through her kitchen drawer for an elastic band. "If I see another jar of calves' foot jelly," she exclaimed with unusual vigour, "I shall scream. That's the fourth one this week. Not to mention three pots of jam, two dozen eggs and goodness knows how many bunches of grapes."

Mrs Bird gave a snort. "If you ask me," she said grimly, "Mr Curry will be coming out of hospital when it suits *him* and not a minute before. He knows when he's on to a good thing. Free board and lodging and everyone at his beck and call. He has a relapse every time the doctor says he's getting better."

The Browns' housekeeper took the elastic band from Mrs Brown and gave it a hard ping as she released it round the neck of the jar. From the expression on her face it looked as if Mr Curry could consider himself lucky that he wasn't within range.

It was a little over a week since the Browns' neighbour had been admitted to hospital after his accident on the golf course and although X-rays and a number of probings from various doctors had revealed nothing amiss he still maintained he couldn't move his leg.

Since then the Browns had received a constant stream of postcards, notes and other messages containing urgent requests for things ranging from best grapes to newspapers, magazines, writing paper, stamps and other items too numerous to be mentioned.

At first they had been only too pleased to oblige, and with Jonathan and Judy back at school after the summer holidays Paddington in particular had spent a great deal of his time rushing round the market with his shopping basket on wheels seeing to Mr Curry's various wants.

But after a week of visiting and listening to his complaints their enthusiasm was beginning to wear decidedly thin.

Even the hospital staff were becoming restive and the Ward Sister herself had made some very pointed remarks about the shortage of beds.

"I'm not having him here," said Mrs Bird flatly. "That's final. And I'm certainly not having Paddington run about after him once he's home. He'll be wearing that poor bear's paws to the bone."

Paddington, who happened to arrive in the kitchen at that moment, gave a start and looked hastily at his paws, but to his relief there was no sign of anything poking through the pads and so he turned his attention to the basket of food standing on the table.

"Now you're sure you'll be all right?" asked Mrs

Brown as she carefully wedged a fruit cake into the last remaining space.

Paddington licked his lips. "I think so, Mrs Brown," he said.

"And no picking the cherries out of the cake on the way," warned Mrs Bird, reading his thoughts. "If Mr Curry finds any holes we shall be getting another postcard and I've had quite enough for one week."

Paddington looked most offended at the suggestion. "Pick cherries out of Mr Curry's cake!" he exclaimed.

Mrs Brown broke in hastily. "Explain to him that we can't come tonight," she said. "We're all going out. There's no need to stay more than five minutes. They don't usually allow visiting in the morning but Mrs Bird rang the Sister in charge of the ward and she said it would be all right just this once."

Paddington listened carefully to all his instructions. In his heart of hearts he wasn't too keen on visiting Mr Curry by himself. All his visits since the accident had been with other members of the family and he had a nasty feeling that the Browns' neighbour might have one or two things to say on the subject of the golf match so he brightened at the news that he wouldn't have to stay long.

Mrs Brown had arranged for a taxi to call and take Paddington to the hospital and a few minutes later, armed with the basket together with a small parcel of sandwiches and a Thermos flask of hot cocoa in case he got delayed and missed his elevenses, he put on his duffle coat and hat and set off.

As the taxi disappeared round the corner of Windsor Gardens Mrs Brown and Mrs Bird turned and went back inside the house.

"I do hope we're doing the right thing, letting him go by himself," sighed Mrs Brown, as she closed the front door.

"I shouldn't worry about that bear," said Mrs Bird decidedly. "He knows how to look after number one."

Mrs Brown gave another sigh. "It wasn't Paddington I was thinking of," she replied. "It's the hospital."

Mr Curry had been admitted to a hospital not far from Windsor Gardens. It was a busy establishment and Mrs Brown shuddered to think of what might happen if Paddington took the wrong turning and got lost in one of its many corridors.

However, it was much too late to worry for it was only a matter of minutes before Paddington's taxi swung off the main road, passed through some large gates, and drew to a halt at the main entrance to a large brick building.

Paddington didn't often have the chance to travel in a taxi, especially by himself, and he was slightly disappointed that it was all over so quickly. Nevertheless, he felt most important as he climbed out on to the forecourt, and after thanking the driver for the ride, made his way through the entrance doors towards a desk marked RECEPTION.

"Mr Curry?" said the uniformed man behind the desk. He ran his finger down a long list clipped to a board. "I don't recollect anyone of that name. Have you an appointment?"

"Oh, yes," said Paddington. "Mrs Bird made one specially."

The receptionist scratched his

head. "Any idea what he does?" he asked. "This is a big hospital, you know. We have all sorts of people here."

Paddington thought for a moment. "I don't think he does anything very much," he said at last. "Except grumble."

"That doesn't help a lot," said the man. "We've got one or two like that round here I can tell you. What's your name, please?"

"Brown," said Paddington promptly. "Paddington Brown. From number thirty-two Windsor Gardens."

The receptionist riffled through some more papers. "I can't find any bears down for an appointment either, let alone brown ones," he said at last. "I think I'd better pass you on to our Mr Grant. He deals with all the difficult cases."

"Thank you very much," said Paddington gratefully. "Is he the head man?"

"That's right," said the receptionist, picking up a telephone. He was about to dial a number when he paused and looked at Paddington. "The *head* man," he repeated, his face clearing. "Bless me! Why didn't you say so before? You want the psychiatrist."

Seeing Paddington's look of surprise he leaned over his desk. "That's the chap who looks after things up here," he said, tapping his own head as he lowered his voice confidentially. "What we call the 'head-shrinker'."

Paddington began to look more and more astonished as he listened. Although he was very keen on long words he'd never heard of one as long as 'psychiatrist' before, and even if his hat did feel a bit tight sometimes, particularly when he had a marmalade sandwich inside it, he wasn't at all sure that he wanted to cure it by having his head shrunk.

"I think I'd rather have my hat stretched instead," he announced with growing alarm.

It was the man's turn to look surprised as he took in Paddington's words. From where he was standing there was a very odd look about the figure on the other side of the desk, and although he couldn't find any trace of an appointment in the name of Brown, he felt sure, if the present conversation was anything to go by, that for once the rules could be bypassed.

Paddington had a very hard stare when he liked

and, backing away slightly, the receptionist hastily consulted another list.

"There, there," he said. "There's nothing to worry about. I'll try and arrange for you to see our Mr Heinz."

"Mr Heinz!" exclaimed Paddington hotly. "But I wanted to see Mr Curry. I've brought him one of Mrs Bird's cherry cakes."

Reaching for a walking stick the man looked anxiously over his shoulder as he came round to the front of the desk. "I think you'll find Mr Heinz much nicer," he said, eyeing Paddington warily. Realising the expression 'head-shrinker' had been a bit upsetting, not to mention the word 'psychiatrist', he tried hard to think of another name. "He's our best 'trick-cyclist'," he added soothingly. "Just follow me."

Apart from the time when he'd spilt some hot toffee down his front by mistake and then had been unable to stand up again after it set, Paddington hadn't had a lot to do with hospitals. Even so he looked most surprised to hear they had such things as 'trick-cyclists' for the entertainment of visitors. It sounded very good value indeed and he looked around with interest as he followed the man towards a door at the far end of a long corridor.

Motioning Paddington to wait, the man disappeared into the room. For a few moments there was the sound of a muffled conversation and then the door opened again.

"You're in luck's way," whispered the receptionist. "Mr Heinz can see you straight away. He's got a free period."

Taking hold of Paddington's spare paw he propelled him through the door and then hastily closed it behind him.

After the brightness of the corridor the room seemed unusually dark. The slatted blinds were drawn over the windows and the only light came from a green shaded lamp on a desk at the far side. Apart from some cabinets and several chairs there was a long couch, rather like a padded table, in the middle of the room, and behind the desk itself Paddington made out the dim figure of a man in a white coat who appeared to be examining him through a pair of unusually thick-lensed glasses.

"Come in… come in," said the man, turning the

lamp so that it shone on Paddington's face. "Take off your coat and make yourself comfortable."

"Thank you very much," said Paddington, blinking in the strong light. He felt very pleased that he was the first one in and, taking off his duffle coat and hat, he placed them on top of his basket and then settled himself down in a nearby chair.

"Have I got long to wait?" he asked, unwrapping his sandwiches.

"Oh, no," said the man in the white coat. He picked up a pen. "In fact, I'll start right away."

"I'm sorry about the cherry cake," said Paddington cheerfully.

Mr Heinz put his pen down again. Taking off his glasses he breathed on the lenses, polished them with a handkerchief and then replaced them on his nose. "You are sorry about your *cherry cake*?" he repeated carefully.

Paddington nodded. "I'm afraid I can't let you have a slice," he said, "because Mrs Bird doesn't want any more postcards from Mr Curry. But you can have one of my marmalade sandwiches if you like."

Mr Heinz gave a slight shudder as he waved aside

the open bag. "Very kind of you," he said briefly, "but..." He paused. "Is anything the matter?" he enquired, as Paddington began peering anxiously around the room.

"It's all right, thank you, Mr Heinz," said Paddington, turning his attention back to the man behind the desk. "I was only wondering where you keep your bike."

"My *bike*?" Mr Heinz rose from his chair and came round to the front of the desk. "This really is a most interesting case," he exclaimed, rubbing his hands together. "The receptionist said... er..." He broke off as Paddington gave him a hard stare. "Er... that is... I may even write an article about it," he continued hastily. "I don't think I've had any bear patients before."

Helping Paddington to his feet Mr Heinz motioned him towards the couch in the middle of the room. "I'd like you to lie on that," he said. "And then look up towards the ceiling and try to make your mind a blank."

Paddington examined the couch with interest. "Thank you very much," he exclaimed doubtfully as he clambered up, "but shall I be able to see your tricks?"

"My *tricks*?" repeated Mr Heinz.

"The man in the hall said you were going to do some tricks," explained Paddington, beginning to look rather disappointed that nothing much was happening.

"I expect he was trying to humour… er… that is, keep you happy," said Mr Heinz, making his way back to the desk.

"As a matter of fact," he continued casually, "I'd like to play a little game. It's really to test your reactions."

"A game to test my reactions?" repeated Paddington, looking more and more surprised. "I didn't know I had any."

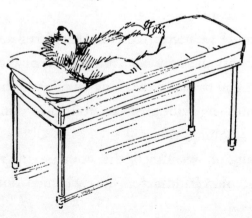

"Oh, yes," said Mr Heinz. "Everyone has reactions. Some people have fast ones and some have slow." He picked up his pen again. "Now I'm going to call out some words – quite quickly – and each time I call one out I want you to give me another one which has the opposite meaning... Right?"

"Wrong," said Paddington promptly.

Mr Heinz paused with his pen halfway to the paper. "What's the matter?" he asked crossly. "Aren't you comfortable?"

"Oh, yes," said Paddington, "but you told me to say the opposite every time you gave me a word." He sat up and gave the man behind the desk another hard stare. For someone who was supposed to be testing reactions he didn't think much of Mr Heinz's own ones at all.

For some unknown reason Mr Heinz appeared to be counting under his breath. "That wasn't the word, bear," he said, breathing heavily. "Wait until I give you the go-ahead. Once you start I don't want to hear anything else. I'll give you a countdown, beginning... now. Three... two... one... go!"

"Stop!" said Paddington.

Mr Heinz opened his mouth and then appeared to change his mind. "Very good," he said grudgingly.

"Very bad," replied Paddington eagerly.

"Look here!" began Mr Heinz, a note of panic in his voice.

"Look there!" cried Paddington wildly. Much as he had been looking forward to seeing Mr Heinz do some tricks on his bicycle he was beginning to think the present game was much more interesting and he looked most disappointed when his last reply was greeted with silence. "Can't you think of any more words, Mr Heinz?" he asked.

The psychiatrist spent a moment or two drumming on his desk with his fingers. He looked as if there were a number of words he would like to have said, but ignoring the temptation he picked up his pen again.

"White," he said wearily.

"Black," said Paddington, settling down again on the couch with his paws crossed and a pleased expression on his face.

"Big," said Mr Heinz hopefully.

"Small," said Paddington promptly.

"Fast," said Mr Heinz.

"Slow," said Paddington.

Trying several more words in quick succession Mr Heinz began to look better pleased with the way things were going and for several minutes his pen raced across the paper as he tried to keep pace with Paddington's replies.

"Fine," he said at last, leaning back in his chair.

"Wet," exclaimed Paddington.

Mr Heinz gave a chuckle. "We've finished…" he began.

"We've started," said Paddington.

"No, we haven't," said Mr Heinz crossly.

"Yes, we have," cried Paddington.

"No... no... no!" shouted Mr Heinz, thumping his desk.

"Yes... yes... yes!" cried Paddington, waving his paws in the air.

"Will you stop!" yelled Mr Heinz.

"No, I won't!" cried Paddington, nearly falling off the couch in his excitement.

Mr Heinz looked wildly about the room. "Why did I ever take this up?" he cried, burying his face in his hands. "I should have had my head examined!"

Paddington sat up looking most surprised at the last remark. "Perhaps it needs shrinking," he said, peering at Mr Heinz's head with interest. "I should go and see the man in the hall. He might be able to help you. He knows all about these things."

As Paddington began clambering down off the couch Mr Heinz made a dash for the door. "I shall be gone for five minutes," he announced dramatically. "Five minutes! And if you're still here when I get back..."

A Visit to the Hospital

Mr Heinz left his sentence unfinished but from the way he punctuated it with the slam of the door even Paddington could see that he wasn't best pleased at the way things had gone.

He peered at the closed door for several moments and then hastily gathered up his belongings. There was another door leading out of Mr Heinz's room and after considering the matter Paddington decided to investigate this one instead of the door he'd come in by. There had been rather a nasty expression on Mr Heinz's face when he'd left, one which he hadn't liked the look of at all, and whatever lay on the other side of the second door, Paddington felt sure it couldn't be worse than the possibility of meeting the hospital's 'trick-cyclist' again.

Chapter Four

PADDINGTON FINDS A CURE

PADDINGTON CLOSED THE door behind him and stood for a moment mopping his brow. All in all he felt he'd had a narrow escape. He wasn't quite sure what he'd escaped from but he hadn't liked the look of things in the next room at all, and he was glad he'd decided to retire from the scene.

He felt even more pleased a few seconds later

when the muffled sounds of voices broke out on
the other side of the wall. From what he could
make out through the keyhole there appeared to be
some kind of argument going on and several times
he distinctly heard Mr Heinz thumping his desk.
Gradually, however, the noise died away and at
long last he was able to turn his attention to his new
surroundings.

After the previous room it was slightly
disappointing. Apart from an old hat stand laden
with white coats, the only items of furniture were a
desk, on top of which was an open bag containing
a number of instruments, a swivel chair, and a
big steel rack which seemed to hold a lot of large
photographic negatives, and which occupied most
of one wall alongside a second door.

It wasn't a bit like some of the rooms he'd seen
in hospital programmes on television, with people
rushing in and out pushing trolleys and barking out
orders. That apart, it was also a very cold room.
From his few short visits to hospitals Paddington
had noticed they were very keen on fresh air and
Mr Curry's was no exception. There were three

windows in the room, all much too high to reach, and all of them wide open.

Paddington began to feel pleased that Mrs Bird had thought to provide him with the Thermos flask full of hot cocoa in case he got delayed, and after several minutes had passed with no sign of anything happening he undid the top and poured some of the liquid into the cup.

A moment later Paddington let out a yell which echoed and re-echoed around the room as he danced up and down waving the cup with one paw and clutching his mouth with the other. Mrs Bird was a great believer in making hot things as hot as possible and for once even she had excelled herself.

Hastily pouring the remains of the cocoa back into the Thermos, Paddington replaced the top and then began peering inside the bag on the desk in the hope of finding a mirror so that he could examine the end of his tongue.

It was while he was doing this that a thoughtful expression gradually came over his face. In the past he'd often watched programmes about hospitals on television. In fact, he was very keen on some of them, particularly the ones where there was a lot of action, and he recognised several instruments in the bag as being identical to the ones Grant Dexter always carried when he made his rounds every Monday evening in the 'Daredevil Doctor' series.

Gradually an ominous quiet descended on the room. A quiet broken only by the sound of heavy breathing and an occasional chink as Paddington investigated still deeper into the bag.

It was some while later that the door leading to the corridor slowly opened and a small figure dressed entirely in white peered out through the gap. The corridor was empty, but even if there had been anyone around, little but the closest inspection would have revealed the identity of the face behind the mask as it looked furtively first one way and then the other.

In fact, other than the unusual appearance of the coat, which reached right down to the floor, even

Grant Dexter himself might have been forgiven if he'd met the wearer face to face and thought he was looking at a shortened version of his own reflection in a mirror.

Apart from the mask, the head was almost completely enveloped in a white skullcap, and this in turn was surmounted by a head band and lamp. A stethoscope was draped around the neck, and although a few whiskers, which had obstinately refused to stay folded, poked out through some gaps and might have provided a clue, the rest of the face was almost entirely hidden.

Having carefully made sure no one was coming, Paddington closed the door again and turned his attention to the photographic plates hanging on the wall.

Holding them up to the light in the way he'd seen Grant Dexter do many times before on television he peered at them hopefully, but after a few minutes he changed his mind and decided to sit down in the chair behind the desk instead. As pictures they had been most disappointing. As far as he could make out most of them showed a lot of old bones, and half of those were broken.

The swivel chair was much more interesting and he spent some while swinging it round and round, gradually getting higher and higher until he was almost level with the top of the desk.

Waving his paws wildly in the air in the way that Mr Heinz had done Paddington was about to give the chair a final heave when suddenly the whole world seemed to turn upside down and he found himself flying through the air. Everything went black for a moment and then he landed in a heap on the floor with what appeared to be a ton weight on top of him.

As he struggled to remove the weight, Paddington heard a patter of running feet in the corridor outside and then the door suddenly burst open and a man in uniform rushed into the room.

"Where is it? Where is it?" he cried, taking aim with a large, red fire extinguisher.

Paddington paused in his efforts to free himself. "Where is it?" he repeated in surprise.

"Blimey!" The man looked down at the figure on the floor. "Are you all right, sir? I thought there'd been an explosion or something. One of them gas cylinders going up."

Paddington thought for a moment. "I think *I'm* all right," he said at last. "But the room's still going round."

"I'm not surprised," said the man, examining the wreckage. "Your seat's come off."

Paddington looked round. "My seat's come off!" he repeated in alarm.

"Probably ran out of thread," explained the man as he bent down to lend a helping hand. "I expect you was turning it round and round too quickly and broke the end stop..." He paused as he caught sight of a coloured badge in Paddington's lapel. "'Ere," he said. "Are you one of them gentlemen from overseas?"

Paddington looked at him in amazement. "I come from Darkest Peru," he said.

"Thought so by your badge," said the man. "Oh

well, we all know who you want to see, don't we?"

"Do we?" exclaimed Paddington, looking more and more surprised. "I expect Mrs Bird rang up."

The man paused for a moment as if he hadn't heard aright. "I think you'd best come along with me," he said at last, giving Paddington a very odd look. Working in a large London hospital he'd become used to seeing strange sights, but somehow, now that he was able to get a better view, the figure standing in front of him surpassed even his previous experience. "We don't want to keep 'is nibs waiting," he continued, hastily opening the door. "'E don't like it much."

"I know he doesn't," agreed Paddington, looking pleased that at long last someone understood what he'd come for. "Thank you very much."

The man looked at Paddington in astonishment as he picked up his basket. "'Ere," he said, "you're not taking *that* in with you are you?"

"I've brought it for him," explained Paddington.

"Oh, well," said the man, scratching his head. "'Ave it your own way. But don't say I didn't warn you. And if you want my advice you'll take them gloves off before you go in the ward."

"Take my gloves off!" exclaimed Paddington hotly as the man disappeared up the corridor. "Those aren't gloves. They're paws!"

Taking a firm grip of the basket he hurried after the man in uniform giving the back of his head some very hard stares indeed as they passed through several sets of swing doors, along another corridor, and finally into a large, brightly lit room with a row of beds on either side.

Paddington peered down the ward. "There's Mr Curry," he said excitedly, waving his paw in the direction of a bed at the far end. "I can see his grapes."

"I daresay it is," said his guide, putting a finger to his lips as a tall, imposing figure rose from a group gathered round a nearby bed and fixed his eyes on them. "And that's Sir Archibald. I can see 'is glares!"

"Sir Archibald?" repeated Paddington in surprise.

"That's right," said the man, looking pleased.

"We're just in time. He's still doing 'is rounds.

"Look," he said, as Paddington hesitated. "You comes from overseas – right?"

"Right," said Paddington promptly.

"And you 'as a badge in yer lapel – right?"

"Right," agreed Paddington rather more doubtfully as he looked down at his coat collar.

"In that case," said the man patiently, "you must be one of Sir Archibald's students. 'E takes 'em on 'is rounds every Monday morning. And if I were you," he whispered, giving Paddington an encouraging push, "I'd go and make my apologies to 'im before I was very much older. 'E don't look best pleased to my way of thinking."

Thanking the man for his trouble Paddington picked up his basket again and hurried down the ward. He wasn't at all sure who Sir Archibald was or why he had to apologise to him, but as he drew near and caught sight of the expression on his face he had to admit that the porter was right about the great man's mood and he hastily lifted the top part of his skullcap and let it drop back into place before he bade him good morning.

"Good afternoon's more like it," barked Sir Archibald. He glared at Paddington's outfit with a look of disgust. "It's ward round today – not operations. You'll be frightening the patients out of their wits.

"Now you *are* here," he continued sarcastically, pointing to the patient under examination, "perhaps you can give us the benefit of your advice. Let's have your diagnosis."

"My diagnosis!" exclaimed Paddington in alarm as he began unloading his basket. "There's a cherry cake and some calves' foot jelly, but I don't think Mrs Bird mentioned one of those."

"Calves' foot jelly," repeated Sir Archibald, as if in a dream. "Did you say *calves' foot jelly*?"

"Grant Dexter always says it's very good if you're ill," said Paddington.

"Grant Dexter!" spluttered Sir Archibald. "And who might he be?"

"You don't know Grant Dexter!" exclaimed Paddington, looking most surprised. "He's in 'Daredevil Doctor' every Monday. He's very good at curing people. All his patients get better."

"I think he'd like to know what you feel about *this* patient," hissed one of the other doctors, pointing to the man on the bed as a loud snort came from the direction of Sir Archibald.

"Have a listen on your stethoscope," murmured someone else, reaching over to undo the man's pyjama jacket. "Do *something*!"

Paddington grew more and more confused as he listened to the crumbs of advice. Picking up a headset off the bed he took the end of the stethoscope which someone else handed him and began hastily poking it on the man's chest as he listened hopefully.

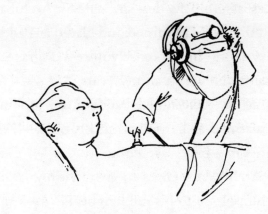

"Well," said Sir Archibald testily. "May we have your considered opinion?"

Paddington removed the headset. "I can hear someone talking," he announced, looking most surprised. "It sounds like Mrs Dale's Diary."

"Mrs Dale's Diary!" bellowed Sir Archibald.

"You've picked up the radio headphones by mistake," hissed someone behind Paddington. "You're supposed to use the other end of the stethoscope."

The patient sat up in bed and stared at Paddington with growing alarm. "'Ere," he exclaimed. "'E's not going to operate, is he? 'Cause if 'e is I'm going off 'ome smartish."

"Rest assured, my dear sir," said Sir Archibald, "it's most unlikely." He turned and glared at Paddington. "As a doctor," he barked, "you're a disgrace to your profession. Never in all my years…"

"A *doctor*," exclaimed Paddington, looking even more alarmed as he pulled off his mask. "I'm not a doctor. I'm a bear. I've come to visit Mr Curry."

Sir Archibald seemed to grow visibly larger as he drew himself up to his full height. He took in a deep breath as if about to explode, and then something in Paddington's words caused him to pause.

"Curry," he repeated. "Did you say Curry?"

"That's right," said Paddington.

"Are you a friend of his?" asked Sir Archibald suspiciously.

"Well, he lives next door," said Paddington carefully. "But I'm not really a friend. I've brought him something to be going on with."

Sir Archibald snorted. "That's the last thing he needs," he exclaimed. "That man's entirely without scruples."

"Mr Curry's without scruples!" repeated Paddington, looking most upset. "I thought he'd only hurt his leg."

Sir Archibald took a deep breath. "Scruples, bear," he said, "are things that stop some people taking advantage of others."

"Oh, I don't think Mr Curry's got any of those, Sir Archibald," agreed Paddington. "Mrs Bird's always grumbling because he takes advantage of others."

Sir Archibald and the others listened carefully as Paddington went on to explain all about the golf match and how Mr Curry had persuaded him to act as caddie. Gradually, as the story unfolded, Sir Archibald's expression changed. When it was over he gave a snort and then, as he looked first up the ward towards Mr Curry's bed and then at Paddington, a twinkle came into his eyes.

"Are you any good at tricks, bear?" he asked thoughtfully.

"Oh, yes, Sir Archibald," said Paddington. "Bears are very good at tricks."

"Thought you might be." Sir Archibald rubbed his hands together briskly and then turned to the others. "I have a feeling this is one of those occasions when we don't stick to the book. We'll make the medicine fit the patient!"

Bending down to adjust Paddington's mask he began whispering in his ear. It was difficult to tell what Paddington was thinking because his face was almost completely hidden again, but he nodded his head vigorously several times and then a few moments later followed the famous surgeon up the ward in the direction of Mr Curry's bed.

Mr Curry was reading a newspaper but when he caught sight of Sir Archibald he lowered it and gave vent to a loud groan.

"How's the patient today?" asked Sir Archibald, removing a large bowl of grapes from the bed so that he could inspect Mr Curry's leg.

"Worse," groaned Mr Curry. "Much worse."

"I thought you might be," said Sir Archibald cheerfully. "That's why we've decided to operate."

"Operate?" echoed Mr Curry, suddenly growing rather pale. "Did you say operate?"

Sir Archibald nodded. "No good playing around with these things," he said. "I'd like to introduce you to... er... a colleague of mine from overseas. He specialises in legs. Does something or other to the knee. Nobody quite knows what but it seems to work very well in the rainforest. Quite a few of his patients still manage to get around after a fashion."

Mr Curry stared uneasily at the small figure hovering by the side of the bed. "It's all right," said Sir Archibald, following his glance. "There's no need to worry. We give him a box to stand on.

"I don't suppose he'll want to shake hands," he added hastily, as Mr Curry leaned over the side of the bed. "His own are a bit shaky."

But it was too late. A gleam of recognition came into Mr Curry's eyes as he caught sight of Paddington's paw.

"Bear!" he roared, recovering himself in record time. "Bear! Up to your tricks again!"

Mr Curry glared first at Paddington, who was looking slightly crestfallen behind his mask now that the plan had misfired, and then at Sir Archibald. "Tricks like this are very bad for patients," he said slowly and loudly for the benefit of everyone else in the ward. "I think I'm going to have another relapse."

As Mr Curry lay back, Paddington hastily pulled off his mask and lifted the basket of food on to the bed in an effort to make amends.

"Careful, bear," growled Mr Curry. "Mind what you're doing with that cake. I don't want any crumbs in the bed. And no taking any of the grapes when I'm not looking. If I find any empty stalks I shall know the reason why." He peered down his bed to where Paddington was busy unloading the basket. "Have you brought the…"

Whatever else Mr Curry had been about to say was lost for all time as suddenly, to everyone's surprise, the ward shook with a tremendous roar of pain and the sheets flew into the air as he jumped out of bed and started dancing up and down in the middle of the floor.

"Bear!" he roared, lifting his injured leg into the air like an acrobat as he tried to rub his foot. "What have you done, bear? I'll… I'll…" Mr Curry's voice trailed away and for the second time within the space of as many seconds he left a sentence unfinished as he gazed sheepishly round at the sea of faces.

Sir Archibald turned to the Sister in charge. "It seems to me," he said, breaking the silence which followed Mr Curry's performance, "we have another bed free in the ward after all."

"Bear's cocoa," said Sir Archibald, holding up the empty Thermos. "I must remember this. Haven't seen quite such a remarkable cure in years. Must be boiling hot though!"

"I don't think I'd screwed the top of my flask on properly, Mrs Bird," explained Paddington. "It went all over Mr Curry's foot."

Mrs Brown and Mrs Bird exchanged glances. So much had happened in the space of a few minutes they were feeling somewhat confused.

First their house had shaken to the sound of Mr Curry's front door being slammed. Then a large black car had drawn up outside number thirty-two Windsor Gardens and to their amazement Paddington had emerged from the back seat, closely followed by a distinguished-looking gentleman, carrying the basket of food and the Thermos flask.

"All the best discoveries are made by accident," said Sir Archibald, seeing their look of puzzlement. "And in my experience some of them take quite a lot of explaining afterwards."

Sir Archibald turned to Paddington and as he did so a look of concern came over his face. "Are you all right, bear?" he asked.

Paddington felt under his coat with the end of the

stethoscope he'd been given as a souvenir. "I think I'm having trouble with my beats, Sir Archibald," he announced faintly.

Sir Archibald began to look even more concerned, and then he followed Paddington's eyes as they gazed hungrily at the shopping basket.

"I think there's hope," he said gravely, turning back to the others. "Given plenty of cake and biscuits. And some hot cocoa. That's most important."

"It's funny you should say that," remarked Mrs Bird. "I was just about to make some." She paused as Sir Archibald hovered wistfully in the doorway. "Would you care for a cup?"

"I should not only care for one," said Sir Archibald. "I should consider it a great honour. After all," he added, "inventing cures is thirsty work and bears aren't the only ones who like their elevenses."

Chapter Five

PADDINGTON AND THE 'FINISHING TOUCH'

MR GRUBER LEANED on his shovel and mopped his brow with a large spotted handkerchief. "If anyone had told me three weeks ago, Mr Brown," he said, "that one day I'd have my own patio in the Portobello Road I wouldn't have believed them.

"In fact," he continued, dusting himself down as he warmed to his subject, "if you hadn't come across that article I might *never* have had one. Now look at it!"

At the sound of Mr Gruber's voice Paddington rose into view from behind a pile of stones. Lumps of cement clung to his fur like miniature stalactites, his hat was covered in a thin film of grey dust, and his paws – never his strongest point – looked for all the world as if they had been dipped not once but many times into a mixture of earth, brick dust and concrete.

All the same, there was a pleased expression on his face as he put down his trowel and hurried across to join his friend near the back door of the shop so that they could inspect the result of their labours.

For in the space of a little over two weeks a great and most remarkable change had come over Mr Gruber's back yard. A change not unlike that in the transformation scene of a Christmas pantomime.

It had all started when Paddington had come across an article in one of Mrs Brown's old housekeeping magazines. The article in question had been about the amount of wasted space there was in a big city like London and how, with some thought and a lot of hard work, even the worst rubbish dump could be turned into a place of beauty.

The article had contained a number of photographs showing what could be done and Paddington had been so impressed by these that he'd taken the magazine along to show his friend.

Mr Gruber kept an antique shop in the Portobello Road and, although his back yard wasn't exactly a dumping ground, over the years he had certainly collected a vast amount of rubbish and in the event he'd decided to make a clean sweep of the whole area.

For several days there had been a continual stream of rag and bone men and then soon afterwards builders' lorries became a familiar sight behind the shop as they began to arrive carrying loads of broken paving-stones, sand, gravel, cement, rocks and other items of building material too numerous to be mentioned.

Taking time off each afternoon, Mr Gruber had set about the task of laying the crazy-paving while Paddington acted as foreman in charge of cement-mixing and filling the gaps between the stones – a job which he enjoyed no end.

At the far end of the yard Mr Gruber erected a

fence against which he planted some climbing roses, and in front of this they built a rockery which was soon filled with various kinds of creeping plants.

In the middle of the patio, space had been left for a small pond containing some goldfish and a miniature fountain, while at the house end there now stood a carved wooden seat with room enough for two.

It was on this seat that Paddington and Mr Gruber relaxed after their exertions each day and finished off any buns which had been left over from their morning elevenses.

"I must say we've been very lucky with the weather," said Mr Gruber, as Paddington joined him and they took stock of the situation. "It's been a real Indian summer. Though without your help I should never have got it all done before the winter."

Paddington began to look more and more pleased as he sat down on the seat and listened to his friend, for although Mr Gruber was a polite man, he wasn't in the habit of paying idle compliments.

Mr Gruber gave a sigh. "If you half close your eyes and listen to the fountain, Mr Brown," he said, "and then watch all the twinkling lights come on as it begins to get dark, you might be anywhere in the world.

"There's only one thing missing," he continued, after a moment's pause.

Paddington, who'd almost nodded off in order to enjoy a dream in which it was a hot summer's night and he and Mr Gruber were sipping cocoa under the stars, sat up in surprise.

"What's that, Mr Gruber?" he asked anxiously, in case he'd left out something important by mistake.

"I don't know," said Mr Gruber dreamily. "But there's something missing. What the whole thing needs is some kind of finishing touch. A statue or a piece of stonework. I can't think what it can be."

Mr Gruber gave a shiver as he rose from his seat, for once the sun disappeared over the roof tops a chill came into the air. "We shall just have to put our thinking caps on, Mr Brown," he said, "and not take them off again until we come up with something. It's a pity to spoil the ship for a ha'p'orth of tar."

"'Adrian Crisp – Garden Ornaments'," exclaimed Mrs Bird. "What's that bear up to now?" She held up a small piece of paper. "I found this under his bed this morning. It looks as if it's been cut from a magazine. *And* my best carrier bag is missing!"

Mrs Brown glanced up from her sewing. "I expect it's got something to do with Mr Gruber's patio," she replied. "Paddington *was* rather quiet when he came in last night. He said he had his thinking cap on and I noticed him poking about looking for my scissors."

Mrs Bird gave a snort. "That bear's bad enough when he *doesn't* think of things," she said grimly. "There's no knowing what's likely to happen when he really puts his mind to it. Where is he, anyway?"

"I think he went out," said Mrs Brown vaguely. She took a look at the scrap of paper Mrs Bird had brought downstairs. "'Works of art in stone bought and sold. No item too small or too large'."

"I don't like the sound of that last bit," broke in Mrs Bird. "I can see Mr Gruber ending up with a statue of the Duke of Wellington in his back garden."

"I hope not," said Mrs Brown. "I can't picture even Paddington trying to get a statue on to a London bus. At least," she added uneasily, "I don't think I can."

Unaware of the detective work going on at number thirty-two Windsor Gardens, Paddington peered around with a confused look on his face. Altogether he was in a bit of a daze. In fact he had to admit that he'd never ever seen anything quite like Mr Crisp's establishment before.

It occupied a large wilderness of a garden behind a ramshackle old house some distance away from the Browns', and as far as the eye could see every available square inch of ground was covered by statues, seats, pillars, balustrades, posts, stone animals – the list was endless. Even Adrian Crisp himself, as he followed Paddington in and out of the maze of pathways, seemed to have only a very vague idea of what was actually there.

"Pray take your time, my dear chap," he exclaimed, dabbing his face with a silk handkerchief as they reached their starting point for the third time. "Some of these items are hundreds of years old and I think they'll last a while yet. There's no hurry at all."

Paddington thanked Mr Crisp and then peered thoughtfully at a pair of small stone lions standing near by. They were among the first things he'd seen on entering the garden and all in all they seemed to fit most closely with what he had in mind.

"I think I like the look of those, Mr Crisp," he exclaimed, bending down in order to undo the secret compartment in his suitcase.

Adrian Crisp followed the direction of Paddington's gaze and then lifted a label attached to one of the lion's ears. "Er… I'm not sure if you'll be able to manage it," he said doubtfully. "The pair are five hundred and seventy pounds."

Paddington remained silent for a moment as he tried to picture the combined weight of five hundred and seventy jars of marmalade. "I quite often bring all Mrs Bird's shopping home from the market," he said at last.

Adrian Crisp allowed himself a laugh. "Oh, dear me," he said. "I'm afraid we're talking at cross-purposes. That isn't the weight. That's how much they cost."

"Five hundred and seventy pounds!" exclaimed Paddington, nearly falling over backwards with surprise.

Mr Crisp adjusted his bow tie and gave a slight cough as he caught sight of the expression on Paddington's face. "I might be able to let you have a small faun for one hundred pounds," he said reluctantly. "I'm afraid the tail's fallen off but it's quite a bargain. If I were to tell you where it came from originally you'd have quite a surprise."

Paddington, who looked as if nothing would surprise him ever again, sat down on his suitcase and stared mournfully at Mr Crisp.

"I can see you won't be tempted, my dear fellow,"

said Mr Crisp, trying to strike a more cheerful note. "Er... how much did you actually think of paying?"

"I was *thinking* of ten pence," said Paddington hopefully.

"*Ten pence!*" If Paddington had been taken by surprise a moment before, Adrian Crisp looked positively devastated.

"I could go up to forty pence if I break into my bun money, Mr Crisp," said Paddington hastily.

"Don't strain your resources too much, bear," said Mr Crisp, delicately removing a lump of leaf mould from his suede shoes. "This isn't a charitable institution, you know," he continued, eyeing Paddington with disfavour. "It's been a lifetime's work collecting these items and I can't let them go for a song."

"I'm afraid I've only got forty pence," said Paddington firmly.

Adrian Crisp took a deep breath. "I suppose I might be able to find you one or two bricks," he said sarcastically. "You'll have to arrange your own transport, of course, but..." He broke off as he caught Paddington's eye. Paddington had a very hard stare when he liked and his present one was certainly one of the most powerful he'd ever managed.

"Er…" Mr Crisp glanced round unhappily and then his face suddenly lit up as he caught sight of something just behind Paddington. "The very thing!" he exclaimed. "I could certainly let you have *that* for forty pence."

Paddington turned and looked over his shoulder. "Thank you very much, Mr Crisp," he said doubtfully. "What is it?"

"*What is it?*" Mr Crisp looked slightly embarrassed. "I think it fell off something a long time ago," he said hastily. "I'm not sure what. Anyway, my dear fellow, for forty pence you don't ask what it is. You should be thankful for small mercies."

Paddington didn't like to say anything but from where he was standing, Mr Crisp's object seemed a rather large mercy. It was big and round and it looked for all the world like a giant stone football. However, he carefully counted out his forty pence and handed the money over before the owner had time to change his mind.

"Thank you, I'm sure," said Mr Crisp, reluctantly taking possession of a sticky collection of coins made up of several five-penny pieces, a number of twopences, and a large pile of pennies. He paused as Paddington turned his attention to the piece of stone. "I shouldn't do that if I were you," he began.

But it was too late. Almost before the words were out of his mouth there came the sound of tearing paper. Paddington stood looking at the two string handles in his paw and then at the sodden remains of brown paper underneath the stone. "That was one of Mrs Bird's best carrier bags," he exclaimed hotly.

"I did try to warn you, bear," said Mr Crisp. "You've got a bargain there. That stone's worth forty pence of anybody's money just for the weight alone. If you'd like to hang on a moment I'll roll it outside for you."

Paddington gave Mr Crisp a hard stare. "You'll roll it outside for me," he repeated, hardly able to believe his ears. "But I've got to get it all the way back to the Portobello Road."

Mr Crisp took a deep breath. "I might be able to find you a cardboard box," he said sarcastically, "but

I'm afraid we expect you to bring your own string for anything under fifty pence."

Mr Crisp looked as if he'd had enough dealings with bear customers for one day and when, a few minutes later, he ushered Paddington out through the gates he bade him a hasty farewell and slammed the bolts shut on the other side with an air of finality.

Taking a deep breath, Paddington placed his suitcase carefully on top of the box, and then, clasping the whole lot firmly with both paws, he began staggering up the road in the general direction of Windsor Gardens and the Portobello Road.

If the stone object had seemed large among all the other odds and ends in Mr Crisp's garden, now that he actually had it outside it seemed enormous. Several times he had to stop in order to rest his paws and once, when he accidentally stepped on a grating outside a row of shops, he nearly overbalanced and fell through a window.

Altogether he was thankful when at long last he peered round the side of his load and caught sight of a small queue standing beside a familiar-looking London Transport sign not far ahead.

He was only just in time for as he reached the end of the queue a bus swept to a halt beside the stop and a voice from somewhere upstairs bade everyone to "hurry along."

"Quick," said a man, coming to his rescue, "there's an empty seat up the front."

Before Paddington knew what was happening he found himself being bundled on to the bus while several other willing hands in the crowd took charge of the cardboard box for him and placed it in the gangway behind the driver's compartment.

He barely had time to raise his hat in order to thank everyone for their trouble before there was a sudden jerk and the bus set off again on its journey.

Paddington fell back into the seat mopping his brow and as he did so he looked out of the window in some surprise. Although, as far as he could remember, it was a fine day outside, he distinctly heard what sounded like the ominous rumble of thunder.

It had seemed quite close for a second or two and he peered anxiously up at the sky in case there was any lightning about, but as far as he could make out there wasn't a cloud anywhere in sight.

At that moment there came a clattering of heavy feet on the stairs as the conductor descended to the bottom deck.

"'Ullo, 'ullo," said a disbelieving voice a second later. "What's all this 'ere?"

Paddington glanced round to see what was going on and as he did so his eyes nearly fell out of their sockets.

The cardboard box, which a moment before had stood neatly and innocently beside him, now had a gaping hole in its side. Worse still, the cause of the hole was now resting at the other end of the gangway!

"Is this yours?" asked the conductor, pointing an accusing finger first at the stone by his feet and then at Paddington.

"I think it must be," said Paddington vaguely.

"Well, I'm not 'aving no bear's boulders on my bus," said the conductor. He indicated a notice just above his head. "It says 'ere plain enough – 'Parcels may be left under the staircase by permission of the conductor' – and I ain't given me permission. Nor likely to neither. Landed on me best corn it did."

"It isn't a bear's boulder," exclaimed Paddington hotly. "It's Mr Gruber's 'finishing touch'."

The conductor reached up and rang the bell. "It'll be your finishing touch and all if I have any more nonsense," he said crossly. "Come on – off with you."

The conductor looked as if he'd been about to say a great deal more on the subject of bear passengers in general and Paddington and his piece of stonework in particular when he suddenly broke off. For as the bus ground to a halt the stone suddenly began trundling back up the gangway, ending its journey with a loud bang against the wall at the driver's end.

A rather cross-looking face appeared for a moment at the window just above it. Then the bus surged forward again and before anyone had time to stop it the stone began rolling back down the gangway, landing once more at the conductor's feet.

"I've 'ad just about enough of this!" he exclaimed, hopping up and down as he reached for the bell.

"We've gone past two requests and a compulsory as it is."

The words were hardly out of his mouth when a by now familiar thundering noise followed by an equally familiar thump drowned the excited conversation from the other passengers in the bus.

For a moment or two the bus seemed to hover shaking in mid-air as if one half wanted to go on and the other half wanted to stay. Then, with a screech of brakes, it pulled in to the side of the road and as it ground to a halt the driver jumped out and came hurrying round to the back.

"Why don't you make up your mind?" he cried, addressing his mate on the platform. "First you rings the bell to say you want to stop. Then you bangs on me panel to say go on. Then you rings the bell again. Then it's bang on me panel. I don't know whether I'm on me head or me heels, let alone driving a bus."

"I like that!" exclaimed the conductor. "*I* banged on your panel. It was that blessed bear with 'is boulder what done it."

"A bear with a boulder?" repeated the driver disbelievingly. "Where? I can't see him."

The conductor looked up the gangway and then his face turned white. "He *was* there," he said. "And he had this boulder what kept rolling up and down the gangway.

"There he is!" he exclaimed triumphantly. "I told you so!"

He pointed down the road to where, in the distance, a small brown figure could be seen hurrying after a round, grey object as it zigzagged down the road. "It must have fallen off the last time you stopped."

"Well, I hope he catches it before it gets to the Portobello Road," said the driver. "If it gets in among all them barrows there's no knowing what'll happen."

"Bears!" exclaimed the conductor bitterly, as a sudden thought struck him. "He didn't even pay for 'is fare let alone extra for 'is boulder."

Paddington and Mr Gruber settled themselves comfortably on the patio seat. After all his exertions in the early part of the day Paddington was glad of a rest and the sight of a tray laden with two mugs, a jug of cocoa and a plate of buns into the bargain was doubly welcome.

Mr Gruber had been quite overwhelmed when Paddington presented him with the piece of stone.

"I don't know when I've had such a nice present, Mr Brown," he said. "Or such an unexpected one. How you managed to get it all the way here by yourself I really don't know."

"It was rather heavy, Mr Gruber," admitted Paddington. "I nearly strained my resources."

"Fancy that conductor calling it a boulder," continued Mr Gruber, looking at the stone with a thoughtful expression on his face.

"Even Mr Crisp didn't seem to know quite what it was," said Paddington. "But he said it was a very good bargain."

"I'm sure he was right," agreed Mr Gruber. He examined the top of the stone carefully and ran his fingers over the top, which appeared to have a flatter surface than the rest and was surrounded by a rim, not unlike a small tray. "Do you know what I think it is, Mr Brown?"

Paddington shook his head.

"I think it's an old Roman cocoa stand," said Mr Gruber.

"A Roman cocoa stand," repeated Paddington excitedly.

"Well, perhaps it isn't exactly Roman," replied Mr Gruber truthfully. "But it's certainly very old and I can't think of a better use for it."

He reached over for the jug, filled both mugs to the brim with steaming liquid and then carefully placed them on top of the stone. To Paddington's surprise they fitted exactly.

"There," said Mr Gruber with obvious pleasure. "I don't think anyone could find a better finishing touch for their patio than that, Mr Brown. Not if they tried for a thousand years."

Chapter Six

EVERYTHING COMES TO THOSE WHO WAIT

MRS BIRD GAVE a groan as the sound of several voices raised in song followed almost immediately by a sharp rat-tat-tat on the front door echoed down the hall.

"Not again," she said, putting down her sewing. "That's the fifth lot of carol singers in half an hour. I shall be glad when Christmas is here."

"I'll go," said Mr Brown grimly.

"I should be careful what you say, Henry," warned Mrs Brown. "Don't forget Paddington's out doing the same thing."

Mr Brown paused at the lounge door. "What!" he exclaimed. "Paddington's out *carol singing*? You don't mean to say you let him go!"

"He seemed very keen on the idea," replied Mrs Brown. "Jonathan and Judy are with him so he should be all right."

"I think they're collecting for some kind of party," broke in Mrs Bird, coming to her rescue. "It's all rather secret."

"Well, I hope whoever they are they're not relying on Paddington's efforts for their Christmas entertainment," said Mr Brown, feeling in his pocket. "Otherwise they're in for a pretty bleak time. Have you ever heard him sing?"

"He went out by himself the other evening before Jonathan and Judy broke up for their holidays," said Mrs Brown. "And he did quite well, considering."

"Two bananas, a button and some French francs,"

replied Mr Brown. "And the bananas looked as if they'd seen better days."

"I wouldn't say singing was exactly his strong point," agreed Mrs Brown reluctantly, "but he's been practising quite hard up in his bedroom just lately."

"There's no need to tell me *that*," remarked Mr Brown feelingly. "He had me out of bed twice last night. I thought it was the blessed cats!" He turned to go as once again the familiar strains of *Good King Wenceslas* filled the air, and then his face brightened as a sudden thought struck him. "I suppose," he said, "it is *one* way of getting our own back!"

Had they been able to overhear the last remark not only Paddington, but both Jonathan and Judy would have been most upset, but fortunately for the sake of peace in the Browns' household they were much too far away at that moment, and in any case they had other more important problems to occupy their minds.

In particular there was the matter of the amount they had been able to collect from their evening's work.

"Thirty-five pence," said Jonathan bitterly, as he

shone his torch into the cardboard box which they'd been using for the takings. "A measly thirty-five pence."

"It's not too bad," said Judy, "considering only six people have answered the door."

"They can't have *all* been out," said Jonathan. "I wish we'd started our school holidays earlier. The trouble is everyone's getting fed up by now. I reckon we've left it a bit late."

"Perhaps we could say we're collecting for *next* Christmas," said Paddington hopefully.

It had been Paddington's idea to collect some money for the annual children's party at the hospital and he was beginning to feel a bit guilty about the whole affair, especially as they'd set themselves a target of twenty pounds.

Judy squeezed his paw. "I don't think they'd be very pleased if we said that," she confided. "Never mind. We'll think of something. We mustn't give up now."

"Suppose we all separate," said Jonathan thoughtfully. "If we do that we ought to collect three times as much."

"We needn't go far away," he added, reading Judy's thoughts. "In fact, we needn't really lose sight of each other. Paddington can have the torch – then he can signal if he wants anything."

"All right," said Judy reluctantly. She glanced at the surrounding houses. "I'll take that one on the corner."

"Bags I have a go at the one over there with the Christmas tree in the window," exclaimed Jonathan. "Which one are you going to do, Paddington?"

Paddington considered the matter for a moment as he peered round at all the houses. "I think I'd like to try that one over there," he announced, pointing towards an imposing-looking house standing slightly apart from the rest, and from which there came the distinct sounds of a party in full swing.

"Come on, then," exclaimed Jonathan impatiently. "We shan't get anywhere if we don't make a start. We'll meet back here in half an hour."

"Don't forget," called Judy. "If you get into any trouble signal with the torch."

"Send an S.O.S.," shouted Jonathan. "Three short flashes, then three long ones and three short ones to follow."

After testing his torch carefully in order to make sure it was working, Paddington hurried up the path towards the front door of the house he'd chosen, cleared his throat several times, and then knocked loudly on the front door. He wasn't the sort of bear who believed in taking too many chances and with so much noise going on inside the house he didn't want to knock *after* he'd sung his carol and then find no one had heard him.

He opened his mouth and was about to launch forth into *Hark the Herald Angels Sing* when to his surprise the door suddenly opened and a lady stood framed in the light from the hall.

"Thank goodness you've come," she exclaimed. "I was beginning to get quite worried. I'm Mrs Smith-Cholmley," she added, as she opened the door wider and motioned Paddington to enter.

Paddington raised his hat politely as he stepped into the hall. "Thank you very much," he exclaimed. "I'm Paddington Brown."

For some reason the welcoming expression on

Mrs Smith-Cholmley's face began to fade. "Have you done much waiting?" she asked.

"Oh, no," said Paddington, looking round with interest. "I've only just got here."

"I mean have you had any previous experience of waiting?" said Mrs Smith-Cholmley impatiently.

Paddington considered the matter for a moment. "I had to wait for a bus the other day when Mrs Bird took me out shopping," he said thoughtfully.

Mrs Smith-Cholmley gave a rather high-pitched laugh. "Mr Bridges at the agency said waiters were a bit short this year," she remarked, looking down at Paddington, "but I didn't think he meant... I mean... I thought he meant they were a job to get... that is..." Her voice trailed away.

"Oh, well, at least they've sent *someone*," she continued brightly, avoiding Paddington's gaze. "We're having a little dinner-party and it's long past time to serve the first course. You'd better go straight to the kitchen and see Vladimir. He's beside himself."

"Vladimir's beside himself!" exclaimed Paddington, looking most surprised.

"He's the chef," explained Mrs Smith-Cholmley.

"And if he doesn't get some help soon I'm sure he'll do something nasty with his chopper. He was looking very gloomy the last time I saw him." She glanced down at Paddington's paw. "Let me take your torch. I'm sure you won't want that."

"I think I'll keep it if you don't mind," said Paddington firmly. "I may want to send some signals."

"Just as you wish," said Mrs Smith-Cholmley, giving him a strange look. She led the way down a long corridor and then paused before a door at the end as she opened her handbag. "Here's your ten pounds."

"My ten pounds!" Paddington's eyes nearly popped out of his head as he stared at the crisp new note in his paw.

"That's what I usually pay," said Mrs Smith-Cholmley. "But I'd like you to start straight away."

"Thank you very much," said Paddington, still hardly able to believe his good fortune. Ten pounds seemed a great deal of money to pay for a carol even if it was nearly Christmas and he hastily put the note into the secret compartment of his suitcase in case

Mrs Smith-Cholmley changed her mind when she discovered he only knew one verse.

As Paddington stood up, opened his mouth, and the first few notes of *Hark the Herald Angels Sing* rang through the hall the colour seemed to drain from Mrs Smith-Cholmley's face. "That's all I need," she cried, putting her hands to her ears. "A singing waiter!"

Paddington broke off in the middle of his opening chorus. "A singing waiter!" he repeated, looking most upset. "I'm not a singer – I'm a bear."

Mrs Smith-Cholmley gave a shudder. "I can tell that," she said, opening the kitchen door. "And I shall certainly have something to say to Mr Bridges about it in the morning. In the meantime you'd better start earning your money. Everyone's absolutely ravenous."

Without waiting for a reply she pushed Paddington through the door and hastily closed it behind him.

"Hah!"

Paddington jumped as a figure in white overalls and a tall white hat rose from behind a pile of saucepans and advanced towards him. "So! You have come at last. Quick... off viz your duffle coat and out viz your arms."

Paddington stood blinking in the strong white light of the kitchen, hardly able to believe his eyes let alone his ears. In fact he was so taken aback at the sudden strange turn of events that before he knew what was happening he found his duffle coat had been removed and he was standing with his arms outstretched while the man in white overalls balanced a row of bowls on each of them.

"Quick! Quick!" shouted Vladimir, snapping his fingers. "Get cracking viz your mulligatawnies."

"Get cracking with my mulligatawnies!" repeated Paddington carefully, finding his voice at last but hardly daring to breathe in case any of the bowls overbalanced.

"Zee soup," said Vladimir impatiently. "It is getting cold and on such short arms it is difficult to balance so much."

Paddington blinked several times to make sure he wasn't dreaming and then closed his eyes in order to count up to ten but before he had time to reach even two he found himself being bundled back out of the kitchen and when he opened them again he was standing outside yet another door behind which could be heard the chatter of voices.

"Quick," hissed Vladimir, giving Paddington a firm push. "In here."

A buzz of excitement broke out in the room as Paddington entered, and several of the guests applauded.

"What a delightful idea, Mabel," said one lady. "Having a bear for a waiter. Trust you to think up something unusual."

Mrs Smith-Cholmley gave a sickly smile. "Oh, it wasn't really my idea," she said truthfully. "It's just happened. But it makes a nice change."

She eyed Paddington warily as he arrived at the table with his load of bowls, but to her relief, apart from the fact that he was breathing rather heavily down the neck of one of her guests who happened to be in the way, there was little she could find fault with.

"I think we'd better give you a hand," she said hastily, when nothing happened. "We don't want any nasty accidents."

"Thank you very much," said Paddington gratefully as one by one the various diners relieved him of his burden. "It's a bit difficult with paws."

"Talking of paws," said the man Paddington had been standing behind, "you've got one of yours in my soup."

"Oh, that's all right," said Paddington politely. "It isn't very hot."

The man eyed the bowl distastefully. "May I give you a tip?" he asked.

"Oh, yes please," said Paddington eagerly. Now

that he was getting used to the idea of being a waiter he was beginning to enjoy himself and after giving his paw a hasty lick in order to remove some soup which had accidentally overflowed he held it out hopefully.

"Don't carry quite so much next time," said the man sternly, as he helped himself to a roll, "then it won't happen."

Mrs Smith-Cholmley gave a nervous giggle as she caught sight of the expression on Paddington's face. "I think I should see how Vladimir's getting on with the next course," she called out hastily.

Paddington gave the man with the roll one final, long hard stare and then, after collecting several empty soup dishes, he made his way towards the door. The carol singing, not to mention the waiting, had made him feel more than usually hungry and Mrs Smith-Cholmley's words reminded him of the fact that during his brief spell in the kitchen he'd noticed some very interesting smells coming from beneath the lids of Vladimir's saucepans.

Although he still wasn't entirely sure what was happening, Paddington didn't want to run the risk of it all coming to an end before he'd had time to investigate the matter. What with one thing and another serving the first course had taken rather longer than he'd expected and he hurried back down the corridor as fast as his legs would carry him.

To his surprise, when he got back to the kitchen Vladimir was no longer dressed in white. His chef's hat was lying in a crumpled ball in the middle of the floor and Vladimir himself was standing by the back door clad in a black overcoat and muffler.

"I may go back to Poland," he announced gloomily when he caught sight of Paddington.

"Oh dear," said Paddington. "I hope nothing's wrong."

"*Everything* is wrong," said Vladimir. He thumped his chest. "I, Vladimir, I who have cooked for ze crowned 'eads of Europe. I, who have 'ad princes wait while I add ze final touches to my creations. I, Vladimir, am reduced to zis. Waiting... all ze time I am kept waiting." He waved his hand disconsolately in the air. "My soup, she is cold. My entrecots, zey are cold..."

"Your entrecots are col !!" repeated Paddington, looking most upset.

Vladimir nodded. "My beautiful steak – ruined!" He pointed towards a grill laden with slowly congealing pieces of meat which stood on a nearby table.

"I 'ad to take them from the stove or they would 'ave been burned to a cinder." He reached out and clasped Paddington's paw. "They are yours, my friend. In the saucepans you will find the vegetables. You may serve it as you think fit. I, Vladimir, no longer care. Goodbye, my friend… and good luck!"

Worn out by his long speech, Vladimir paused by the back door, waved his hand dramatically in the air, and then disappeared from view, leaving Paddington rooted to the spot in astonishment.

But if Paddington was upset by the sight of Vladimir's sudden departure, Mrs Smith-Cholmley looked even more upset when, some while later, she caught sight of her steak.

By the time he'd got around to serving all the various vegetables and carried all the plates into the dining-room things had gone from bad to worse.

Even putting some of the pieces of steak in an electric toaster hadn't helped matters, particularly as several of them had popped out and fallen on the floor before he'd had a chance to catch them.

Looking at his offering Paddington had to admit that he didn't really fancy it much himself and he felt pleased he'd taken time off to have his own snack before serving the others.

"If there's anything wrong with the Baked Alaska," hissed Mrs Smith-Cholmley, endeavouring to glare at Paddington with one half of her face and smile at her guests with the other, "I shall insist on Vladimir giving me my money back.

"Baked Alaska," she repeated through her teeth as she saw the look of surprise on Paddington's face. "It's a special surprise for my guests and I want it to be absolutely perfect."

If Paddington's spirits sank as he made his way slowly back down the corridor towards the kitchen they fell still more during the next few minutes as he peered hopefully at first one cookery book and then another.

Although Mrs Smith-Cholmley had only spoken

of asking the chef for his money back he had a nasty feeling that when it came down to it and she found Vladimir had disappeared, his own ten pounds might not be too safe.

Mrs Smith-Cholmley had a large collection of cookery books from many different parts of the world, but not one of them so much as mentioned the dish he was looking for.

It was as he closed the last of the books that Paddington caught sight of a nearby low hanging shelf which he hadn't noticed before and as he did so he gave a sudden start. For there, right in front of his eyes, was a row of tins one of which was labelled with the very words he'd been looking for.

Hardly daring to close his eyes in case the tin disappeared Paddington spent the next few minutes hastily making his preparations. First he turned the knob over the oven to read 'high', then he looked around for a suitable dish. After carefully checking the thermometer in order to make sure the oven was hot enough he emptied the contents of the tin into the dish and placed it inside the cooker.

Normally the only thing Paddington had against

cooking was the amount of time it took for anything to happen, but on this occasion he hadn't long to wait. In fact, he'd hardly had time to settle down on his suitcase and make himself comfortable before several whiffs of black smoke rose from the cooker and the pleased expression on his face was rapidly replaced by a look of alarm as a most unappetising smell began to fill the kitchen.

Hurrying across the room he tore open the oven door only to stagger back as a cloud of thick, black smoke poured out.

Holding his nose with one paw he picked up his torch with the other and peered mournfully at the contents of the baking dish as it sizzled and bubbled inside the oven.

Paddington was a hopeful bear at heart, but although Mrs Smith-Cholmley had definitely said she wanted to surprise her guests, he couldn't help feeling as he trundled a trolley laden with portions of his sweet down the corridor some while later that his efforts might prove rather more than she'd bargained for.

Giving vent to a deep sigh he took a firm grip of his torch as he tapped on the dining-room door. Jonathan had told him to send out a distress signal if he was in trouble and he had a nasty idea in the back of his mind that the moment to take his advice was not too far away.

Mr Brown stared at Paddington as if he could hardly believe his eyes. "Do you mean to say," he exclaimed, "that you actually served this Mrs Smith-Cholmley baked *elastic*?"

Paddington nodded unhappily. "I found some

rubber bands in a tin, Mr Brown," he explained.

"He didn't realise Mrs Smith-Cholmley said 'Baked *Alaska*'," said Judy. "That's a sort of ice cream dish cooked in the oven."

"It was just after that he sent out his S.O.S.," added Jonathan.

"I'm not surprised," exclaimed Mrs Bird. "It's a wonder some of the guests didn't send one as well."

"They were jolly nice about it all," said Judy. "When the real waiter turned up and they discovered Paddington had really only come to sing a carol they made us all stay."

"He'd met Vladimir on the way too," added Jonathan.

"*Vladimir?*" echoed Mr Brown. He was rapidly losing track of the conversation. "Who's Vladimir?"

"The chef," explained Judy. "When he discovered the mistake he came back after all and he made some real Baked Alaska so everyone was happy."

"We sang some carols afterwards," said Jonathan. "And we collected over five pounds. That means we've nearly reached our target."

Judy gave a sigh. "The Baked Alaska was super," she said dreamily. "I could eat some more."

"So could I," agreed Jonathan.

Paddington licked his lips. "I expect I could make you some if you like, Mr Brown," he exclaimed.

"Not in *my* kitchen," said Mrs Bird sternly. "I'm not having any young bear's elastic baked in my oven!"

She paused at the door. "Mind you," she added casually, "as it happens, we were having some ice cream for supper..."

"I must say it sounds rather nice," said Mrs Brown.

Mr Brown stroked his moustache thoughtfully. "I could toy with some myself," he agreed. "How about you, Paddington?"

Paddington considered the matter for a moment. If one thing stood out above all others in his mind from the evening's adventure it was the memory of Vladimir's Baked Alaska and he felt sure that an Alaska baked by Mrs Bird would be nicer still.

The Browns' housekeeper looked unusually pink about the ears as she raised her hands at the noisy approval which greeted Paddington as he gave voice to his thoughts.

"Compliments are always nice," she said. "Especially genuine ones.

"But if you ask me," she continued, pausing at the door, "bears' compliments are the nicest ones of all and they certainly deserve the biggest helpings!"

Chapter Seven

PADDINGTON GOES TO TOWN

MR BROWN LOWERED his evening paper and looked around the room at the rest of the family. "Do you realise something?" he said. "It's nearly Christmas and we haven't been up to town to see the decorations yet!"

Paddington pricked up his ears at Mr Brown's words. "I don't think I've *ever* been to see them,

Mr Brown," he said. "Not the Christmas ones."

The Browns stopped what they were doing and stared at him in wide-eyed amazement. Paddington had been with them for so long, and was so much a part of their lives, they'd somehow taken it for granted that he'd seen the Christmas decorations at some time or another and it didn't seem possible for such an important matter to have been overlooked.

"Mercy me, I do believe that bear's right," said Mrs Bird. "We've seen the ordinary lights several times, and we've seen the decorations during daylight when we've been doing our Christmas shopping, but we've never been up specially. Not at night."

"Gosh, Dad," exclaimed Jonathan. "Can we go tonight? It's years since we went."

Mr Brown looked first at his watch and then at his wife and Mrs Bird. "I'm game," he said. "How about you?"

Mrs Brown looked at Mrs Bird. "I've done everything I want to do," said their housekeeper. "I'm very well advanced this year. I only have to take my mince pies out of the oven and I shall be ready."

"May we go, Daddy?" implored Judy. "*Please?*"

Mr Brown glanced round the room with a twinkle in his eye. "What do you say, Paddington?" he asked. "Would you like to?"

"*Yes, please*, Mr Brown," exclaimed Paddington eagerly. "I should like that very much indeed."

Paddington was always keen on trips, especially unexpected ones with the whole family, and when Mr Brown announced that he would call in on the way and pick up Mr Gruber into the bargain he grew more and more excited.

For the next half an hour there was great pandemonium at number thirty-two Windsor Gardens as everyone rushed around getting ready for the big event and even Paddington himself went so far as to rub a flannel over his whiskers while Judy gave his fur a brush down.

It was a very merry party of Browns that eventually set off in Mr Brown's car and shortly afterwards the hilarity was increased still further as Mr Gruber emerged from his shop carrying a camera and some flashbulbs, several of which he used in order to take photographs of the assembly.

"You're not the only one who hasn't been to see the Christmas decorations, Mr Brown," he said, addressing Paddington as he squeezed into the back seat alongside Mrs Bird, Jonathan and Judy. "I've never been either and I want to make the most of it."

If the Browns had been surprised to discover that Paddington had never seen the lights they were even more astonished at this latest piece of information and Paddington himself was so taken aback he quite forgot to give his usual paw signal as they swung out of the Portobello Road.

Mr Gruber chuckled at the effect of his words. "People never do see things that are on their own doorstep," he said wisely. "I must say it'll be a great treat. I've heard they're particularly good this year."

As they drove along Mr Gruber went on to explain to Paddington how each year all the big shops in London got together in order to festoon the streets with huge decorations made up of hundreds of coloured lights, and also how each year an enormous Christmas tree was sent from Norway as a gift to the people of London, and how it was always placed in a position of honour in Trafalgar Square.

It all sounded most interesting and the excitement mounted as they drew nearer and nearer to the centre of London.

Mr Gruber coughed as Paddington jumped up in his seat and began waving his paws in the direction of a cluster of green lights some distance ahead.

"I have a feeling those are traffic lights, Mr Brown," he said tactfully, as they changed to amber. "But just you wait until you see the real thing."

At that moment the lights suddenly changed again, this time to red, and the car screeched to a halt. "I'm not surprised he mistook them," grumbled Mr Brown. "It's a wonder he could see anything at all. If we're not careful we shall have a nasty accident." Rather pointedly he picked up a duster and began wiping the glass in front of him. "Bear's steam all over my windscreen! People will begin to think we're boiling a kettle in here or something."

"It's always worse when he's excited, Henry," said Mrs Brown, coming to Paddington's rescue as he sank back into his seat looking most offended.

"If I were you," she continued, "I'd stop somewhere. We shall see much more if we walk."

Mrs Brown's suggestion met with whole-hearted approval from the rest of the family. They were beginning to feel a bit cramped, and some while later, having disentangled the car from the maze of traffic and found somewhere to park, even Mr Brown had to agree that it was a good idea as they climbed out and set off on foot down one of the busy London thoroughfares.

It was a crisp, clear night and the pavement on either side of the street was thronged with people gazing into shop windows, staring up at the decorations which seemed to hang overhead like a million golden stars in the sky, or simply, like the Browns, strolling leisurely along drinking it all in.

Nearby, on the Browns' side of the street, a long queue of people were waiting to go into a cinema, and somewhere in the background there was the sound of a man's voice raised in song – a song punctuated every now and then by a rhythmic clicking like that of castanets.

"I do believe it's someone playing the spoons, Mr Brown," exclaimed Mr Gruber. "I haven't seen that for years."

Paddington, who'd never even heard
of anyone playing the spoons
before let alone seen it happen,
peered around with interest
while Mr Gruber explained
how some people, who called
themselves 'buskers', earned
their living by entertaining
the theatre and cinema queues
every evening while they were
waiting to go in.

To his disappointment the
owner of the spoons appeared to be somewhere out
of sight round a corner and so rather reluctantly he
turned his attention back to the lights.

There were so many different things to see it
was difficult to know which to investigate first and
he didn't want to run the risk of missing anything,
but the Christmas lights themselves seemed very
good value indeed. After considering the matter for
a moment or two he took off his hat so that the
brim wouldn't get in the way and then, holding it
out in front of him, he hurried along the pavement

after the others with his neck craned back so that he would have a better view.

A little way along the street he was suddenly brought back to earth when he bumped into Mr Gruber, who'd stopped outside the entrance to the cinema in order to set up his camera on a tripod and make a record of the scene.

Paddington was just staggering back after his collision when to his surprise a man in the front of the nearby queue leaned over and dropped a small, round, shiny object into his hat.

"There you are," he said warmly. "Merry Christmas."

"Thank you very much," exclaimed Paddington, looking most surprised. "Merry Christmas to you."

Peering into his hat to see what the man had given him he nearly fell over backwards on to the pavement in astonishment and his eyes grew rounder and rounder as they took in the sight before them.

For inside his hat was not just one, but a whole pile of coins. There were so many, in fact, that the latest addition – whatever it had been – was lost for all time among a vast assortment of pennies, five-pence pieces, ten pences; coins of so many different shapes, sizes and values that Paddington soon gave up trying to count them all.

"Is anything the matter, dear?" asked Mrs Brown, catching sight of the expression on his face. "You look quite…" Her voice broke off as she too caught a glimpse of the inside of Paddington's hat. "Good gracious!" She put a hand to her mouth. "What *have* you been up to?"

"I haven't been *up* to anything," said Paddington truthfully. Still hardly able to believe his good fortune he gave his hat a shake and several five pences and a penny fell out through some holes in the side.

"Crikey!" exclaimed Jonathan. "Don't say you've been collecting money from the queue!"

"They must have thought you were with the man playing the spoons," said Judy in alarm.

"Look here," said the man who'd just made the latest contribution to Paddington's collection. "I thought you were a busker."

"A busker!" exclaimed Paddington, giving him a hard stare. "I'm not a busker – I'm a bear!"

"In that case I'd like my ten pence back," said the man sternly. "Collecting money under false pretences."

"'Ear, 'ear," said a man with a muffler as he pushed his way to the front. "Came round with 'is 'at 'e did. What about my five pence?"

Mrs Brown looked round desperately as the murmurings in the front of the queue began to grow and several people farther down the street began pointing in their direction. "Do something, Henry!" she exclaimed.

"*Do something!*" repeated Mr Brown. "I don't see what *I* can do."

"Well, it was your idea to come up and see the lights in the first place," said Mrs Brown. "I knew something like this would happen."

"I like that!" exclaimed Mr Brown indignantly. "It's not my fault." He turned to the queue. "People ought to make sure they know what they are giving their money to before they part with it," he added in a loud voice.

"Came round with 'is 'at 'e did," repeated the man who was wearing the muffler.

"Nonsense!" said Mrs Bird. "He only happened to be holding it in his paw. It's coming to something if a bear can't walk along a London street with his hat in his paw when he wants to."

"Oh dear," said Judy. "Look!" She pointed towards the tail end of the queue where another argument appeared to be developing. It was centred around a man dressed in an old raincoat. He was holding an obviously empty hat in one hand while shaking his other fist at a group of people who, in turn, were pointing back up the street towards the Browns.

"Crikey! We're for it now," breathed Jonathan, as the man, having been joined by two stalwart policemen who'd been drawn to the scene by all the noise, turned and began heading in their direction.

"That's 'im! That's 'im!" cried the busker, pointing an accusing finger at Paddington. "Trying to earn an honest bob to buy meself a loaf of bread for Christmas Day I was… and what 'appens? 'E comes round with 'is 'at and robs me of all me takings!"

The first policeman took out his notebook. "Where do you come from, bear?" he asked sternly.

"Peru," said Paddington promptly. "*Darkest* Peru!"

"Number thirty-two Windsor Gardens," replied Mrs Brown at the same time.

The policeman looked from one to the other. "No fixed abode," he said ponderously as he licked his pencil.

"No fixed abode!" repeated Mrs Bird. She took a firm grip of her umbrella and glared at the speaker. "I'll have you know that young bear's abode's been fixed ever since he arrived in this country."

The second policeman viewed Mrs Bird's umbrella out of the corner of his eye and then glanced round at the rest of the Browns. "I must say they don't look as if they've been working the queues," he said, addressing his colleague.

"Working the queues!" said Mr Brown indignantly. "We most certainly have been doing nothing of the sort. We came up to show this young bear the lights."

"What about my takings then," interrupted the busker. "'Ow do they come to be in 'is 'at?"

"Deliberate it was," shouted the man with the muffler. "Took my five pence 'e did."

"It certainly wasn't deliberate," said Mr Gruber, stepping into the breach. "I saw the whole thing through my viewfinder.

"I happened to be taking a photograph at the time, officer," he continued, turning to the first policeman in order to explain the matter, "and I'm quite sure that when it's developed you'll see this young bear is in no way to blame."

Mr Gruber looked as if he would like to have said a good deal more on the subject but at that moment to everyone's relief a commissionaire appeared at the cinema doors and the queue began to move.

"That's all very well," said the busker. "But what about my takings?

"Two choruses of *Rudolph the Red Nosed Reindeer* I gave 'em on me spoons," he continued plaintively, "and all for nothing."

As the last of the queue disappeared into the cinema and the rest of the crowd began to disperse, the first policeman put his notebook away. "It seems to me," he said, turning to his colleague as they made to leave, "if this young bear here gives up his collection everyone'll be happy and we can call it a night. Only look slippy, mind," he continued, addressing himself to Paddington. "Otherwise if certain people are still here when we get back they may find themselves in trouble for causing an obstruction."

Thanking the policeman very much for his advice Paddington began hastily emptying the contents of his hat into the one belonging to the busker.

As the pile of coins cascaded down in a shower of bronze and silver he began to look more and more disappointed. It was difficult to tell exactly how much was in the collection but he felt sure it would have been more than enough to enable Jonathan, Judy and himself to reach their target for the Children's Christmas Party Fund.

"I don't know about no bear's targets," said the busker as Paddington explained what he'd been hoping to do with the money. "I've got me own targets to worry about."

"Never mind, Paddington," said Judy, squeezing his paw. "We've done very well. You never know – something may turn up."

"Tell you what," said the busker, catching sight of the expression on Paddington's face. "I'll give you a tune on me spoons to cheer you up before you go."

Lifting up his hand he was about to break into the opening bars when to everyone's surprise Mr Gruber, who had been listening to the conversation with a great deal of interest, suddenly stepped forward. "May I see those spoons a moment?" he asked.

"Certainly, guv'," said the busker, handing them over. "Don't tell me you play 'em as well."

Mr Gruber shook his head as he took a small spyglass from his pocket and held the spoons up to a nearby lamp so that he could examine them more closely. "You know," he said, "these could be quite valuable. They may even be very rare Georgian silver…"

"What!" began the busker, staring open-mouthed at Mr Gruber. "*My* spoons..."

"I have an idea," said Mr Gruber briskly, silencing the busker with a wave of his hand before he had time to say any more. "If I give you ten pounds for this pair of spoons will you let young Mr Brown keep the collection? After all, he did make it in a way, even if it was an accident."

"Ten pounds!" exclaimed the busker, eyeing Mr Gruber's wallet. "For them spoons? Lor' bless you, sir. Why, 'e can 'ave me 'at as well for that!"

"No, thank you," broke in Mrs Brown hastily. Paddington's own hat was bad enough at the best of times but from where she was standing it looked as if the busker's might well have matched up to it, give or take a few marmalade stains.

"Tell you what, guv'," said the busker hopefully, as he took Mr Gruber's ten-pound note in exchange for the spoons and began transferring the money back into Paddington's hat. "There's some more where them two came from. 'Ow about..."

Mr Gruber gave him a hard look. "No," he said firmly. "I think these two will do admirably, thank you."

A few minutes later, bidding a rather dazed-looking busker goodbye, the Browns resumed their stroll, with Paddington keeping very much to the outside this time.

"Well," said Mr Brown, "I'm not quite sure what all that was about, but it seems to have worked out all right in the end."

"Four pounds and ten pence," exclaimed Jonathan a few minutes later as he finished counting the money. "That's more than enough to reach our target. I bet they'll be jolly pleased at the hospital."

"I didn't know you were collecting for a children's party," said Mrs Brown. "You should have said. We could have given you some towards it."

"It was really Paddington's idea," said Judy, giving the paw by her side another squeeze. "Besides, it wouldn't have been the same if you'd given it to us. Not the same at all."

Mr Brown turned to Mr Gruber. "Fancy you noticing those spoons," he said. "Isn't it strange how things work out."

"Very strange," agreed Mr Gruber, taking a sudden interest in some decorations just overhead.

Only Mrs Bird caught a faint twinkle in his eye – a twinkle not unlike the one she'd noticed when he'd been conducting his deal with the busker, and one moreover which caused her to have certain suspicions on the matter – but wisely she decided it was high time the subject was changed.

"Look," she said, pointing ahead. "There's the Christmas tree in Trafalgar Square. If we hurry we may be in time for the carols."

Mr Brown gave a sniff. "I'll tell you something

else," he said. "I can smell hot chestnuts."

Paddington licked his lips. Although it wasn't long since he'd had his tea, all the excitement was beginning to make him feel hungry again. "Hot chestnuts, Mr Brown," he exclaimed with interest. "I don't think I've ever had any of those before."

The Browns stopped in their tracks and for the second time that day, stared at Paddington in amazement.

"You've never had any hot chestnuts?" repeated Mr Brown.

Paddington shook his head. "Never," he said firmly.

"Well, we can soon alter that," said Mr Brown, leading the way towards a coke brazier at the side of the road. "Seven large bags, please," he announced to the man who was serving.

"What a good thing I brought my camera," exclaimed Mr Gruber. "Two firsts in one evening," he continued, as he set up his tripod. "The decorations and now this. I shall have to make some extra copies for your Aunt Lucy in Peru, Mr Brown. I expect she'll find them most interesting."

Paddington thanked his friend happily through a mouthful of hot chestnuts. In the distance he could still see some decorations in the busy shopping part of London, while in front, the biggest tree he'd ever seen in his life rose up into the night, supporting a myriad of brightly coloured fairy lights, and from somewhere nearby the sound of a Christmas carol filled the air. All in all, he thought it had been a lovely evening out and it was nice, not only to think that Christmas Day itself was still to come, but to round things off in such a tasty manner.

"Are you having trouble with your exposures, Mr Gruber?" he asked hopefully, as he came to the end of his chestnuts.

Mr Gruber looked up in some surprise. "I only wondered," said Paddington hastily, eyeing the brazier before his friend had time to reply, "because if you are I thought perhaps you'd like me to have another bag just to make sure!"

"There's one thing about bears," said Mrs Bird, joining in the laughter which followed Paddington's last remark. "They certainly don't believe in taking any chances!"

Mr Brown reached into his pocket. "And for once," he said, amid general agreement, "I'm entirely on their side. Seven more bags, please!"

Paddington
Takes the Air

CONTENTS

Chapter One

A VISIT TO THE DENTIST

PADDINGTON STARED AT Mrs Brown as if he could hardly believe his ears. "You've dropped my tooth down the waste disposal!" he exclaimed. "I shan't even be able to put it under my pillow now!"

Mrs Brown peered helplessly into the gaping hole at the bottom of her kitchen sink. "I'm awfully sorry, dear," she replied. "It must have been in the leavings when I cleared up after breakfast. I think you'll have to leave a note explaining what happened."

It was a tradition in the Browns' household that anyone who lost a tooth and left it under their pillow that night would find it replaced by fifty pence the next morning, and Paddington looked most upset at being deprived of this experience.

"Perhaps we could try looking under the cover outside," suggested Judy hopefully. "It might still be in the drain."

"I shouldn't think so," said Jonathan. "Those waste disposals are jolly good. They grind up anything. It even managed that everlasting toffee Paddington gave me yesterday.

"It was a super one," he added hastily, as he caught Paddington's eye. "I wish I could make one half as nice. It was a bit big, though. I couldn't quite finish it."

"Well," said Mr Brown, returning to the vexed question of Paddington's tooth, "at least it didn't jam the machine. We've only had it a fortnight."

But if Mr Brown was trying to strike a cheerful note, he failed miserably, for Paddington gave him a very hard stare indeed.

"I've had my tooth ever since I was born," he said. "And it was my best one. I don't know what Aunt Lucy's going to say when I write and tell her."

And with that parting shot, he hurried out of the kitchen and disappeared upstairs in the direction of his room leaving behind a very unhappy group of Browns indeed.

"I don't see how anyone can have a *best* tooth," said Mr Brown, as he made ready to leave for the office.

"Well," said Mrs Bird, their housekeeper, "best or not, I must say I don't blame that bear. I don't think I'd be too happy at the thought of one of my teeth going down a waste disposal – even if it was an accident."

"It would have to be Paddington's," said Judy. "You know how he hates losing anything. Especially when it's something he's cleaned twice a day."

"We shall never hear the last of it," agreed Mrs Brown. She looked round the kitchen at the remains of the breakfast things. "I do hate Mondays. I don't know why, but there always seems to be more dried egg on the plates than any other day."

The others fell silent. It was one of those mornings at number thirty-two Windsor Gardens. Things had started badly when Paddington announced that he'd found a bone in his boiled egg, but remembering a similar occurrence some years before with a Christmas pudding, the Browns had pooh-poohed the idea at first and it wasn't until a little later on, when he'd gone upstairs to do his Monday morning accounts that the trouble had really begun.

A sudden cry of alarm had brought the rest of the family racing to the scene only to find Paddington on his bed with a pencil stuck between a large gap where one of his back teeth should have been.

Immediately the whole house had been in an uproar. The bed was stripped, carpets were turned back, the vacuum cleaner emptied, pockets turned out; Paddington even tried standing on his head in case he'd swallowed the lost half by mistake, but all to no avail... it was nowhere to be seen.

It wasn't until Mrs Bird remembered the episode with the boiled egg that they suddenly put two and two together and went scurrying back downstairs again as fast as their legs would carry them.

But they were too late. Before they were halfway down, they heard a loud grinding noise coming from the kitchen and they arrived there just in time to see Mrs Brown switch the machine off.

The waste disposal was still a new toy in the household. Everything from used matchsticks to old bones was fed into its ever-open mouth, but never in her wildest moments would Mrs Brown have dreamed of disposing of one of Paddington's teeth and she was as upset as anyone when she realised what had happened.

"I can't see them taking him on the National Health," she said. "Perhaps he'd better go to the vet."

"Certainly not," said Mrs Bird decidedly. "He'll have to go as a private patient. I'll ring Mr Leach straight away."

Although the Browns' housekeeper kept a firm hand on Paddington's 'goings-on', she was always quick to come to his aid in time of trouble and she bustled out of the room in a very determined manner.

All the same, the others awaited her return with

some anxiety, for although Mr Leach had looked after the family's teeth for more years than they cared to remember, he'd never actually been asked to deal with one of Paddington's before. They weren't at all sure how he would view the matter and their spirits rose when Mrs Bird reappeared wearing her coat and hat.

"Mr Leach will see him as soon as we can get there," she announced. "He keeps a free period for emergencies."

Mrs Brown heaved a sigh of relief. "How nice," she said. "It's not as if we've ever registered Paddington with him."

"Who said anything about Paddington?" replied Mrs Bird innocently. "I simply said we have an emergency in the house." She glanced up at the ceiling as a loud groan came from somewhere overhead. "And if you ask me, there's no one who'll deny the truth of that! I'd better order a taxi."

While Mrs Bird got busy on the phone again, the others hurried upstairs to see how Paddington was getting on. They found him sitting on the side of his bed wearing a very woebegone expression on his face indeed. Or rather, the little of his face that could be seen, for most of it was concealed behind a large bath towel. Every so often a low groan issued from somewhere deep inside the folds, and if the news of his forthcoming visit to the dentist did little to raise his spirits, they received a further setback a few minutes later when he was ushered into the back of a waiting taxi.

"'Aving trouble with yer choppers, mate?" asked the driver, catching sight of the towel.

"My *choppers*?" exclaimed Paddington.

"I only 'ope he's not a strong union man,"

continued the driver as they moved away. "One out – the lot out!"

Mrs Brown hastily closed the window between the two compartments. "Don't take any notice, dear," she said. "I'm sure you're doing the right thing. Mr Leach is very good. He's been practising for years."

"Mr Leach has been *practising*?" repeated Paddington with growing alarm. "I think I'd sooner pay extra and have someone who knows what he's doing."

The Browns exchanged glances. It was sometimes very difficult explaining things to Paddington – especially when he had his mind firmly fixed on something else – and they completed the rest of the journey in silence.

However, if Paddington himself was beginning to have mixed feelings on the subject of his tooth, Mr Leach had no such problems when they reached the surgery a short while later.

"I'm afraid I shall have to charge extra," he said, as the situation was explained to him. "Bears have forty-two teeth."

"I've only got forty-one," said Paddington. "One of mine's been disposed of."

"That's still nine more than I normally deal with," said Mr Leach firmly, ushering Paddington into his surgery. "None of my charts cover it for a start. I shall have to get my nurse to draw up a completely new one."

"I do hope we *are* doing the right thing," said Mrs Brown anxiously, as the door closed behind them. "I feel it's all my fault."

Mrs Bird gave a snort. "More likely that bear's everlasting toffees," she said grimly. "They're well named. It's almost impossible to get rid of them. It's no wonder he's lost a tooth. He was testing them all day yesterday. I had to throw the saucepan away and there were toffees all over the kitchen floor. I nearly ricked my ankle twice."

Paddington's home-made toffees were a sore subject in the Brown household. It wasn't so much that they had set hard. In fact, had they done so there might have been fewer complaints, but they'd ended up as a pile of large glutinous balls which stuck to everything they came in contact with, and Mrs Bird spent the next few minutes holding forth on what she would like to do with them.

However, it was noticeable that all the while she was talking, the Browns' housekeeper kept her gaze firmly fixed on the door leading to the surgery, rather as if she wished she had X-ray eyes.

But as it happened, for once Mrs Bird's worst fears weren't being realised, for Paddington was beginning to have second thoughts about dentists.

Looking around Mr Leach's surgery, he decided it was all very much nicer than he'd expected. Everything was gleaming white and spotlessly clean, with not a marmalade stain to be seen anywhere. And although it wasn't what Mrs Bird would have called 'over- furnished', the one chair Mr Leach did possess more than made up for the fact.

Paddington had never come across anything quite like it before. It was like a long couch which rose into the air and took on all kinds of shapes simply at the press of a button. It seemed very good value indeed and Paddington was most impressed.

Above his head there was a nice warm lamp and just beside his left paw there was a glass of pinkish liquid and a basin, while on the other side, next to Mr Leach, there was a table fixed to an arm on which a number of instruments were laid.

Paddington hastily averted his gaze from these as he settled back in his chair, but he liked anything new, and despite his aching tooth, he dutifully opened his mouth and eyed Mr Leach with interest as the latter picked up a small rod-like object and what looked like a mirror on the end of a stick.

Mr Leach gave several grunts of approval as he peered into Paddington's mouth, tapping the teeth one by one with the end of the rod, and several times he broke into song as he delved deeper and deeper.

"We've got a good one there, bear," he said, standing up at last. "I'm glad you came along."

Paddington sat up looking most relieved. "Thank you very much, Mr Leach," he exclaimed. "That didn't hurt a bit."

Mr Leach looked slightly taken aback. "I haven't done anything yet," he said. "That was only an inspection – just to see what's what. We've a long way to go yet. I'm afraid you have a fractured cusp."

"What!" exclaimed Paddington hotly. "My cusp's fractured!" He peered at the rod in Mr Leach's hand. "It was all right when I came in," he added meaningly. "I think it must have happened when you tapped it."

"A fractured cusp," said Mr Leach stiffly, as he busied himself with a tray of instruments, "merely means you have a broken tooth." He wagged his finger roguishly. "I have a feeling we've been eating something we shouldn't."

Paddington sank back in his chair and looked at the dentist with renewed interest. "Have you been making toffee too, Mr Leach?" he exclaimed.

Mr Leach gave Paddington a strange look. "You have quite a large piece of double tooth missing," he said, slowly and carefully, "and I shall have to make you a new top to replace it."

Looking most upset at this latest piece of news, Paddington reached out a paw for the nearby glass of pink liquid. "I think I'll have my orangeade now, Mr Leach, if you don't mind," he exclaimed.

"That," said Mr Leach sternly, "is *not* orangeade. It's not even for drinking. It's put there so that you can swill your mouth out and get rid of the bits and pieces after I've finished drilling. If I kept every

A Visit to the Dentist

young bear who came in here supplied with free drinks I'd soon be out of business."

He looked distastefully at Paddington's front where the fur had already become rather soggy from the drips and then signalled his nurse to tie a plastic bib round Paddington's neck. "Would we like an injection?" he asked. "It may hurt otherwise."

"Yes, please," said Paddington promptly. "I'll have two if you like."

"I think one will be sufficient," replied Mr Leach, holding a syringe up to the light. "Now, open your mouth wide, please," he continued. "And don't forget, this is going to hurt me more than it hurts you."

Paddington dutifully obeyed Mr Leach's instructions and, in fact, apart from a slight prick, it was much less painful than he had expected.

"Shall I do yours now, Mr Leach?" he asked.

Mr Leach gave him a strange look. "Mine?" he repeated. "I don't have one."

Paddington gave Mr Leach an equally strange look in return. "You said *we* were going to have one," he persisted. "*And* you said yours would hurt more than mine."

Mr Leach stared at Paddington for a moment as if he could hardly believe his ears and then turned to his nurse. "I think," he said, breathing heavily, "we'll try putting a wedge in his mouth. It may make things easier.

"Now," he continued, turning to Paddington as the nurse handed him a piece of plastic-looking material. "I want you to open your mouth again, say 'ah', and when I've put this in, take a good, hard bite."

Paddington opened his mouth and let out a loud "aaaah".

"Good," said Mr Leach approvingly, as he reached into the opening. "Now, one more 'aah' like that and then a good hard bite. And whatever happens from now on – don't let go."

"Aaaaah," said Paddington.

Mr Leach's face seemed to change colour suddenly. "Ooooooooh," he cried.

"Ooooooooooooh," repeated Paddington, biting harder than ever.

"Owwwwwwwwwwwwwww," shouted Mr Leach, as he began dancing up and down.

A Visit to the Dentist

"Owwwwwwww," called Paddington, nearly falling out of the chair in his excitement. "Owwwww-wwwwww!"

"Ouch!" shrieked Mr Leach. "Owwwwwwwwwwww! Oooooooooooooo! Aaaaaaaaaaa!"

Outside in the waiting-room, the Browns looked anxiously at one another. "Poor old Paddington," said Jonathan. "It sounds as if he's going through it."

"I do hope it doesn't take much longer," said Mrs Brown. "I don't know about Paddington, but I'm not sure if I can stand a lot more."

As it happened, Mrs Brown's prayers were answered almost before the words were out of her mouth, for at that moment, the surgery door burst open and a white-faced nurse appeared in the opening.

"Can you come quickly?" she cried.

Mrs Brown clutched at her throat. "Paddington!" she cried. "He's not..."

"No," said the nurse, "he's not! We haven't even started on *him* yet. It's Mr Leach we're having trouble with."

Mrs Bird hurried into the surgery clutching her

umbrella. "Whatever's going on?" she demanded.

"Aaaaaaaaaaaah," replied Paddington.

"Oooooooooooh!" shrieked Mr Leach. "Ooooh! Ouch! Aaaaaaaah!"

"Crikey!" exclaimed Jonathan, as he and Judy dashed towards the chair where Paddington and Mr Leach appeared to be inextricably locked together.

"You grab Mr Leach," cried Judy. "I'll pull Paddington."

A moment later Mr Leach staggered back across the room. "My thumb," he said slowly and distinctly as he glared at the occupant of the chair, "my thumb – or what's left of it – was caught under your wedge, bear!"

Paddington put on his injured expression. "You said bite hard and not let go whatever happened, Mr Leach," he explained.

Mrs Brown gazed anxiously at the dentist as he stood in the middle of the surgery nursing his injury. "Would you like us to come back another day?" she asked doubtfully.

Mr Leach appeared for a moment to be undergoing some kind of deep internal struggle and then he took a grip of himself. "No," he said at last. "No! When I became a dentist I knew there would be days when things wouldn't always go right." He looked at Paddington and then reached for his drill. "I've had twenty most enjoyable years. I suppose it had to come to an end some time and I'm certainly not letting a bear's cusp get the better of me now!"

It was some time before Paddington emerged again from Mr Leach's surgery, and although all had remained quiet, the Browns were relieved to see him looking none the worse for his experience. Instead, as he hurried into the waiting-room holding his mouth open for all to see, he looked positively excited.

"Mr Leach is going to give me a new gold tooth," he announced importantly. "My cusp's so large he doesn't think an ordinary one would stand the strain."

Mr Leach permitted himself a smile as he hovered in the doorway nursing a bandaged thumb. "I think we're winning at long last," he said. "I'd like to see young Mr Brown again next week for a final fitting."

"Thank you very much, Mr Leach," said Paddington gratefully. Bending down he undid his suitcase, withdrew a large paper bag and held it out. "Perhaps you'd like to try one of these?"

Mr Leach hesitated. "I... er... I don't normally indulge," he said, peering into the bag. "It doesn't set a very good example. But I must say they look tempting. It's very kind of you. I... er..."

As he placed one of Paddington's everlasting toffees into his mouth, Mr Leach's voice trailed away and for the second time that morning his face took on a glazed expression.

"Grrrrrr," he gurgled, pointing to his mouth. "Glug!"

Paddington peered at him with interest. "I hope you haven't fractured one of *your* cusps now, Mr Leach," he said anxiously.

Mr Leach glared at him for a moment and then staggered back into his surgery, clutching his jaw. Far from being fractured, his cusps gave the impression they were cemented together for all time, and the look on his face as he slammed the door boded ill for the next patient on his list that morning.

Paddington looked most upset. "I only thought he would like one to be going on with," he exclaimed.

"Going on with is right," said Mrs Bird grimly, as a series of muffled exclamations reached their ears. "By the sound of things it'll be going on until this time next week."

She held out her hand. "I know something else that's due to be disposed of just as soon as we get home. We've had quite enough bear's everlasting toffee for one day."

Judy squeezed Paddington's paw as they climbed into a taxi to take them home. "Never mind," she whispered. "There can't be too many bears who are able to say they're having a gold tooth made for them."

"I'll tell you something else," said Mrs Brown. "It'll make you even more valuable than you are at the moment. While you have a gold tooth in your head you'll never be completely without – whatever happens."

Paddington digested this latest piece of information for a moment or two as he settled back in his seat. So much had happened that morning he felt he'd have a job to remember it all let alone put it down on a postcard when he next wrote to his Aunt Lucy in Peru. But all in all he was beginning to feel rather pleased at the way things had turned out and he felt sure she would be equally delighted by the news.

Mrs Bird glanced across at him with the suspicion of a twinkle in her eye. "If this morning's events are anything to go by," she said, "it strikes me that a tooth in the sink is worth two under the pillow any day of the week."

Paddington nodded his agreement. "I think," he announced at last, amid sighs of relief, "I'll always have my old teeth disposed of in future."

Chapter Two

A STITCH IN TIME

MRS BIRD HELD a large square of chequered cloth up to the light and examined it with an expert eye. "I must say, Paddington's made a first-class job of it," she declared approvingly.

"I've seen worse in some shops," agreed Mrs Brown. "What is it?"

"I think he said it's a tablecloth," replied Mrs Bird.

"But whatever it is, I'm sure it'll come in very handy."

Mrs Brown glanced up at the ceiling as a steady rhythmic clanking came from somewhere overhead. "At least we can leave him on his own for the day without worrying too much," she said thankfully. "We may as well make the most of it. At the rate he's going, that sewing machine won't last much longer."

Mrs Brown was never too happy about leaving Paddington on his own for too long. Things had a habit of going wrong – especially on days when he was at a loose end – but with Jonathan and Judy back at school after the Easter holiday it couldn't always be avoided. It happened to be one of those days and she was most relieved to know he was occupied.

Paddington's interest in sewing had been something of a nine-day wonder in the Brown household. It all came about when he lost his fifty pence a week bun money down a drain one morning as he was on his way to the baker's to pick up his standing order.

The coin had slipped through a hole in one of his duffle coat pockets, and even the combined efforts of several passing dustmen and a road sweeper had failed to locate it.

Although Mr Brown took pity on him and replaced the money, Paddington had been upset for several days afterwards. He still felt he was going to be fifty pence short for the rest of his life and when some men arrived a few days later to swill out the drains, he gave them some very hard stares indeed.

It was Mr Gruber who finally took his mind off the matter. Mr Gruber kept an antique shop in the nearby Portobello Market and over the years he and Paddington had become firm friends. In fact, most mornings they shared some buns and a cup of cocoa for their elevenses.

One morning, shortly after his loss, Paddington arrived at the shop only to find a mysterious cloth-covered object standing on a table just inside the door.

At Mr Gruber's bidding he lifted the cloth, and then nearly fell over backwards with surprise, for there, lo and behold, was a sewing machine. And even more exciting, on the side there was a label – with *his* name on it!

Mr Gruber waved Paddington's thanks to one side. "We don't want another day like 'the one we don't talk about' in a hurry, Mr Brown," he said, referring to 'bunless' Friday as they'd come to know it.

"I'm afraid it's rather an old one," he continued, as Paddington examined the machine with interest. "It came in a job lot I bought at a sale many years ago and it's been lying under a chair at the back of my shop ever since. But there's a book of instructions and it may do a turn if you want to go over some of your old seams."

Paddington didn't know what to say. Although Mrs Bird had unpicked the join on his duffle coat pocket and inserted a double-strength calico lining to make doubly sure for the future, he didn't want to take any more chances and after thanking Mr Gruber very much, he hurried home with the present safely tucked away in his shopping basket on wheels.

Paddington had often watched Mrs Bird in action with her machine, and once she'd even let him turn the handle, but never in his wildest dreams had he pictured actually owning one himself.

Threading the needle by paw had been his biggest problem and the first time it had taken him the best part of a day, but once the cotton was safely through the eye of the needle there was no holding him and soon the steady clickety-clack of the machine had begun to echo round the house.

At first he'd contented himself with joining together some old bits of cloth Mrs Bird had found  in her sewing box, but when these ran out he turned his attention to more ambitious things and really and truly he'd been most useful. A new tea towel for Mrs Bird; a set of curtains for Judy's doll's house; a bag for Jonathan's cricket bat, and a smaller one for Mr Brown's pipe; now the tablecloth – there seemed no end to his activities.

"Just so long as he doesn't do anything nasty to his new eiderdown," said Mrs Bird, as they went upstairs to give Paddington his instructions for lunch.

"I don't want to come back and find it turned into a tea cosy."

Although the Browns' housekeeper was as pleased as anyone over Paddington's new-found industry, she didn't entirely share Mrs Brown's optimism about leaving him alone for the day.

Nevertheless, even Mrs Bird gave a nod of approval as they entered his room and she caught sight of a pile of old handkerchiefs he was busy repairing.

"That reminds me," said Mrs Brown as they said goodbye, "the laundry man is due this morning. I've put the things by the front door. Mr Curry might call in later – he's got a pair of trousers he wants altered."

Mrs Bird gave a snort. "I shouldn't worry too much about that," she said meaningly. "It's only because there's a special offer of one pound off this week if repairs go with the laundry. If he's so mean he can't send any washing of his own then it's too bad."

There was little love lost between Mrs Bird and the Browns' next-door neighbour. Mr Curry had a reputation not only for his meanness but for the way he seized every opportunity to take advantage of others, and the latest example lasted Mrs Bird as a topic of conversation all the way to the bus stop.

It seemed just a matter of seconds after the front door closed behind them that another loud bang sent Paddington hurrying downstairs only to find Mr Curry waiting impatiently on the front step.

"Good morning, bear," he said gruffly. "I'd like you to put these with your laundry.

"I want two inches off the waist," he continued, handing over a pair of grey flannel trousers, "no more, and certainly no less. The instructions are all on a sheet of paper in one of the pockets. I lost a lot of weight when I was in hospital last year and I've never put it on again. All my clothes are the same."

"Oh dear, Mr Curry," said Paddington. "I'm sorry to hear that."

In saying he was sorry to hear about Mr Curry's loss of weight, Paddington was speaking the truth, for ever since the unfortunate incident on the golf course when he'd stepped on a marmalade sandwich and ended up in hospital, the Browns' neighbour had let no opportunity of mentioning the matter go by.

But to Paddington's relief, for once Mr Curry seemed to have his mind on other things. "I want you to make sure they go in your name," he said. "It's most important. They're doing waistbands for one pound this week and it's the last day of the offer."

A thoughtful expression came over Paddington's face as he took the trousers from Mr Curry. "I know someone who would do it for fifty pence," he said hopefully. "*And* give it back to you today!"

"*Fifty pence?*" repeated Mr Curry. "It seems remarkably cheap. Are you sure they'll do them in a day?"

Paddington nodded. "It isn't a *they*, Mr Curry," he confided. "It's a *he*."

"Is this person completely reliable, bear?" asked Mr Curry suspiciously. "I can hardly believe it."

"Oh yes," said Paddington confidently. "I've known him all my life. He lost his bun money down a drain the other day and now he's trying to make up for it."

Fortunately Paddington's last words were lost on Mr Curry, who seemed to be busy with his own thoughts. He hesitated for a moment and then came to a decision. "Wait there, bear," he said, turning to go. "This is too good an opportunity to miss."

The Browns' neighbour was gone for several minutes and while he was away the man arrived to collect the weekly wash. Paddington hesitated over the trousers. Although the idea of doing them himself had seemed a very good one at the time, now that he'd taken a closer look he was beginning to have second thoughts on the matter, and he was about to chase after the van when he caught sight of Mr Curry glaring at him through his bedroom window and hurriedly changed his mind again.

A few moments later, the Browns' neighbour emerged from his front door and headed back towards number thirty-two. To Paddington's surprise he was wearing a dressing gown and carrying a large brown paper parcel in his arms.

"I've decided to go the whole hog, bear," he announced, as he came up the path. "If this person's as good as you say he is it'll be well worth while."

Paddington's face grew longer and longer as Mr Curry unwrapped his parcel and revealed not one pair of trousers, but a great pile. In fact, outside of a shop, Paddington couldn't remember ever having seen quite so many pairs of trousers before.

"I'm having the whole lot done," explained Mr Curry. "Including," he added ominously, "the ones from my best suit."

"You wouldn't like to keep a pair in case of an emergency would you, Mr Curry?" asked Paddington anxiously.

"An *emergency*?" barked Mr Curry, catching sight of the look on Paddington's face. "I don't like the sound of that, bear! Are you sure this person will do a good job? If not I'd rather send them with your laundry."

"I'm afraid it's too late now, Mr Curry," said Paddington unhappily. "It's gone!"

Mr Curry looked at Paddington sternly. "In that case," he warned, "I shall hold you personally responsible for the safety of my trousers from now on. *And* I shall look forward to their prompt return. I can't go out until they come back, so woe betide you if anything goes wrong.

"I may give you fifty pence for going," he added, as Paddington held out his paw hopefully. "It all depends. But I'm certainly not paying the full amount until I see some results."

With that, the Browns' neighbour turned on his heels and disappeared in the direction of his house leaving Paddington with a very woebegone expression on his face indeed. For some reason which he could never quite fathom, things always got out of hand when Mr Curry was around and he was apt to find himself agreeing to do things before he knew what they actually were.

Heaving a deep sigh Paddington gathered up Mr Curry's parcel and made his way back upstairs in order to consult the instruction book.

Up to now he'd concentrated on the mechanical side of the booklet, which explained the workings of the various parts, but towards the back there were several chapters devoted to what one could do with the needle once it was threaded, and it was to this section that he turned when he'd settled down.

But in the event it proved rather disappointing. As far as he could make out, when the machine was first made, very few people seemed to wear trousers, or if they did they were so well made they were seldom in need of repair. Most of the illustrations dealt with some very odd situations indeed. There was a picture of a lady who'd caught her dress on a penny-farthing cycle and another, called DRAMA IN THE DESERT, which showed a man with a large moustache and shorts repairing what was left of his tent after a camel had trodden on it. But any hints and tips to do with trousers as such were conspicuous only by their absence.

Although Paddington was very keen on instruction books he'd noticed in the past that they had a habit of dealing with every kind of situation except the one he most wanted, and the present one was no exception.

According to the closing paragraph anyone who owned a SEW-RITE sewing machine had unlimited horizons, but Paddington could see only two good things on his particular horizon; the Browns were out and unlikely to return for some while, and Mr Curry was in and unlikely in his present state to venture out.

However, Paddington wasn't the sort of bear to let things get the better of him if he could possibly help it, and picking up a pair of scissors, he poked hopefully at one of Mr Curry's seams.

To his surprise, his efforts were rewarded much sooner than he expected, for without any warning at all the waistband suddenly parted in the middle. In fact, it was even more successful than he'd intended, for when he pulled at the loose thread there was a rending sound and it travelled right down to the turn-ups at the bottom.

Paddington wasn't quite sure whether it was the direct result of pulling that thread or whether he'd pulled another one by mistake, but when he picked the trousers up to examine them more closely one of the legs fell off.

After drawing his bedroom curtains to be on the safe side, Paddington held the remaining leg up to his bedside light and peered at it uneasily. Now that matters had finally come to a head he rather wished he'd sorted through the pile and picked on something other than the trousers from Mr Curry's best navy-blue pinstripe suit to practise on.

On the other hand, when he looked at some of his efforts a little later on he began to wonder if perhaps his first choice hadn't been the best one after all. At least the two halves had come apart cleanly, which was more than could be said for some of the older pairs of trousers.

But it was when he tried sewing some of the halves together again that his troubles really started. It was much more difficult than he had expected. In the past most of the material he'd used had been thin and easy to work, whereas Mr Curry's trousers seemed unusually thick. There were so many folds in his waistbands he soon lost count of them, and the handle of the machine became very hard to turn. In desperation, Paddington tried jamming it in one of his dressing table drawers and turning the machine

itself, but the only result of that was an ominous
'ping' as the needle snapped.

It was all most disappointing. After working
away as hard as he could, with barely a pause for a
marmalade sandwich at lunch, Paddington had to
admit that the results fell somewhat short of even his
own expectations, and he shuddered to think how
far short they would be of Mr Curry's.

As far as he could see, all he could offer the Browns'
neighbour was a choice between a pair
of trousers with thirty-centimetre
hips and pockets on the outside,
one with a large gap in the back,
a pair of grey flannel shorts with
one leg longer than the other,
some trousers with different
coloured legs, or a kind of
do-it-yourself selection from
the pieces that were left over.
Whichever Mr Curry chose,
Paddington couldn't picture him being exactly
overjoyed let alone paying fifty pence a time.

He looked at the pile of material mournfully. For

a wild moment he toyed with the idea of disguising his voice and ringing the Browns' neighbour to try and explain matters to him, but then he remembered Mr Curry wasn't on the phone anyway.

All the same, the thought triggered off another idea in Paddington's mind, and a moment later, after consulting his instruction book again, he hurried downstairs.

In the back of the SEW-RITE booklet was a note headed WHAT TO DO IF ALL ELSE FAILS! and this was followed by an address to write to in case of an emergency.

Paddington hoped very much that they'd had enough emergencies over the years to keep their service going *and* to have a telephone installed into the bargain, though he doubted very much if they could ever have had one quite as bad as his present one.

The man from the SEW-RITE emergency service stared round Paddington's room in amazement. "You're in a bit of a mess, and no mistake," he said sympathetically. "What on earth's been going on?"

"I'm afraid I've been having trouble with Mr Curry's seams," said Paddington. "I've got rather a lot of his legs left over."

"I can see that," said the man, picking up a handful. "This sort of thing isn't really our pigeon," he continued doubtfully, "but I suppose I might be able to pull a few strings for you."

"I've tried pulling some threads," said Paddington, "but it only seemed to make things worse."

The man gave Paddington an odd look and then, glancing round the room again, he gave a sudden start. "Is that yours?" he asked, pointing to the machine on the floor.

"Well, yes," began Paddington. "Mr Gruber gave it to me. I'm afraid it's rather an old one so you may not like it very much."

"Not like it?" cried the man, dashing to the door. "*Not like it?* Jim!" he shouted. "Jim! There's a young bear up here with one of our Mark Ones!"

Paddington grew more and more mystified as a pounding of feet on the stairs heralded the approach of a second man. He wasn't at all sure what was going on but he was thankful to see something happening at long last. It had taken him several telephone calls and some long conversations to get the men from SEW-RITE to come in the first place. Even then he hadn't been at all hopeful about the results, but as he listened to their comments his eyes grew rounder and rounder.

"Just you wait till our Mr Bridges hears about this," exclaimed the first man, as they made to leave. "He'll go berserk. You'll never hear the like again."

"I expect I shall," said Paddington unhappily. "You wait until Mr Curry hears about his trousers!"

Although the long-term prospects had begun to look much better than he'd dared expect, Paddington didn't view the immediate future at all hopefully and as things turned out, his forecast proved all too correct. The roar of rage which issued from Mr Curry's house a short while later when the men from SEW-RITE broke the news about his trousers followed him all the way down Windsor Gardens, lasting almost as far as the Portobello Road, and he was very thankful indeed to reach the safety of Mr Gruber's shop.

While Paddington sat on the horsehair sofa mopping his brow, Mr Gruber hastily made some cocoa, and a few minutes later they adjourned to their usual deck chairs on the pavement outside.

Once there, Mr Gruber settled back and listened patiently while Paddington did his best to explain all that had taken place that day.

It was a long story and at the finish Mr Gruber looked as surprised at the outcome as Paddington had done.

"What a bit of luck that old sewing machine I gave you turned out to be so valuable," he said. "I would never have guessed it. It only goes to show that even in this business there's always something to learn."

"The man from SEW-RITE said it's one of their Mark Ones, Mr Gruber," replied Paddington impressively. "He told me it must have been one of the first they ever made. They've been trying to find one like it for years to put in their museum so it's probably worth a lot of money."

"It's a good job they offered to repair Mr Curry's trousers free of charge," chuckled Mr Gruber, pouring out a second cup of cocoa by way of celebration. "We should never have heard the last of it otherwise. It seems to me you struck a very lucky bargain, Mr Brown.

"Just think," he mused, "if you hadn't accidentally dropped your bun money down a drain, all this might never have happened. Big things sometimes have very small beginnings indeed."

Paddington nodded his agreement behind the cocoa steam and then hesitated as he felt in his duffle coat pocket.

Mr Gruber read his thoughts. "I don't think it would be quite the same if you deliberately put some money down a drain, Mr Brown," he said tactfully. "After all, I know lightning seldom strikes twice in the same place, but fate plays funny tricks sometimes."

Paddington considered the matter for a moment. All in all he decided Mr Gruber was quite right and it wasn't worth taking any unnecessary risks. "I don't think I should like to see even Mr Curry's trousers struck by lightning," he announced. "Especially while they're still at the menders!"

Chapter Three

RIDING HIGH

PADDINGTON REINED IN his horse and stared at the judge's rostrum as if he could hardly believe his ears.

"I've got four hundred and fifty-two faults?" he exclaimed hotly. "But I've only been round once!"

"There are twelve fences," said Guy Cheeseman, measuring his words with care, "and you went straight through all of them – that's forty-eight for a start. Plus another four for going back over the last one.

"*And*," he added, bringing the subject firmly to a close as he glared down at the battered remains of what had once been a hat, "your horse trampled all over my best bowler – the one I intended wearing at the presentation this afternoon – that's another four hundred!"

Mr Cheeseman wasn't in the best of moods. In fact, the look on his face as he made an entry alongside Paddington's signature on the clipboard he was carrying was what Mrs Bird would have called "a study". He gave the distinct impression that he wished he'd never heard of St Christopher's School and its teachers and parents in general, not to mention Paddington in particular.

The occasion was the end of term celebrations at Judy's school and instead of the usual speech-making, Miss Grimshaw, the headmistress, had decided to hold a gymkhana in aid of a new swimming pool.

There were a number of events on the programme, and the two main items at the beginning and end were open to all and sundry – including the parents, relations and friends of the pupils.

The competitors were given 'sponsor sheets' and each had to collect as many signatures as possible from people who were prepared to pay a small sum for every successful jump.

The Browns arrived quite early in the day and Paddington – who had decided to enter for both the events – had been kept very busy hurrying round the grounds collecting names for his sheet.

He was already a familiar figure at Judy's school and almost the entire upper and lower fourth, fifth and sixth forms had persuaded their nearest and dearest to sponsor him at anything between fifty pence and one pound a jump. In view of the number of signatures Paddington had managed to collect, the swimming pool fund stood to benefit by a tidy amount.

Guy Cheeseman, the famous Olympic rider, had very

kindly agreed to judge the contests and act as commentator, and with the sun shining down from a cloudless sky, the sound of horses' hooves pounding the turf, the murmur of the large crowd which had gathered round the sports field, and the creaking of innumerable picnic baskets, it promised to be a memorable occasion.

The roar of excitement as Paddington mounted his horse was equalled only by the groan of disappointment which went up as he disappeared from view over the other side. And when he eventually reappeared facing the wrong way an ominous silence fell over the field; a silence broken only by the crash of falling fences and a cry of rage from Mr Cheeseman as he watched his best hat being ground to pulp.

Paddington was more upset than anyone, for although he'd never actually been on a horse before, let alone a jumping one, Mr Gruber had lent him several very good books on the subject and he'd spent the last few evenings sitting astride a pouffe in the Browns' sitting room practising with a home-made whip and some stirrups made from a pair of Jonathan's old handcuffs.

It was all most disappointing. In fact, he rather wished now he'd chosen something else to practise on. To start with, the horse was very much taller and harder than he'd expected – more iron and steel than flesh and blood – and whereas by gripping the pouffe between his knees he'd been able to hop around the house at quite a speed it was nothing compared with Black Beauty once she got going. That apart – aside from when he'd unexpectedly bumped into Mrs Bird in the hall – he'd never attempted any kind of jumps on the pouffe, and no matter what he shouted to Black Beauty she seemed to have it firmly fixed in her mind that the shortest distance between two points was a straight line, regardless of what happened to be in the way.

According to Mr Gruber's book, one of the first requirements in horse riding was complete confidence between rider and mount, and Paddington would have been the first to admit that as far as he was concerned he was a nonstarter in this respect. He completed the round clinging helplessly to Black Beauty's tail with his eyes tightly closed, and the trail of damage they left behind made the hockey pitch at St Christopher's resemble the fields of Belgium immediately after the battle of Waterloo.

"Never mind, Paddington," said Judy, grabbing hold of the reins. "We all thought you did jolly well. Especially as it was your first time out," she added, amid a chorus of sympathetic agreement from the other girls. "Not many people would have dared to try."

"Th... th... thank you v... v... very m... m... much," stuttered Paddington. He was still feeling as if he'd been for a ride on a particularly powerful pneumatic drill and he gave Mr Cheeseman a very hard stare indeed as he was helped down to the ground.

"It's a shame really," said Mrs Brown, as they watched his progress back to the horse enclosure. "It would have made such a nice start to the day if he'd had a clear round."

"Perhaps he'll do better in the 'Chase me Charley'," said Jonathan hopefully. "He's down for that as well at the end."

"Four hundred and fifty-two faults indeed!" snorted Mrs Bird, as the commentator's voice boomed through the loudspeakers.

"It's a good job *he* didn't tread on *Paddington's* hat. He'd have lost a good deal more than that!"

Giving a final glare in the direction of the judge's rostrum, the Browns' housekeeper began busying herself with the picnic basket in a way which boded ill for Mr Cheeseman's chances of a snack if he found he'd left his own sandwiches at home.

"That's a good idea," said Jonathan enthusiastically. "I'm so hungry I could eat a horse."

"Pity you didn't eat Paddington's," said Mr Brown gloomily. "Especially after that last round."

"Ssh, Henry," whispered Mrs Brown. "Here he comes. We don't want to upset him any more."

Mr Brown hastily turned his attention to the important matter of lunch and as the fences were put back and the next event got under way he began setting up a table and chairs in the shade of a nearby oak tree. Mr Brown didn't believe in doing things by halves, especially where picnics were concerned, and he shared the French habit of turning such affairs into a full-scale family occasion.

Mrs Bird had packed an enormous hamper of jars and plastic containers brimful with sliced tomatoes, cucumber, beetroot, ham, beef, liver sausage, and seemingly endless supplies of mixed salads. What with these and strawberries and cream to follow, not to mention two sorts of ice cream, lemonade, tea, coffee, various cakes and sweetmeats, and a jar of Paddington's favourite marmalade into the bargain, the table was soon groaning under the weight.

Even Mr Brown, who wasn't normally too keen on equestrian events, had to admit that he couldn't think of a more pleasant way of spending a summer afternoon. And as event followed event and the contents of the hamper grew less and less, the bad start to the day was soon forgotten.

Paddington himself had worked up quite an appetite, though for once he seemed more interested in Mr Gruber's book on riding, which he'd brought with him in case of an emergency, rather than in the actual food itself. Several times he dipped his paw into the bowl of salad dressing in mistake for the marmalade as he studied a particularly interesting chapter on jumping which he hadn't read before, and apart from suddenly rearing up into the air once or twice as he went through the motions, he remained remarkably quiet.

It wasn't until nearly the end of the meal when he absent-mindedly reached into the basket and helped himself to one of Mrs Bird's meringues that he showed any signs of life at all.

"Aren't they delicious?" said Mrs Brown. "I don't think I've ever tasted better."

"Don't you like them, Paddington?" asked Mrs Bird, looking most concerned at the expression on his face.

"Er... yes, Mrs Bird," said Paddington politely. "They're... er... they're very unusual. I think I'll put some marmalade on to take the taste... to er..."

Paddington's voice trailed away. Although not wishing to say so he didn't think much of Mrs Bird's meringue at all and he was glad it was particularly small and dainty. It was really most unusual, for Mrs Bird was an extremely good cook and her cakes normally melted in the mouth, whereas the present one not only showed no signs of melting but was positively stringy.

And it wasn't just the texture. Paddington couldn't make up his mind if it was because he'd followed the ice cream with another helping of Russian salad or whether Mr Brown had accidentally spilled some paraffin over it when he'd filled the picnic stove, but whatever the reason, Mrs Bird's meringue was very odd indeed and not even a liberal splodge of marmalade entirely took the taste away.

However, Paddington was a polite bear and he had no wish to offend anyone, least of all Mrs Bird, so he dutifully carried on. Fortunately he was saved any farther embarrassment by Guy Cheeseman announcing that the final event on the programme was about to take place and asking the competitors to come forward.

Hastily cramming the remains of the meringue into his mouth, Paddington gathered up his book and sponsor sheet and hurried off in the direction of the saddling enclosure closely followed by Judy and several of her friends.

"I know one thing," said Mr Brown, as he disappeared from view into the crowd, "if he manages to get over *one* fence the swimming pool fund won't do too badly. He's got enough signatures now to float a battleship."

For various reasons Paddington's sponsor sheet had grown considerably during the course of the afternoon. Apart from a number of people who'd added their names a second time to show they hadn't lost faith, there was a considerable new element who had signed for quite a different reason – sensing that in backing Paddington they could show willing without too great an expense, and his sheet was now jam-packed with signatures.

"It would serve some of them right if he did do well," said Mrs Bird darkly. "It might teach them a lesson."

Mrs Bird looked as if she'd been about to add

a great deal more but at that moment a burst of applause heralded the first of the long line of competitors.

The 'Chase me Charley' event was one in which all the contestants formed up in a circle, their horses nose-to-tail, and took it in turns to jump a single pole. Only one fault was allowed and each time a round had been completed, those with faults dropped out and the pole was raised another inch until the final winner emerged.

Practically everyone who could ride was taking part and the circle of horses stretched right round the field so that it was some time before Paddington came into view on Black Beauty.

There was a nasty moment when he came past the Browns and tried to raise his hat, which he'd insisted on wearing on top of his compulsory riding one, but he soon righted himself and disappeared from view again, holding the reins with one paw and anxiously consulting Mr Gruber's book which he still held in the other.

"Oh dear," said Mrs Brown nervously. "I do hope he takes care. I didn't like to say so in his presence but it must be terribly difficult with short legs. No wonder his paws keep coming out of the stirrups."

"I shouldn't worry," said Mrs Bird. "There's one thing about bears – they always fall on their feet no matter what happens."

Mrs Bird did her best to sound cheerful but she looked as worried as anyone as they waited for Paddington to make his first jump. Judy arrived back just in the nick of time and in the excitement only Mrs Bird's sharp eyes noticed that she, too, was now wearing a very odd expression on her face. An expression, moreover, which was almost identical to the one Paddington had worn a little earlier when he'd had trouble with his meringue. But before she had time to look into the matter her attention was drawn back to the field as a great roar went up from the crowd.

The Browns watched in amazement as Paddington and Black Beauty literally sailed over the pole. One moment they'd been trotting gently towards it, then Paddington appeared to lean forward and whisper something in the horse's ear. The very next instant, horse and rider leapt into the air and cleared the hurdle with several feet to spare. Admittedly the pole was at its lowest mark but even so the performance drew a gasp of astonishment from the onlookers.

"Bravo!" cried someone near the Browns. "That bear's done it at last. And not even a sign of a refusal!"

"Heavens above!" exclaimed Mr Brown, twirling his moustache with excitement. "If he carries on like that he'll be up among the leaders in no time. Did you see it? He went higher than anyone!"

Jonathan listened to his sister as she whispered in his ear. "*If* he does it again," he said gloomily.

"Well, even if he doesn't, he's certainly not bottom this time," said Mrs Brown thankfully, as a following rider brought the pole down with a clatter.

And as it happened, Jonathan's worst fears went unrealised, for seeming miracle began to follow miracle as Paddington and Black Beauty made one effortless clear round after another and one by one the other competitors began to drop out.

Each time they drew near to the jump, Paddington leaned over and appeared to whisper something in

Black Beauty's ear and each time it had a magical effect as she bounded into action and with a whinny which echoed round the cloisters, cleared the hurdle with feet to spare.

Paddington was so excited he discarded Mr Gruber's book in order to raise his hat in acknowledgement of the cheers, and even those who'd signed his sheet rather late in the day, although they'd worn long faces at first, began applauding with the rest.

And when it came to the final round, with Paddington pitted against Diana Ridgeway, the head girl, the excitement was intense. Even with loyalties so divided, the cheer which rang out as Paddington emerged the victor practically shook the school to its foundations, and Diana Ridgeway herself set the seal on the occasion by dismounting and running over to offer her congratulations.

Guy Cheeseman so far forgot the unpleasantness earlier in the day that phrases like 'superb horsemanship', 'splendid display' and 'supreme example of rider and mount being as one', floated round the grounds with scarcely a pause for breath.

For some reason or other Diana Ridgeway appeared

to have second thoughts as Paddington leaned down to speak to her, but with an obvious effort she overcame them and in the general excitement the moment passed practically unnoticed.

"What an incredible business!" exclaimed Mr Brown, mopping his brow as he settled down again. "I wonder what on earth Paddington kept whispering to Black Beauty? It must have been something pretty good to make her want to jump like that."

Jonathan and Judy exchanged glances, then Judy took a deep breath. "I'm not sure he *whispered* anything," she began, only to break off again as she suddenly caught sight of Paddington and the headmistress about to converge a short distance away.

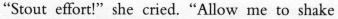

"Crikey! That's torn it," said Jonathan, as Miss Grimshaw began pumping Paddington's paw up and down.

"Stout effort!" she cried. "Allow me to shake

you by the paw. You've given our swimming pool a tremendous fillip."

Paddington began to look more and more surprised as he listened to the headmistress. He had no idea they'd dug the hole even, let alone filled it up. "I hope I haven't filled it too full, Miss Grimshaw," he exclaimed politely.

Miss Grimshaw's smile seemed to become strangely fixed, then she paused and gave a sniff. "I really must get Birchwood to look at the drains," she said, eyeing Paddington even more doubtfully. "I... er... I hope we shall meet again at the presentation."

"Crumbs!" said Judy, as the headmistress hurried on her way. "The presentation! We'd better do something before then."

Dashing over to Paddington she grabbed hold of his paw and then turned to her brother. "Come on, Jonathan," she called. "We'll take him to see Matron. She's just over there in the First Aid tent. She may be able to give him something."

"Matron?" echoed Mrs Brown, as Judy began whispering in Paddington's ear. "What on earth are they on about?"

"It's all right, Mrs Brown," cried Paddington. "It's nothing serious. I'm afraid I'm having trouble with one of Mrs Bird's meringues."

"Trouble with one of my *meringues*?" Mrs Bird began to look thoughtful as Judy and Jonathan whisked Paddington away. "How many did the children have?" she asked, rummaging in her picnic basket.

"Three each, I think," replied Mrs Brown. "I remember them talking about it. Jonathan wanted another but there weren't any left. I had two – the same as you." She turned to her husband. "How many did you have, Henry?"

"Er... four," said Mr Brown. "They were a bit moreish."

"That makes fourteen altogether," said Mrs Bird, as she began emptying the contents of the picnic basket. "And that's all I made," she added ominously. "So whatever that bear ate it certainly wasn't a meringue!"

Mr Brown wound down the window of his car to its fullest extent and then glanced across at Paddington. "How anyone could mistake a head of garlic for a meringue I just don't know," he said.

"Especially one of Mrs Bird's," said Judy. "Matron couldn't believe her ears."

"Or her nose!" added Jonathan.

Paddington looked at them sheepishly. "I'm afraid I was busy reading about my cavalletti's," he explained. "That's to do with jumping. I didn't notice I'd made a mistake until it was too late."

"But a whole head," said Mrs Brown from behind her handkerchief. "I mean... a clove would have been bad enough but a *whole head*!"

"No wonder Black Beauty was jumping so well," said Judy. "Every time you leaned over her she must have got the full force."

"It's a wonder she didn't go into orbit," agreed Jonathan.

The Browns were making all possible speed in the direction of Windsor Gardens, but even with all the windows open there was a decided 'air' about the car.

Paddington had been standing on the front seat with his head poking out of the sunroof for most of the way, and every time they stopped they got some very funny looks indeed from any passer-by who happened to be down wind.

"I'll say one thing," remarked Mr Brown, as they drew to a halt alongside a policeman who hastily waved them on again, "it soon clears the traffic. I don't think we've ever made better time."

"Perhaps I could eat some garlic when we go out again, Mr Brown?" said Paddington, anxious to make amends.

Mr Brown gave a shudder. "No, thank you," he said. "Once is quite enough."

"Anyway," broke in Judy, "all's well that ends well. There were over two hundred signatures on Paddington's sheet and Miss Grimshaw reckons it must be worth at least as many pounds to the fund."

"Mr Cheeseman said he'd never seen anything like it before," said Jonathan.

"Nor will he again if I have anything to do with it," said Mrs Bird grimly. "That's the last time I make any meringues."

In the chorus of dismay which greeted this last remark, Paddington's voice was loudest of all.

"Perhaps you could make them extra large, Mrs Bird," he said hopefully. "Then they won't get mistaken."

The Browns' housekeeper remained silent for a moment. All in all, despite everything, it had been a most enjoyable day and she was the last person to want to spoil it. "Perhaps you're right," she said, relenting at last. "But you must promise not to go riding on the pouffe when we get home."

Paddington didn't take long to make up his mind. Although he was much too polite to say so, the events of the day were beginning to catch up on him and sitting down, even on the softest of pouffes, was the last thing he had in mind.

"I think," he announced, amid general laughter as he clambered up on the seat again, "I shall go to sleep standing up tonight!"

Chapter Four

PADDINGTON STRIKES A BARGAIN

NEXT MORNING MR Gruber had a good laugh when he heard about Paddington's exploits at the gymkhana.

"It's strange that you should have spent your day riding a horse, Mr Brown," he said. "I spent most of mine tinkering with what's known as a *horseless* carriage."

Leading the way across the patio at the back of his shop towards a nearby mews stable which he normally reserved for emergency supplies of antiques during the busy tourist season, Mr Gruber threw open the wide double doors and then stood back and waited patiently while Paddington accustomed his eyes to the gloom.

"It's what's known as an 'old crock', Mr Brown," he said impressively.

"Is it really?" said Paddington politely.

Although he didn't like to say so, the object of Mr Gruber's fond gaze seemed very aptly named. From the little he could make out it looked for all the world like a very old boiler on wheels to which an enormously tall pushchair had been added as a kind of afterthought.

Mr Gruber chuckled as he caught sight of the expression on Paddington's face. "I thought it might puzzle you, Mr Brown," he said. "I don't suppose you've ever seen anything quite like it before. It's a very early steam-driven motor car. One of the first ever made, in fact. I came across it quite by chance the other week and I've been keeping it as a surprise."

Paddington's eyes grew wider and wider as Mr Gruber went on to explain about early motor cars and how valuable some of them had become over the years, and he listened with growing interest to the story of the first 'horseless carriages'. Knowing how crowded the present-day London streets were it was difficult to picture the scene as Mr Gruber described it, and he was most surprised to learn that cars used to have someone walking in front of them carrying a red flag.

Mr Gruber, who was obviously very proud of his stroke of good fortune, turned to his new machine and gave it a fond pat. "I doubt if there's another one quite like it in the whole of England, Mr Brown," he said impressively. "I'm afraid it's in a bit of a state at the moment because it's spent most of its life in a hay barn, but if you can spare the time I did wonder if we could do it up between us."

For once in his life, Paddington was at a loss for words. Although Mr Brown sometimes let him clean the family car, and on very rare occasions gave him a spanner to hold, he'd never before been asked to actually help in doing one up. "Oooh, yes please, Mr Gruber!" he exclaimed at last.

But Mr Gruber had kept his most exciting piece of news until last.

"There's a big Festival taking place in the Portobello Road in September," he continued, closing the stable door as he led the way back to his shop. "It's called INTERNATIONAL WEEK and it's for the benefit of all the overseas visitors. On the last day there's even going to be a Fair and a Grand Parade through the market."

As they settled down again Mr Gruber looked at Paddington thoughtfully over the top of his glasses. "If we manage to get the car finished in time," he said casually, "I did wonder if we could enter it."

Paddington stared at his friend in amazement. Over the years Mr Gruber had sprung a good many surprises but this one surpassed all his previous efforts, and shortly afterwards, bidding him goodbye, he hurried back in the direction of Windsor Gardens in order to tell the others.

Paddington's news met with a mixed reception in the Brown household. Jonathan and Judy were most impressed at the thought of knowing anyone who actually owned an 'old crock', and when Paddington announced that Mr Gruber had promised to reserve them two seats in the car if it was ready in time for the Grand Parade, their excitement knew no bounds. But Mrs Bird, with thoughts of oily paws on her best towels, looked less enthusiastic about the whole idea.

Nevertheless, it was noticeable during the next few weeks that as Paddington began to arrive home with descriptions of the work in progress even the Browns' housekeeper began to take an interest in the matter, and on several occasions she was seen hovering at the end of the mews when she was out doing the morning shopping.

What with dismantling the engine and rebuilding it, rubbing down the coachwork ready for repainting and varnishing, polishing the boiler and refurbishing the leather seats, time flew by at an alarming rate and the gap between Mr Gruber's first announcement and the day of the actual Parade rapidly narrowed.

Towards the end practically everyone became involved in one way or another, and most nights found Paddington spreading newspapers on his bedroom floor so that he could catch up on polishing some of the many smaller bits and pieces before he went to bed.

During all this time a great change came over the market itself. Shop windows that had remained untouched for years suddenly took on a new lease of life, and some of the more recent establishments dealing in old army uniforms and other colourful relics of a bygone era began to look very festive indeed. Flags and bunting blossomed from bedroom windows and coloured lights appeared across the narrow street, so that altogether it was not unlike the transformation scene in a Christmas pantomime.

One evening Paddington arrived home later than usual and his news that Mr Gruber's 'old crock' was ready at long last gave rise to great excitement in the Brown household.

"I know one thing," said Mrs Bird, when the clamour had died down, "if you're going to be in the Grand Parade tomorrow you'd better have a good bath and get rid of all that oil and grease. You'll never win a prize otherwise."

"You can use some of Mr Brown's bubble-mixture as a treat if you like," said Mrs Brown, ignoring the dark glances from her husband.

Paddington, who wasn't normally too keen on baths, brightened considerably at the news.

He'd had his eye on Mr Brown's jar of bubble-mixture for some time. According to the label on the side even a single cupful of the secret ingredients produced undreamed of magical results, and although Mr Brown himself had managed to get through almost half the bottle with little outward sign of change, Paddington felt sure it was worth a go, particularly if it helped Mr Gruber win a prize.

Carefully making sure no one was around he added several extra helpings to his bath water that night in order to make sure the effect lasted until the following day.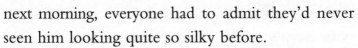

When he arrived down for breakfast next morning, everyone had to admit they'd never seen him looking quite so silky before.

"It almost seems a pity to cover it up," said Mrs Brown as she helped him on with his duffle coat. "If it was a shiny fur competition you'd be bound to win first prize."

The Browns weren't the only ones to be impressed by Paddington's appearance and as Mr Gruber's 'old crock' steamed into position a little later on, its polished paint and brasswork gleaming in the morning sun, quite a few of the early morning spectators gave him a special round of applause.

A large area of waste ground near the Portobello Road had been set aside for the festivities and already it was a scene of great activity. The centre of the area had been roped off for some games that were to start the proceedings, while almost the whole of one side was occupied by a travelling Fair, and as the various floats and vehicles arrived to take up their position for the Grand Parade the picture grew livelier with every passing moment.

Mr Gruber gave a tactful cough as they dismounted. "Why don't you have a look round, Mr Brown?" he said. "I have to take one of the front wheels off to make some last-minute adjustments, but I shall be quite all right on my own."

Paddington hesitated for a moment, torn between helping his friend and investigating some of the other exciting things that were going on around him, but Mr Gruber clinched the matter by helping him off with his coat. "I should make the most of it, Mr Brown," he said. "You're only young once."

Paddington needed no second bidding and a few moments later he joined the crowds already thronging the area.

Hoping to find out about Mr Gruber's chances of winning a prize he tried visiting a fortune-teller first. But the lady inside the tent seemed to spend most of the time blowing her nose violently into a large coloured handkerchief and when he inquired about his own future, all she forecast was that he would probably get a nasty cold, so he decided to turn his attention to the important matter of the games which were about to get under way. A number of the local shops had presented prizes for the various events and Paddington consulted his programme with interest. Although he couldn't quite picture himself shining in the high jump – or even the long one come to that – there were several other items which interested him, including one called TOSSING THE CABER. The prize for this particular event was a free supply of buns for a month at his local baker's.

It seemed very good value indeed and although

Paddington wasn't at all sure what a caber was he felt quite certain he could toss one given half a chance.

Going up to a man wearing a kilt, he tapped him importantly on the shoulder. "Excuse me," he said politely, "I'd like to toss your caber if I may."

The man in charge looked Paddington up and down. "I hope ye ken what you're takin' on," he said dolefully. "It's no' for the like o' young Sassenach bears."

"Sassenach bears?" repeated Paddington, giving the man a hard stare. "I'm not a Sassenach bear. I'm from Darkest Peru. Besides, Mrs Bird often lets me have a go with her pancakes."

"*Pancakes?*" The man stared at Paddington as if he could hardly believe his ears. "Och, weel," he said at last. "Be it on your own head.

"So long as it's no' on mine," he added. "Put your paws together, bend your knees, close your eyes, and take it steady. We're no' wanting to start the day with a young bear's rupture."

Looking more and more surprised, Paddington did as he was bidden. For a while all he could hear was a lot of grunting and groaning and he was about to stand up again when what seemed like a tonne weight suddenly landed on his paws.

Opening his eyes in order to see what was going on, he nearly fell over backwards in astonishment. Or rather, he would have fallen over if his paws hadn't been pinned to the ground by what appeared to be an enormous telegraph pole.

But if the whole thing looked frightening at first sight, it was nothing compared to the situation a few seconds later when he heaved the pole in the air in order to try and free himself.

For a brief moment, all was well and a ripple of applause ran round the assembly, but almost at once things started to go wrong.

Hearing the cries of alarm as the pole began to fall, Paddington hurried after it as fast as he could, only to feel it start to topple in the opposite direction.

The man in charge jumped back. "Och aye!" he shouted. "Take it away. It's all yours!"

"I don't think I want it any more, thank you very much," gasped Paddington, turning to the speaker.

But it was too late. The man had disappeared and instead, words of advice and encouragement began to rain on him from all sides.

"Watch out!"

"Brace yourself!"

"Left paw down a bit!"

There were so many different instructions he couldn't even begin to remember half of them, let alone decide which one to act on first.

He would have liked very much to give the pole away to someone but as fast as he ran with it in one direction, the crowd scattered in the other.

It was all like some terrible nightmare, or rather all the nightmares he had ever known rolled into one, with the pictures flitting back and forth across his vision like some gigantic television screen that had gone wildly out of control.

And then, just as he was beginning to give up all hope of ever being saved, he heard a familiar voice rising above the others.

"Over here, Mr Brown!" shouted Mr Gruber. "Over here!"

Like a drowning man clutching at a straw, Paddington closed his eyes, heaved the pole for all it was worth and then let go.

He wasn't quite sure what happened next. For an

instant everything went black and the whole world seemed to turn upside down, then there was a tremendous thud and a clang followed by silence.

"Oh dear, Mr Brown," said a voice, as a willing pair of hands helped him to his feet. "I'm afraid this is all my fault. If I hadn't called you when I did, it would never have happened."

Paddington opened his eyes and stared round in alarm, but to his relief, Mr Gruber's car still seemed to be in one piece.

"It's a good job the pole hit this wheel and not the car itself," said Mr Gruber, picking up a twisted piece of metal, "otherwise it really would have been an 'old crock'. But I'm very much afraid it's put paid to our chances of entering the Grand Parade," he added ruefully.

Paddington's face grew longer and longer as he took in Mr Gruber's words. "Perhaps we could try running it on *three* wheels?" he suggested hopefully.

Mr Gruber shook his head. "It's been known," he said. "In fact, I do believe there's someone who holds the record for running a car on two wheels, but we would need a very large weight on the back seat to balance things up and I doubt if we'll get one in time. Jonathan and Judy certainly won't be heavy enough and there's only ten minutes to go before the start..."

Mr Gruber broke off, for much to his surprise his words seemed to be having a strange effect.

One moment Paddington was standing in front of him forlornly eyeing the squashed remains of the wheel, the next moment he was galvanised into action rather as if he'd suddenly received an electric shock.

"I shan't be a moment, Mr Gruber," he called. "I've just had an idea!" And before Mr Gruber had time to open his mouth, let alone reply, he'd disappeared into the crowd with a very determined expression on his face indeed.

Despite his friend's assurances on the matter, Paddington still felt most upset about his unfortunate accident. He was anxious to make amends and Mr Gruber's remarks about needing a large weight in a hurry had triggered off an idea in the back of his mind.

The object of Paddington's attention was a large stage which lay towards the back of the Fair. However, it wasn't so much the stage or the ropes surrounding it that had set his mind to work, but a large poster hanging overhead. It was labelled TWO-TONNE 'MUSCLES' GALORE and it showed a view of the largest man he could ever remember seeing.

Paddington didn't know what 'Muscles' Galore did for a living or why he was at the Fair, but if his picture was anything to go by and he sat in the back of Mr Gruber's car there would be absolutely no possibility whatsoever of it ever falling over.

As he climbed through the ropes on to the stage, Paddington was surprised to hear a cheer ring out and he paused for a moment in order to raise his hat at the crowd below before hurrying across to the far corner where a man in leopard-skin tights was sitting.

"Excuse me, Mr Galore," he began, politely holding out his paw. "I was wondering..."

The rest of Paddington's words died before they even reached his lips.

He wasn't quite sure how it happened or why for that matter, but somewhere a bell clanged and he suddenly found himself flying through the air towards the ropes on the far side of the stage almost as if he'd been shot from a cannon. It felt like a ride on a helter-skelter, a moon-rocket, and a dodgem car all rolled into one, and to his alarm, no sooner had he recovered from his first shock than he caught sight of 'Muscles' Galore advancing towards him again with a most unfriendly look in his eye.

"Would you like a second?" whispered a hoarse voice in his ear.

Paddington looked around and found he was being addressed by a man with a towel round his neck. "I didn't even want the first, thank you very much," he said hotly.

"If you want my advice," said the man, "you'll go in there fighting and give him 'what for' while you've got the chance. I should watch it though, he's got a chip on his shoulder."

"Mr Galore's got a chip on his shoulder?" repeated Paddington, licking his lips. Although he didn't think much of his new friend's advice, he found the last piece of information much more to his liking. All the activity that morning had made him feel hungry and he peered hopefully at the advancing figure.

But his interest was short-lived. There wasn't so much as a potato peeling on Mr Galore's shoulders let alone any chips, and as he loomed nearer and nearer, snorting and baring his teeth, it was all too easy to see how he'd earned his name. In fact, he seemed to have muscles on top of his muscles and Paddington didn't like the look of the way some of them were rippling at all.

"Lay in to 'im!" shouted someone in the crowd. "Tear 'im apart!"

Paddington wasn't sure whether the remark was intended for him or Two-Tonne 'Muscles' Galore, but he didn't stop to find out. Pulling his hat firmly down over his head, he slithered past his opponent and hurried round the ring in an effort to find the nearest exit. He was only just in the nick of time for there was a loud 'twang' behind him as 'Muscles' Galore landed against the ropes and bounced off again, landing with a heavy thud on the floor.

The roar which greeted Paddington's narrow escape was equalled only by the growl from Two-Tonne 'Muscles' as his outstretched hands grasped at the empty air.

"First rate," said someone, pushing Paddington back into the ring as he tried to clamber through the ropes. "I don't think I'd want to stay in the ring with a great brute like that just for the sake of a pound a minute."

"Not for fifty pounds," agreed someone else. "I'd like to live to spend it. Still, it's the best so far today. By my reckoning, that young bear's two quid up already."

Paddington stared at the speaker in amazement. Far from wanting to earn a pound for every minute spent in the ring with 'Muscles' Galore, he would willingly have foregone quite a few weeks' bun money in order to stay out.

But before he had time to think too deeply about the matter, he felt a vice-like grip encircle his waist and for a second time in as many minutes, he found himself hurtling through the air.

"'Ere!" called 'Muscles' Galore, as he staggered back against the ropes. "'E's all slippery. He's coated 'isself with something."

"Get on with it!" shouted someone in the crowd.

Two-Tonne 'Muscles' Galore turned and glared at the audience. "I can't fight 'im," he yelled. "It's like trying to wrestle with a pussycat."

"Meeow," called a voice, as the crowd dissolved into laughter. "Meeeow."

"Puss, puss, puss," echoed more voices as they took up the cry.

The chanting of the crowd seemed to act like a red rag to a bull on 'Muscles' Galore and for the next ten minutes Paddington was hard put to keep ahead of him let alone make good his escape from the ring as they tore round and round.

How long it would have gone on was impossible to say, for as fast as Two-Tonne 'Muscles' Galore caught up with Paddington and grabbed hold of him, he slipped from his grasp again, and it was really more a question of who would hold out the longest.

But as it happened, matters were suddenly decided for them in the shape of a stern figure emerging from the crowd brandishing an umbrella.

Ignoring the boos from the rougher element who would willingly have seen the contest go on all day, Mrs Bird climbed into the ring.

"Stop these 'goings-on' at once!" she commanded, glaring at Paddington's opponent. " 'Muscles' Galore indeed! You ought to be ashamed of yourself – chasing a young bear like that!"

"It wasn't really Mr Galore's fault, Mrs Bird," gasped Paddington urgently. "And it wasn't his muscles I was after – it was his tonnes!"

With only seconds to go before the start of the Grand Parade, Paddington wasn't at all sure if he could get Two-Tonne 'Muscles' Galore to the car in time let alone explain why he wanted him.

He gave a deep sigh as he tried to gather his breath. "If you'd like to come and sit on Mr Gruber's back seat, Mr Galore," he announced generously, "I'll give you back my winnings!"

Two-Tonne 'Muscles' Galore needed no second bidding. In fact, he looked quite pleased to leave the ring, and a moment later, with Paddington leading and Mrs Bird bringing up the rear, they were pushing their way through the crowd in the direction of Mr Gruber's car as fast as they could go.

After all the excitement, the events which followed – even the strange sight of Mr Gruber's 'old crock' heading the procession on three wheels, its bonnet adorned by an enormous blue 'winner's' rosette and the back seat by the equally huge figure of Mr Galore – proved something of an anticlimax.

Both Paddington and Mr Gruber were well-known figures in the market and it was a popular result, but long after the Parade was over and the last of the Fair was being packed up ready to leave, the main talking point was Paddington's exploits in the ring.

Even 'Muscles' Galore himself made a special point of shaking him warmly by the paw before he left.

"Such a nice gentleman," said Mrs Bird surprisingly, as she waved goodbye.

"Quite one of the old school," agreed Mr Gruber. "I think he and young Mr Brown were very well matched. With odds-on Mr Brown, of course," he added hastily.

"Fancy staying in the ring with him for *ten* whole minutes though," exclaimed Jonathan admiringly. "I wouldn't have fancied it."

"The man who ran the booth announced it was a record," broke in Judy.

"Mr Galore said I'm what they call a South Paw," explained Paddington. "That's most unusual."

The Browns exchanged glances. There was a peculiar gleam in Paddington's eye and it was noticeable that they were being given an extra wide berth by the other passers-by as they made their way home.

"I must say it's nice to feel in such safe paws," said Mrs Bird, as Paddington aimed a particularly hard stare at a nearby shadow. "Especially late at night."

"What are you going to do when you get home, Paddington?" asked Mr Brown jokingly. "Have half an hour with a medicine ball or do some press-ups?"

Paddington directed his stare in Mr Brown's

direction. "I think," he said, to everyone's astonishment, "I shall have a nice hot bath."

"Good gracious!" exclaimed Mrs Brown. "Wonders will never cease."

But Paddington had other things on his mind. Thinking back over the day's events he'd decided that the thing that had impressed him most of all was the outcome of the previous night's bubble bath. The result of only a few capfuls had surpassed anything forecast on the side of the jar and there was no knowing what might happen if he used the rest in one go.

"My fur's got very dusty, Mr Brown," he announced hopefully, "so I think I shall need plenty of your mixture to put it right!"

Chapter Five

THE CASE OF THE DOUBTFUL DUMMY

MR BROWN LOWERED his evening newspaper and glanced up at the dining-room ceiling as a strange wailing sound, half-human, half-animal, rang out from somewhere overhead.

"What on earth was that?" he asked.

"It's only Paddington," replied Mrs Brown soothingly. "I let him borrow Jonathan's old violin to play with. I expect he's got caught up in the strings again. It's a bit difficult with paws."

"Jonathan's old violin?" repeated Mr Brown. "It sounds more like someone putting a cat through a mangle!" He gave a shiver as another banshee-like note echoed round the house. "Don't tell me he's taking up music now."

"I don't think so, Henry," replied Mrs Brown vaguely. "He said it had something to do with his detective work."

"Oh, Lord!" Mr Brown gave a groan as he settled back in his armchair. "Well, I wish he would hurry up and solve something. Perhaps we shall have a bit of peace and quiet then."

"At least it keeps him out of mischief," said Mrs Brown.

Mrs Bird looked up from her knitting. "It all depends on what you mean by mischief," she said meaningly. "If you ask me, it's more eating than detecting. I caught him looking for clues in my larder this morning."

The Browns' housekeeper tended to view most of Paddington's activities with suspicion and his latest one was no exception. Indeed, when he'd finally emerged from the larder, his face had worn an unusually guilty expression for someone who was supposed to be on the side of law and order.

Paddington's interest in detective work had started several weeks earlier when he'd had to spend some time in bed.

Shortly after the Fair, the fortune-teller's warning had come true and he'd caught a cold. It had been a particularly nasty one; for a while he'd been completely off marmalade sandwiches – always a sure sign that things were not as they should be, and when the worst was over, Mrs Bird had insisted on his staying indoors for a few extra days just to be on the safe side.

With Jonathan and Judy back at school, Mrs Brown had been hard put to keep him amused and in desperation, she'd lent him some of her husband's library books. Mr Brown liked detective stories and in no time at all, Paddington began to share his enthusiasm. Even though he was a slow reader, he managed to get through quite a number and after some discussion with the local librarian, Mrs Brown made arrangements for him to have his own ticket for a trial period.

From that moment on, Paddington visited the library several times a week and he soon became quite a familiar figure in the 'mystery' section.

One of his favourite characters was a private detective called Carlton Dale – partly because his books were on the bottom shelf and easy to get at and partly because there seemed to be a never-ending supply. Mr Dale solved many of his cases from the comfort of his own home and – like Sherlock Holmes before him – he often soothed his nerves with the aid of a violin. In fact, he seemed to spend most of his time sitting up in bed playing selections from *The Desert Song* while baffled officials from Scotland Yard sought his advice on their latest unsolved case.

Unaware of the disturbance he was causing downstairs, Paddington pushed the bow back and forth over his own instrument several times and then gloomily laid it down on his bedside table. He had to admit that the noise was far from soothing, particularly as he hadn't even got a case to work on.

The Case of the Doubtful Dummy

In the books Carlton Dale was never short of cases. If it wasn't the milkman falling down dead on his doorstep, it was someone from the police knocking him up with some urgent problem or other.

Peering out of the front room window early one morning, Paddington came to the conclusion that the Browns' milkman looked unusually healthy, and when he tried ringing up the local police station to see if they had any unsolved crimes they were most unhelpful.

Heaving a deep sigh he turned his attention to a letter he'd just finished writing. It was addressed to Mr Carlton Dale himself and in it Paddington had sought advice on how to look for cases.

According to his books, Carlton Dale lived in a fashionable quarter of London and Paddington felt sure that he must be well known to the Post Office, particularly as he'd once solved *The Case of the Missing Mailbags* for them.

Carefully sealing the envelope, he inscribed Mr Dale's name on the outside, donned his duffle coat and hat, and then made his way downstairs in order to borrow a stamp.

"Oh dear," said Mrs Brown anxiously, when she saw what he was up to. "*Must* it go tonight?" She lifted one of the curtains and peered into the gloom. "It's a thick fog. Not fit for a dog to be out, let alone a bear. I think *you'd* better go, Henry."

"Thank you very much," said Mr Brown from behind his paper. "I've had quite enough fog for one night driving home – without posting bears' letters."

"It's all right, Mrs Brown," broke in Paddington hastily. "I'd rather do it myself, thank you." And before the others had a chance to open their mouths he'd disappeared out of the dining-room.

To be truthful, Paddington didn't really want anyone else to see who he'd been writing to and he was in so much of a hurry to escape, it wasn't until the front door closed behind him that he began to have second thoughts on the matter. For if it had looked murky through the Browns' dining-room window it seemed doubly so now he was outside.

Pulling the duffle coat hood over his hat, he wrapped a handkerchief round his nose in order to keep out the worst of the smog, and after taking a deep breath began edging his way carefully along Windsor Gardens towards the pillarbox at the far end.

Paddington had never been out in a really thick fog before and it wasn't long before he made a strange discovery. The railings which he'd been carefully keeping on his right had suddenly disappeared, and although he must have trodden the same path countless times in the past he hadn't the slightest idea where he was.

Worse still, when he turned round in what he thought was a half circle in order to retrace his steps, he walked headlong into a tree, which certainly hadn't been there on his way out.

Paddington was a brave bear at heart but he began to grow more and more anxious as he groped his way along and not a single familiar landmark came into view.

Even the roads were strangely silent, with only the occasional outline of an abandoned car or other vehicle to show they were there at all, and as time went by with no sign of any passer-by to advise him he had to admit that he was well and truly lost.

He tried calling out "Help!" several times, first fairly quietly and then in a much louder voice, but it had no effect at all. Indeed, for all the good it did he might just as well have saved his breath.

Lowering the handkerchief from his nose, Paddington felt under his hat, removed the marmalade sandwich he always kept there in case of an emergency, and was just about to sit down in order to consider his next move when he gradually became aware of a faint glow somewhere ahead of him.

Like a lighthouse beam to a lost mariner, the glimmer gave him fresh heart and in no time at all he was making all haste in its direction.

The light seemed to be coming from a building with a number of very large windows and as he drew near, Paddington suddenly recognised it as a large department store he'd visited many times in the past. How he'd got there he didn't know, for it lay in quite the opposite direction to the one he'd expected. But having found his bearings at last he felt sure he would be able to get home again simply by following a main road which ran near to Windsor Gardens. Indeed, even as he stood considering the matter, he distinctly caught the welcome sound of slow-moving traffic in the distance.

There was a lady standing in one of the windows, peering out into the gloom, and he was about to tap on the glass and ask where the nearest bus stop was when he suddenly stopped in his tracks, the marmalade sandwich poised halfway to his mouth and all thoughts of returning home momentarily forgotten.

Pulling the handkerchief over his face, Paddington stepped back a pace into the mist and then watched with ever-growing astonishment as a man with a beard crept through a door at the back of the window, and threw a white sheet over the lady. Before she had time to cry out let alone put up any kind of a struggle, he picked her bodily up and then crept out again, closing the door behind him in what could only be described as an extremely furtive manner indeed.

It was all over in a matter of seconds and
Paddington could hardly believe his eyes. It was *The
Case of the Miserable Mummies* all over again, only
more so because he'd actually seen it happen with
his own eyes.

In the book of that name, Carlton Dale had solved
a particularly dastardly crime to do with kidnapping,
in which the unfortunate victims had been hypnotised
and then left in a shop window disguised as dummies
to await collection during the night.

The likeness of the two stories was uncanny, even
down to the fog and the man with the beard. Most
of the crimes in Carlton Dale's casebook took place
under cover of a thick fog – when the police were
powerless to act, and a great many of them were
committed by men with beards. Indeed, Carlton
Dale himself seemed fascinated by beards of any sort,
and he was forever pulling them off on the final page
in order to unmask the true villain.

Mr Dale had solved *The Case of the Miserable
Mummies* by taking on a job in the store itself, and
if Paddington had entertained any thoughts about
reporting his strange experience to the police, they

disappeared for good and all a moment later when he caught sight of a notice pasted to one of the shop windows near the main entrance. It said, simply:

VACANCIES GOOD PROSPECTS. OWN CANTEEN. APPLY MISS GLORIA. STAFF APPOINTMENTS.

It was unusually late before Paddington finally turned out his bedside light that night, and even then he was much too excited to sleep.

Once or twice he switched it back on again in order to make an entry on a large sheet of paper headed 'CLEWS', and it needed several quite long sessions on his violin before he finally dropped off to sleep.

Fortunately, the Browns were so thankful he'd arrived home safely after his long absence they managed to turn a deaf ear, but on the last two occasions Mr Curry was heard to fling open his bedroom window and empty a jug of water into the garden below. And if the tone of his voice was anything to go by, any tomcat who happened to be passing at the time would have been well advised to turn back without delay.

However, despite his late night, Paddington woke early next morning. When he drew his curtains he was pleased to see the fog had almost cleared and after a quick wash, followed by an even quicker breakfast, he got ready to depart again.

"I do wish I could see into Paddington's mind," said Mrs Brown, as the front door closed behind him. "*I know* something's going on. I can recognise the signs. Besides, it's bonfire night at the weekend and there was a letter from Jonathan this morning asking him to see about the fireworks. He hasn't done a thing yet. It's most unusual."

"If you ask me," said Mrs Bird, "it's a good job we *can't* see into that bear's mind. There's no knowing what we might find sometimes!"

Despite her words the Browns' housekeeper looked as if she would have liked to ask Paddington a few questions as well, but by that time he was much too far away, and busy with problems of his own.

It took him some while to find the Appointments Office of the store where the mysterious goings-on had taken place the night before, and as he approached a lady sitting behind a desk at the far end of the room, a clock was already striking ten somewhere in the distance.

"Excuse me, Miss Gloria," he announced urgently, "I've come about the job in the window. I'd like to be taken on, please."

The lady in charge of appointments appeared to have problems of her own, for she carried on writing. "Are you an 'under ten thousand pounds a year man'?" she asked briefly.

"Oh, yes," said Paddington eagerly. "I'm a pound a week bear."

"A pound a week *bear*?" Miss Gloria gave a start as she glanced up from her work.

"I don't think you're quite what we're looking for," she began, breaking off as Paddington fixed her with a hard stare.

"Er... have you tried the Post Office?" she asked, in a slightly more helpful tone. "Perhaps you could put your name down as a Christmas 'temp'."

"A Christmas *'temp'*?" repeated Paddington hotly. "I don't want to work for the Post Office – I want to work for you. It's a matter of life and death!"

"Oh, really?" Miss Gloria's expression changed

and she began to look quite flustered. "Er... how nice. I... er... I'd like to help you," she continued, patting her hair, "but I don't think I can put you behind a counter. You may have trouble seeing over the top. After all, you are rather... er..." Once again her voice trailed away as she caught Paddington's gaze. "I really don't think I can offer you anything in the way of a *four*-figure job," she said unhappily, riffling through some cards.

"Have you a three-figure one?" asked Paddington hopefully.

Miss Gloria paused and withdrew a card from the file. "There is one here," she said. "And I suppose you *could* call it a three-figure job. It's five pounds fifty a week, actually, and we do supply a free mackintosh."

"A free mackintosh?" repeated Paddington, becoming more and more surprised. "Isn't the job inside?"

"Well," said Miss Gloria uneasily. "It is and it isn't. Most of you is under cover. You'd be in charge of our sandwich board, actually."

Paddington's eyes glistened. It seemed even better than he'd dared hope for. "Do I bring my own sandwiches?" he inquired. "Or do you supply them?"

Miss Gloria gave a shrill laugh. "I'll give you a chit," she said hurriedly. "You'd better go down and see our Mr Waters. He's in charge of the stores and he'll fit you out. That is, if you want the job?"

"Oh, yes, please," said Paddington. He'd never been in charge of any sort of board before, let alone a sandwich one at five pounds fifty a week, and after thanking the lady very much for all her trouble he hurried back downstairs as fast as he could.

The storeman eyed Paddington gloomily as he examined the chit. "I suppose they 'as to take what they can get these days," he said. "But I shouldn't go joining no pension scheme if I were you. I doubt if you'll last that long!"

Mr Waters disappeared behind some metal racks for a moment or two and when he returned he was staggering beneath a pile of what looked like old tables with advertisement slogans painted on them.

"Try this on for size," he said, lifting the conglomeration over Paddington's head. "'Ave a walk up and down and get the feel of it."

Paddington peered at the storeman over the top of his board as if in a trance. Far from needing to walk up and down he knew just what it felt like without even moving.

"What do you think?" asked Mr Waters. "I don't know as we 'ave a smaller one."

Paddington took a deep breath. His hat had been pushed down over his head; his whiskers were ruffled; and to make matters worse, the straps were biting into his shoulders as if he was supporting a tonne weight.

He was about to tell the storeman exactly what he thought about sandwich boards in general and the one belonging to the store in particular when he suddenly froze, hardly able to believe his good fortune. For a new figure had come into view through the door. Or rather, not a new figure, but an all-too familiar one with a beard.

"Hallo, 'Soapy'!" The newcomer nodded towards

the back of the store as he addressed Mr Waters.
"You've still got 'you know who' all right?"

The storeman gave a wink. "She 'asn't moved,
Mr Adrian," he chuckled. "Snug as a bug in a rug.
All right for the weekend, eh? No change of plans?"

The man with the beard nodded again. "There's
a whole gang coming," he said. "Can't stop now.
My turn to get the coffee this morning – all twenty-
three! Just thought I'd check on my way to the
canteen."

Paddington stood rooted to the spot as the voices
died away. It hadn't occurred to him that he might
have a gang to deal with. It was *The Case of the
Dozen Desperadoes* all over again, only with eleven
extra members, and it took him some moments to
digest this new piece of information.

"I 'as to lock up now," said the storeman, breaking
into his thoughts as he came back into the room.
"It's coffee time. If you want my advice you'll get a
cuppa while you've got the chance. It's thirsty work
lugging sandwich boards about. The canteen's just
along on your right. Follow Mr Adrian – you can't
miss it."

But Mr Waters was addressing the empty air, for Paddington was already clumping his way along the corridor in hot pursuit of his suspect.

Regardless of the odd looks being cast in his direction, he pushed his way into the canteen past a row of startled onlookers and made his way along the front of the counter until he was right behind the man with the beard.

Although Carlton Dale had never mentioned having to wear a sandwich board on any of his cases, Paddington was glad he hadn't stopped to remove it, for at least it gave him cover while he considered his next move.

Peering over the top, he racked his brains as the man in front loaded a tray with cups and saucers and then felt in a purse for the money.

It was as the lady behind the cash register handed over the change and slammed the till shut that Paddington had a sudden flash of inspiration; for the sight of all the money reminded him of yet another of Mr Dale's famous cases – *The Affair of the Forged Florins* – in which the criminal had been tracked down with the aid of fingerprints taken from the coins themselves.

"Excuse me," he called, addressing the lady behind the counter. "Have you seen what's on the wall behind you?"

As the cashier looked round, Paddington seized his opportunity. Reaching out from beneath the board he hastily turned the cash register round until it was facing him and then pressed one of the buttons.

He wasn't at all sure what happened next, for it was all over before he had time to blink, let alone see inside the till. There was a 'ping' as the drawer shot out, and a split second later a crash echoed and re-echoed around the canteen as twenty-three cups of coffee went flying in all directions.

"Mr Adrian! Mr Adrian!" The lady behind the cash desk peered under the counter as a cry of mingled pain and astonishment came from somewhere underneath. "Are you all right?

"What a thing to happen," she cried, turning to one of the assistants. "And only two days before Bonfire Night!"

"He's been to so much trouble and all," clucked someone else. "They say he's made a marvellous guy from a dummy out of one of his windows. Been keeping it down in the stores as a surprise."

"He did it!" shouted another assistant, pointing at Paddington. "The one with the whiskers behind that sandwich board. He did it on purpose."

"I knew he was up to no good as soon as he came in," cried a waitress. "He pushed me in my vanilla slices, he was in such a hurry!"

"Help! Bandits!" shouted yet another voice, taking up the call.

Immediately the whole canteen was in an uproar as attention suddenly switched from the unfortunate Mr Adrian, still lying under the counter in a pool of brown liquid, and focused on the sandwich board.

But Paddington was no longer inside it. Like Carlton Dale at his most elusive, he had disappeared. He still hadn't had time to take in all that had been said, but of one thing he was perfectly certain; any working out of the problem which remained was much better done in the quiet of number thirty-two Windsor Gardens rather than the store's canteen.

"There's a funny case in tonight's paper," said Mr Brown, later that same evening. "Quite near here. Apparently they had some sort of to-do in that big store.

"'Sandwich board runs amok in staff canteen,'" he read. "'Bearded window-dresser attacked by mystery coffee-throwing bandit!'"

"What will people get up to next?" asked Mrs Brown from behind her knitting. "You're not safe anywhere these days."

Mr Brown tossed the paper on to the floor for the others to see. "Sounds like a case for you, Paddington," he called jokingly. "I bet you five pounds you can't solve that one!"

Paddington, who'd spent most of the evening busily writing notes in his scrapbook, nearly fell off the pouffe with astonishment.

"Would you really, Mr Brown?" he exclaimed excitedly.

"Er... yes," replied Mr Brown, suddenly looking slightly less enthusiastic about the matter. "That's what I said."

There was a confident note in Paddington's voice he didn't entirely like the sound of, and he looked even more unhappy a moment or so later when Paddington cut a picture out of the paper and began pasting it alongside his notes.

"Don't tell me you've been working on the case already?" he asked.

Paddington nodded as he licked a gummed label to place under the photograph of a coffee-stained Mr Adrian being interviewed with his guy. He suddenly felt very much better about everything. Carlton Dale rarely received any sort of reward for solving *his* crimes, let alone five pounds, and although he didn't think he could possibly make as good a guy as the one in the picture, he was quite certain Mr Brown's money would go a long way towards it, and supply a goodly number of extra fireworks for Jonathan and Judy into the bargain.

"I've called it *The Case of the Doubtful Dummy*," he announced importantly, clearing his throat as everyone gathered round to listen. "It all began yesterday evening when I wrote to Carlton Dale..."

Chapter Six

PADDINGTON RECOMMENDED

MRS BROWN TORE open the first of the morning's mail, withdrew a large piece of white pasteboard, and then stared at it in amazement. "Good gracious!" she exclaimed. "Fancy that! Mrs Smith-Cholmley is holding a Christmas ball in aid of the local children's hospital and we've all been invited."

Paddington peered across the table with a slice of

toast and marmalade poised halfway to his mouth. "Mrs Smith-Cholmley's holding a Christmas ball?" he repeated in great surprise. "I hope we get there before she drops it!"

"It isn't that sort of a ball, dear," said Mrs Brown patiently.

"It means she's having a dance," explained Judy.

"Who's Mrs Smith-Cholmley when she's at home?" asked Mr Brown.

Mrs Brown handed him the card. "Don't you remember, Henry? Paddington met her when he was out Carol Singing last year. She's the one he cooked the baked elastic for by mistake."

"Crikey!" broke in Jonathan, as he read the invitation. "She's either left it a bit late or it's been delayed in the post. It's tomorrow night!"

"And that's not all," added Mrs Brown. "Have you seen what it says at the bottom?"

Paddington hurried round the table and peered over Mr Brown's shoulder. "Ruzzvup!" he exclaimed.

"No, dear," said Mrs Brown. "R.S.V.P. That simply means '*Répondez, s'il vous plaît*'. It's French for 'please reply'."

"You mean the bit about evening dress?" Mr Brown looked around at Paddington, who was waving his toast and marmalade dangerously near his left ear. "Well, that's put the tin lid on it. I suppose we shall just have to say no."

There was a note of relief in Mr Brown's voice. He wasn't too keen on dancing at the best of times and the thought of going to a ball with Mrs Smith-Cholmley filled him with gloom. But any hopes he'd entertained of using Paddington as an excuse were quickly dashed by the chorus of dismay which greeted his last remark.

"I think we ought to try and arrange *something*, Henry," said Mrs Brown. "After all, it's in a very good cause. It's the same hospital Paddington collected for last year, and if it wasn't for him we shouldn't be invited anyway."

"We'll take him along to Heather and Sons and have him fitted out for the evening," said Mrs Bird decidedly, as she bustled around clearing up the breakfast things. "They hire out evening clothes and it says in their advertisements they fit anyone while they wait."

Mr Brown eyed Paddington's figure doubtfully. "We need it *tomorrow* night," he said. "Not next year."

Paddington looked most upset at this last remark. It was bad enough writing things in initials, let alone French ones, but having to wear special clothes simply in order to dance seemed most complicated.

However, he brightened considerably at the thought of going up to London to be fitted out. And when Mr Brown, recognising defeat at last, announced that he would meet them afterwards and take them all out to lunch as a special treat, he joined in the general excitement.

Paddington liked visiting London and he couldn't wait to get started, especially when Mr Brown brought out his copy of a guide to good restaurants and began searching for a likely eating place.

"They have a restaurant at Heather's now," said Mrs Brown. "We could combine the two things. It'll save a lot of trouble."

Mr Brown made a quick check. "It isn't a Duncan Hyde recommended," he said disappointedly. "He doesn't even mention it."

"It only opened last week," replied Mrs Brown, "so it wouldn't be. But not many people know about it yet so at least it won't be crowded."

"All right," said Mr Brown. "You win!" He snapped the book shut and handed it to Paddington. "Perhaps you can test a few of the dishes at lunchtime," he continued, as the others hurried upstairs. "If they're any good we'll send a recommendation to Mr Hyde."

"Thank you very much, Mr Brown," said Paddington gratefully. He'd spent many happy hours browsing through the pages of Mr Hyde's book and he put it away carefully in the secret compartment of his suitcase while he got ready to go out.

Duncan Hyde spent his time visiting restaurants all over the country, awarding them various shaped hats for their cooking, ranging from a very small beret for run-of-the-mill dishes to a giant-size bowler hat for the very best, and some of the dishes he described were very mouthwatering indeed.

Although no one had ever met him, for he preferred to remain anonymous, it was widely agreed that he must be a person of great taste, and when they arrived at Heather and Sons later that morning, Paddington peered through the restaurant window with interest in case there was anyone around carrying a hat.

As they trooped through the main entrance, the Browns were greeted by a man in morning dress.

"We'd like to fit this young bear out for a special occasion," said Mrs Brown. "Can you direct us to the right department, please?"

"Certainly, Modom. Please step this way." With scarcely the flicker of an eyelid, the supervisor turned and led the way towards a nearby lift. "Does the young... er, gentleman, have an appointment at Buckingham Palace?" he asked, glancing down at Paddington as the doors slid shut. "Or is he simply going out?"

"Neither," said Paddington, giving the man a hard stare. "I'm coming in!" After the warmth of the underground, the air outside had struck particularly cold to his whiskers and he didn't want to be sent out again.

"He's going to a ball," explained Mrs Brown hastily. "We want to hire some evening dress."

"A ball?" The man looked slightly relieved. "One

of the Spring functions, no doubt?" he remarked hopefully.

"No," said Mrs Bird firmly. "One of the Christmas ones. It's for tomorrow night, so there's no time to be lost."

"It says in the advertisement you fit anyone," broke in Jonathan.

"While you wait," added Judy imploringly.

"Er... yes," said the supervisor unhappily. He looked down at Paddington again. "It's just that the young... er... gentleman's legs are a bit... ahem... and we may have to do some drastic alterations if it's to be from stock."

"My legs are a bit 'ahem'?" exclaimed Paddington hotly.

He began giving the supervisor some very hard stares indeed, but fortunately the lift came to a stop before any more could be said. As the doors slid open and the man gave a discreet signal to an assistant hovering in the background, Mrs Brown exchanged glances with the others.

"I was wondering," she said, "if it wouldn't be better for the rest of us to carry on with our

Christmas shopping? We can all meet again in the restaurant downstairs at one o'clock."

"A very good idea, Modom!" The supervisor sounded most relieved. "Rest assured," he continued, as he ushered Paddington from the lift, "we will use our best endeavours and leave no stone unturned. I'll get our Mr Stanley to look after the young gentleman. He does all our difficult cases and there's nothing he likes better than a challenge."

"That's as may be," said Mrs Bird ominously, as the gates slid shut again, "but I have a feeling he's going to have to turn over a good few stones before that bear's fitted out. You mark my words!"

The Browns' housekeeper didn't entirely approve of leaving Paddington to the tender mercies of Heather and Sons, impressive though their shop was, but as it happened the supervisor's confidence in his staff was not misplaced, for no sooner had the Browns departed than everyone sprang into action.

"I'll put 'Thimbles' Martin on the job," announced Mr Stanley, making notes as he circled Paddington with a tape measure. "He's the fastest man with a needle and thread in the business. He'll fix you up in no time at all."

Looking suitably impressed, Paddington settled down to read his Duncan Hyde book while he waited, and indeed, it seemed only a very short while before Mr Stanley reappeared proudly carrying an immaculately pressed set of evening clothes.

"You'll look a blade in these and no mistake, sir," he exclaimed enthusiastically, as he led Paddington into a changing cubicle.

"Quite the young bear about town," agreed the supervisor. "Mind you," he continued, allowing himself a smile of satisfaction as he helped Paddington on with the jacket, "you'll have to watch your p's and q's. There's no knowing who you might not get mistaken for dressed like that. Will you be taking them with you, or shall we send them?"

Paddington examined his reflection in the mirror – or rather, since there were mirrors on all four walls, what seemed like a never-ending line of reflections stretching away into the distance.

Although he felt very pleased to get his evening dress so quickly he was looking forward even more to the thought of carrying out Mr Brown's suggestion and investigating some dishes for the guide.

"I think," he announced at last, "I'll wear them, thank you very much." And disregarding the anxious expressions he was leaving behind, he picked up his belongings and headed for the lift.

As Mrs Brown had forecast, not many people knew about Heather's restaurant and what with that and the early hour, it was still practically empty when Paddington entered.

Just inside the door there was an enormous sweet trolley and his eyes nearly popped out with astonishment as he took in the various items. There were so many different shapes, sizes and colours he soon lost count, and it was while he was on his paws and knees examining the mounds of chocolate mousse and the oceans of fruit salads on the bottom shelf that he suddenly realised someone was talking to him.

"May I be of assistance?" asked one of the waiters.

Paddington stood up and raised his hat politely. "No, thank you very much," he said sadly. "I was only looking." Holding up the Duncan Hyde book he ran his eye over the trolley again. "I was hoping I might be able to do some testing later on. I think some of your dishes might be worth a bowler."

To Paddington's surprise, his words seemed to have a magical effect on the waiter. "Pardon me, sir," he exclaimed, jumping to attention. "I didn't realise who you were. If you care to wait just one moment, sir, I'll call the manager."

Bowing low as he backed away, the man disappeared from view, only to return a moment later accompanied by an imposing figure dressed in a black coat and striped trousers.

"I can't tell you," boomed the second man, rubbing his hands with invisible soap, "how delighted we are that you've decided to honour us with your presence. It's just what our restaurant needs." Taking in Paddington's dress suit, hat and whiskers he gave a knowing wink at the book. "I see you've been hiding your light under a bushel!"

"I have?" exclaimed Paddington, looking more and more surprised at the turn the conversation was taking.

"We'll put you in the window, sir," announced the manager, leading the way across the floor. "We have some very special dishes on today," he confided with another wink, as he helped Paddington into a chair. "I'm sure we can find something to titivate your palate."

"I expect you can," said Paddington, politely giving the man a wink in return. "But I'm not sure if I can afford them."

"My dear sir." The man raised his hands in mock horror as he whisked the menu away. "We don't want to bother ourselves with mere money."

"Don't we?" exclaimed Paddington excitedly.

The manager shook his head. "You need only sign the bill," he explained. "Let's think about food first. That's much more important. We want you to feel perfectly at home."

"Oh, I do already," said Paddington, grasping his knife and fork. "When can I start?"

"That's what I like to see," replied the manager, beaming all over his face. "Well," he continued, rubbing his hands in anticipation, "I can certainly recommend our avocado pear filled with sea-fresh prawns and cream sauce.

"After that," he said, "may I suggest either pot-fresh lobster, Dover-fresh sole, farm-fresh escalope of veal, or oven-fresh steak and kidney pudding?"

All the talk of food was beginning to make Paddington feel hungry and it didn't take him long to make up his mind. "I think I'd like to try some of each," he announced rashly.

If the manager was surprised, he concealed his feelings remarkably well. In fact, a look of respect came over his face as he handed Paddington's order to a waiter who was hovering nearby. "I must say," he remarked, "you take your job very seriously, sir. There aren't many people in your position who would take the trouble to try *everything* on the menu. Would you care to test one of our rare old wines?"

Paddington thought for a moment. "I think I'd sooner test some of your tin-fresh cocoa," he said.

"Tin-fresh *cocoa*?" For one brief moment the

manager's calm seemed to desert him, then he brightened. "I have a feeling you're trying to catch us out," he said, wagging his finger roguishly.

"Perhaps," he added, waving in the direction of the trolley, "you would care to contemplate the sweets over the cheese."

Paddington gave him an odd look. "I'd sooner eat them," he said. "But I think I'd better leave a little bit of room. I'm having lunch with someone at one o'clock."

A look of renewed admiration came over the man's face. "Well," he said, bowing his way out as the first of the dishes began to arrive, "I'll leave you to your task, but I do hope you'll see fit to mention us when the time comes."

"Oh, yes," replied Paddington earnestly. "I shall tell all my friends."

Paddington still wasn't sure why he was being treated in such a Royal manner, but he wasn't the sort of bear to look a gift horse in the mouth and as everyone obviously wanted him to enjoy his meal, he was only too willing to oblige.

Already quite a large crowd had gathered on the

pavement outside Heather's. In fact, the window was black with faces and it was getting darker with every passing moment.

Paddington's every move was watched with increasing interest and as he settled down to his gargantuan meal, the applause which greeted each new course was exceeded only by the one which followed.

But if the vast majority of the audience viewed the goings-on inside the restaurant with wonder and delight, there were five newly-joined members who stood watching with horror and dismay on their faces.

The Browns had arranged to meet outside the shop, but like most of the other passers-by, they had been drawn to the crowd gathered around the window, and now, as they pushed their way to the front, their worst fears were realised.

"Mercy me!" cried Mrs Bird. "What on earth is that bear up to now?"

"I don't know what he's *up* to," said Mr Brown gloomily, as a loud groan rose from the audience. "But whatever it is, I think it's coming to an end."

A sudden change had indeed taken place on the other side of the glass, and the Browns watched with sinking hearts.

It all began when a waiter arrived bearing a large sheet of folded paper on a plate. Handing Paddington a pen, he stood over him with a deferential smile on his face while he signed his name. Then gradually the smile disappeared only to be replaced by an expression which the Browns didn't like the look of at all.

"Come on," cried Judy, grabbing her mother's arm. "We'd better do some rescuing."

"Oh, Lord!" groaned Mr Brown, as they pushed

their way back into the crowd. "Here we go again."

Unaware that help was on its way, Paddington stared at the waiter as if he could hardly believe his eyes let alone his ears. "Eighty pounds and sixty-two pence!" he exclaimed. "Just for a meal?"

"Not just for *a* meal," said the waiter, eyeing all the stains. "About ten meals if you ask me. We thought you were Duncan Hyde, the famous gourmet."

Paddington nearly fell backwards off his chair at the news. "Duncan Hyde, the famous gourmet?" he repeated. "I'm not Duncan Hyde. I'm Paddington Brown from Darkest Peru and I'm a bear."

"In that case," said the waiter, handing back the bill. "I'm afraid it's cash. It includes the 'cover-charge'," he added meaningly, "but not the tip."

"A *cover* charge?" exclaimed Paddington hotly. "But I didn't even have one. It was all open." He peered at the piece of paper in his paw. "*Ten pounds and seventy pence for a bombe surprise!*"

"That's all part of the surprise," replied the waiter nastily.

"Well, I've got one for you," said Paddington. "I've only got twenty pence!"

Paddington felt most upset about the whole affair, especially as he hadn't intended eating in the first place. Apart from putting his signature on the bill as he'd been asked, he'd even added his special paw print to show it was genuine, and he looked very relieved when he caught sight of the Browns heading in his direction.

Since he'd arrived, a great change had come over the restaurant and it was now full almost to overflowing. The Browns had to weave a tortuous path in and out of the other diners and before they were able to reach Paddington's table, they found their way barred by the manager.

"Does this young gentleman belong to you?" he asked, pointing in Paddington's direction.

"Er... why do you ask?" queried Mr Brown, playing for time.

"Henry!" exclaimed Mrs Brown. "How could you?"

"I've never seen you before either, Mr Brown," called Paddington, entering into the spirit of things.

Mr Brown heaved a deep sigh as he reached for his wallet. "Since you ask," he said, "I'm afraid he does."

"Afraid?" The manager stared at the Browns. "Did you say *afraid*?" He waved an all-embracing hand round the restaurant. "Why, this is the best thing that's happened to us since we opened. That young bear's attracted so many new customers we don't know whether we're coming or going. There's certainly no charge."

He turned back to Paddington. "I wish we could have you sitting in the window every day of the week. You may not be a Duncan Hyde, but you're certainly worth your weight in Lobster Soufflé..."

The manager broke off and looked at Paddington with concern. For some reason or other, his words seemed to be having a strange effect.

"Are you all right, sir?" he asked. "Your whiskers seem to have gone a very funny colour. Let me help you up. Perhaps you'd like to try some of our bean-fresh coffee with cream."

Paddington gave another groan. If he'd had to make a list of his needs at that moment, getting up would have figured very low while food and drink would have been lucky to get a mention at all.

Dropping his guidebook, he sank back into the chair and felt for the buttons on his jacket. "I'd rather not do any more testing today, thank you very much," he gasped.

Apart from all his other troubles, Paddington had noticed a rather ominous tearing sound whenever he moved, and although he'd minded his 'peas' during lunch he had a feeling that both Mr Stanley and 'Thimbles' Martin were in for a busy afternoon dealing with his q's.

All the same, he had to admit he'd never had *quite* such a meal in his life before.

"I think," he announced, "that if I was a food tester, I would award Heather's one of my uncle's hats!"

Mr Brown smacked his lips in anticipation. "It must be good then," he said, reaching for the menu. "I shall enjoy my lunch.

"After all," he continued, amid general agreement, "one of Paddington's hats must be worth a whole wardrobeful of Duncan Hyde's bowlers any day of the week!"

Chapter Seven

THE LAST DANCE

MR BROWN HUNG his dressing gown on the bedroom door and then sat on the bed rubbing his eyes. "Three times I've been down to the front door," he grumbled, "and all the time it was Paddington banging about in his room!"

"I expect he's practising his dancing," said Mrs Brown sleepily. "He said he was having trouble with his turns last night."

"Well, I'm having trouble with my sleep this morning," said Mr Brown crossly. "I've put my foot down."

"I can see you have," replied Mrs Brown, eyeing her husband's slippers as he took them off. "Right in the middle of Paddington's rosin! I think you'd better scrape it off. He'll be most upset if there's any missing. He bought it specially to stop his paws slipping on the linoleum. He had several nasty falls yesterday."

Mr Brown looked at his soles in disgust. "Only a bear," he said bitterly, "would want to do the tango at half past six on a Saturday morning. I only hope they don't have a bear's 'excuse me' at the ball tonight. Anyone who lands Paddington as a partner is in for a pretty rough time."

"Perhaps he'll have improved by then," said Mrs Brown hopefully. "It can't be easy rehearsing with a bolster."

Mrs Brown turned over and closed her eyes, though more in an effort to blot out the mental picture of events to come than with any hope of going back to sleep. For although one half of her was looking forward to Mrs Smith-Cholmley's ball that evening, the other half was beginning to have grave doubts about the matter, and recent events only served to tip the scales still further on the side of the doubts.

But daylight lends enchantment to the gloomiest of views and some, at least, of Mrs Brown's worst fears were relieved when Paddington arrived downstairs a little later that morning looking unusually spick-and-span despite his disturbed night.

"I must say you look very smart," she remarked, amid murmurs of approval from the others. "There can't be many bears who sit down to breakfast in evening dress."

"There'll be one less," said Mrs Bird, striking a warning note, "if certain of them get any marmalade down their front!"

Mrs Bird had suffered from 'bumps in the night' as well, and with Christmas looming large on the horizon, she didn't want her kitchen turned into a bear's ballroom.

Paddington considered the matter for a moment while he tackled his bacon and egg. He was the sort of bear who believed in getting value for money, and having heard how much Mr Brown was paying for the hire of his suit, he wanted to make the most of it. All the same, if the Browns were having second thoughts on the subject of dancing, he had to admit that he was having third and even fourth ones himself.

In the past he often watched dancing programmes on the television and wondered why people made so much fuss, for it all looked terribly easy – just a matter of jumping about the floor in time to some music. But when he'd tried to do it he soon found that even without a partner his legs got tangled up and he shuddered to think what it might be like when he had someone else's in the way as well.

In the end he'd tried doing it on his bed for safety, but that had been worse still – rather like running round in circles on a cotton-wool covered trampoline.

All in all, he decided dancing was much more difficult than it looked at first sight, and to everyone's relief he announced that he was going out that morning in order to consult his friend, Mr Gruber, on the subject.

The Last Dance

Over the years, Mr Gruber had turned up trumps on a variety of subjects and Paddington felt sure he would be able to find something among the many books which lined the walls of his antique shop. Even so, he was still taken by surprise when he arrived at Mr Gruber's and found his friend doing a kind of jig around his nick-nacks table to the tune from an old gramophone.

Mr Gruber looked at Paddington sheepishly over the top of his glasses as he drew up a chair. "I have a feeling you won't be the only one with problems tonight, Mr Brown," he said, panting a little after his exertions. "It's a long time since I last tripped the Light Fantastic."

As Paddington had no idea that Mr Gruber could dance let alone do a Light Fantastic, the news that he was going to Mrs Smith-Cholmley's ball came like a bolt from the blue, and he grew more and more excited when his friend drew his attention to a large poster in the window.

"Practically anyone who's anyone around here is going tonight, Mr Brown," he said. "They've got Alf Weidersein's orchestra, and Norman and Hilda Church are bringing their Formation Team."

Paddington looked most impressed as Mr Gruber went on to explain that Norman Church was a very famous ballroom dancer indeed, and that apart from bringing his team he would be judging the various competitions to be held during the course of the evening.

And when Mr Gruber, with a twinkle in his eyes, reached up to one of the shelves and took down a book on dancing written by Mr Church himself, Paddington could hardly believe his good fortune. He felt sure if he studied a book written by the man who was actually going to act as judge he ought to do very well indeed.

For the rest of that day, apart from odd strains of the Veleta and an occasional thump from Paddington's room, number thirty-two Windsor Gardens remained remarkably quiet as everyone got ready for the big event.

Paddington himself was waiting in the hall from quite early on in the evening, clutching Mr Gruber's book in one paw and an alarm clock in the other, while he did some last-minute 'promenades' by the front door.

Although Norman Church's book was lavishly illustrated with footprints showing the various steps, none of them seemed to go anywhere, and as some were marked 'clockwise' and others 'anticlockwise', he got very confused trying to work out which ones to follow and watch the hands on the clock at the same time.

The book was called *Learning to Hold Your Own on the Dance Floor in Twenty-Five Easy Lessons*, and with only a matter of minutes to go, Paddington rather wished Mr Church had made do with five hard ones instead, for he found it difficult enough getting through the title let alone read the instructions.

All the same, when they set off shortly afterwards, he soon joined in the general gaiety, and as they drew near the ballroom, he grew more and more excited.

But the journey itself was nothing compared to the atmosphere once they were inside and Paddington peered round with interest as he handed his duffle coat to an attendant.

Strains of music floated out through a pair of double doors at the top of some stairs leading down to the dance floor, and beyond the stairs he could see couples in evening dress gliding about, their faces lit by twinkling reflections from an enormous mirrored globe revolving high above them.

Mr Brown cocked an ear to the music as they joined Mr Gruber and a small queue of other new arrivals. "They're playing 'Goodbye Blues'," he said. "That's one of my favourites."

"'Goodbye Blues'?" repeated Paddington, looking most upset. "But we've only just arrived!"

Mr Gruber gave a tactful cough. "I think there'll be plenty more tunes before we leave, Mr Brown."

Bending down, he drew Paddington to one side as the queue moved forward. "I should put your best paw forward," he whispered. "I think you're about to be announced."

Mr Gruber pointed towards a man in an imposing wig and costume standing at the head of the stairs, and Paddington's eyes nearly popped out as he heard Mr and Mrs Brown's names ring out around the ballroom.

"I don't think I've ever been announced before, Mr Gruber," he replied, hastily stuffing as many of his belongings as possible underneath his jacket.

"Crumbs!" Judy gave a startled gasp as she gave Paddington a quick last-minute check. "You've still got your cycle clips on!"

Catching her daughter's words, Mrs Brown looked anxiously over her shoulder. "Do take them off, dear," she warned. "You won't feel the benefit otherwise."

Mindful of Mrs Bird's remarks about keeping his evening dress clean, Paddington hadn't wanted to take any risks with the trouser bottoms – which tended to slip down rather, and with a forecast of snow in the air, he'd decided to make doubly sure. All the same, he did as he was bidden and as he approached the man doing the announcements he bent down.

"Excuse me," he called in a muffled voice. "I'm Mr Brown and I'm having trouble with my cycle clips."

"Mr Cyclops Brown," called the man in sonorous tones.

"Cyclops Brown!" exclaimed Paddington hotly. He stood up clutching his clips, looking most upset that on the very first occasion of being announced, his name should have been wrongly called. But by that time the man was already halfway through announcing Mr Gruber, and Paddington found himself face to face with Mrs Smith-Cholmley, who was waiting to greet her guests at the foot of the stairs.

"I'm so sorry," said Mrs Smith-Cholmley, trying to pass the whole thing off with a shrill laugh as she took Paddington's paw. "I always thought Cyclops only had one eye…" She broke off as she followed Paddington's gaze towards the middle of the dance floor, for it was all too obvious that Paddington not only had *two* eyes but they were both working extremely well.

"That's Mr Church," she explained, catching sight of a nattily dressed man posing beneath a spotlight. "He's about to lead off."

As the music started up again, Mrs Smith-Cholmley turned back to Paddington. "Er… I see you've been doing your homework," she continued, catching sight of Mr Gruber's book in his other paw. "If Mr Church has trouble with his steps, he'll know where to come…" Once again, Mrs Smith-Cholmley broke off, and a look of alarm came over her face. "I didn't say he has got trouble," she called. "I only said if. It was a joke. I…"

But Paddington was already halfway across the floor. "Don't worry, Mr Church!" he cried, waving his book. "I'm coming. I think it's all on page forty-five."

Paddington reached the centre of the floor in time to meet the first wave of advancing dancers. Norman and Hilda Church's Formation Team were just getting into their stride, and if the smile on Mrs Smith-Cholmley's face had begun to look a trifle fixed, the one Mr Church presented to his public looked as if it had been indelibly etched for all time.

"Go away," he hissed, as Paddington tapped him on the shoulder. "You're upsetting my Alberts."

Norman Church looked as if he'd just thought up a few more choice items for his chapter on ballroom etiquette, but before he had time to put any of them into words a very strange thing happened.

As his team turned to make a sweeping movement back down the floor, a bell started to ring somewhere in their midst.

There was a note of urgency about it which caused the leaders to falter in their stride. In a moment, all was confusion as those in the rear cannoned into the ones in front, and in less time than it takes to form up for a Quadrille, the damage had been done.

A hard core who thought a fire had broken out behind the bandstand jostled with a group who were equally convinced the floor was about to give way, and they, in turn, ran foul of those who simply wanted to see what was going on.

In the middle of all this hubbub, Paddington suddenly reached inside his jacket. "It's all right, Mr Church," he called, holding up a large, round brass object. "It's only my alarm clock!"

In the silence that followed, Mr Brown's voice sounded unusually loud. "Two minutes!" he groaned. "That's all the time we've been here. Two minutes – and look at it!"

There was no need to suggest looking at the scene on the dance floor, for the rest of the Browns were only too painfully aware of what it was like.

Even Paddington, as he made his way back through the dancers, was forced to admit that he rather wished the floor had collapsed, for it would have afforded a quick means of escape from the glances of those around him.

"Never mind," said Judy, going forward to meet him. "We know you meant well."

"Thank you very much," said Paddington gratefully. "But I don't think Mr Church does."

Casting an anxious glance over his shoulder, he allowed himself to be led off the floor in the direction of some tables to one side of the hall.

"I think I'll sit this one out, thank you very much," he announced, after consulting his book.

Although the chapter on ballroom behaviour didn't include any mention of what to do following the kind of disaster he'd just experienced, there were quite a number of phrases Mr Church recommended for use when you didn't want to dance, and Paddington felt it was a good moment to test one or two of them.

"Not that anyone's likely to ask him after what's just happened," said Mr Brown, as he whirled past the table a little later on.

"It's a shame, really," agreed Mrs Brown, catching sight of Paddington deep in his book. "He's been practising so hard. I don't like to think of him being a wallflower and he's been sitting there for ages."

Mr Brown gave a snort. "Anything less like a wallflower than Paddington would be difficult to imagine," he remarked.

Mr Brown was about to add pessimistically that

the evening wasn't over yet, but at that moment there was a roll of drums and all eyes turned in the direction of the band rostrum as Norman Church climbed up and grasped the microphone in order to announce the start of the competitions.

Now that the dance was in full swing, Mr Church seemed to have recovered his good humour. "Now I want everyone, but everyone to join in," he boomed. "There are lots of prizes to be won... lots of dances... and a special mammoth Christmas hamper for the best couple of the evening..."

Mr Church's words had a livening effect on the ball and during the items which followed he proved his worth as a Master of Ceremonies. He kept up such a steady flow of patter, even Paddington began to get quite worked up, and a marmalade sandwich which he'd brought along to pass the time with lay untouched on the table beside him.

It was while the fun was at its height that Mrs Smith-Cholmley suddenly caught sight of him peering through a gap in the crowd.

"Come along," she called. "You heard what Mr Church said. Everyone has to join in."

Paddington gave a start. "Thank you very much, Mrs Smith-Cholmley," he called excitedly. "I'd like to very much."

"Oh!" Mrs Smith-Cholmley's face dropped. "I didn't mean... that is, I... er..." She looked at Paddington uneasily and then glanced down at her programme. "It *is* the Latin America section next," she said. "I believe you come from that part of the world."

"Darkest Peru," agreed Paddington earnestly.

Mrs Smith-Cholmley gave a nervous laugh. "I'm not sure if Mr Weidersein knows any Peruvian dances," she said, "especially dark ones, but we could try our hand at the rumba if you like."

"Yes, please," said Paddington gratefully. "I don't think I've done one of those before."

Paddington was very keen on anything new, and after slipping the cycle clips over one of his sleeves for safety, he hastily thrust the marmalade sandwich behind his back, picked up his book, and rose from the table.

"I see you're 'with it'," said Mrs Smith-Cholmley, mistaking the sudden flurry of movement for a dance step.

Paddington clasped Mrs Smith-Cholmley firmly with both paws. "I'm never without it," he replied.

Peering round his partner's waist, he consulted the etiquette section of Mr Church's book again.

"Do you come here often?" he inquired politely.

Mrs Smith-Cholmley looked down at her feet, both of which were submerged beneath Paddington's paws. "No," she replied, in a tone of voice which suggested she was rather regretting her present visit. "Haven't you got any pumps?" she asked.

Paddington glanced down at his cycle clips. "I haven't even got a bike," he exclaimed, looking most surprised.

Mrs Smith-Cholmley gave him a strange look. "You really ought to have pumps," she said, breathing heavily as she tried to lift her own and Paddington's feet in time to the music. "It would make things so much easier."

Paddington returned her look. He was beginning to get a bit fed up with the way the conversation was going. It wasn't at all like any of the examples in Mr Church's book, most of which were to do with sitting out on balconies eating snacks. "I think Mr Brown's got a spare wheel," he replied helpfully. "Have you got a puncture?"

"No," said Mrs Smith-Cholmley through her teeth, "I haven't. But if you stand on my feet much longer, I'm liable to have one!"

Paddington's claws were rather sharp and they were digging deeper and deeper into her instep with every passing moment. "I'd be obliged if you would find somewhere else to put your paws."

Paddington relaxed his grasp on Mrs Smith-

Cholmley and tried jumping up and down experimentally a few times. "I don't think I can," he gasped at last. "I have a feeling they're caught in your straps."

To his surprise, when he looked up again, Mrs Smith-Cholmley's face seemed to have gone a very funny colour indeed. And not only that, but she had begun to wriggle in a way which certainly wasn't included in any of Mr Church's illustrations for the rumba.

"My back!" she shrieked. "My back! There's an awful creature crawling down my back!" Almost turning herself inside out, Mrs Smith-Cholmley reached behind herself and withdrew something long, golden and glistening, which she gazed at with increasing horror. "It's all wet and sticky... ugh!"

Paddington peered at the object dangling between his partner's forefinger and thumb with interest. "I don't think that's a creature, Mrs Smith-Cholmley," he exclaimed. "It's a chunk. I must have dropped my marmalade sandwich down the back of your dress by mistake!"

Unaware of the drama that was taking place behind their hostess's back, Mr Brown gave his wife a nudge. "Good Lord, Mary," he said. "Look at those two. They're going great guns."

Mrs Brown turned and glanced across the dance floor. "Well I never!" she exclaimed with pleasure. "Who would have thought it?"

But if Mr and Mrs Brown were astonished at the sight of the gyrations on the other side of the floor, the rest of the dancers were positively astounded.

One by one the other couples dropped out in order to take a closer look as Paddington and Mrs Smith-Cholmley, seemingly moving as one, rocked and wriggled in time to the music.

At a signal from Mr Church, the man in charge of the spotlight concentrated his beam on the two figures, and as Alf Weidersein began urging his orchestra to greater and greater efforts, the shouts of encouragement, the clapping and the stamping of feet, began to shake the very rafters of the hall.

Paddington himself became more and more confused as he clung to his partner and, far from needing an alarm clock to show him the way, he found himself wishing he'd brought a compass, for he hadn't the least idea where he'd started from, let alone where he was going.

From the word go, the winners of the mammoth hamper for the best couple of the evening were never in doubt. Indeed, it would have taken a very brave man indeed to have gone in the face of the cheers which rang out as the music came to an end at last.

For some reason, as soon as willing hands had disentangled Paddington's paws from her shoe straps, Mrs Smith-Cholmley beat a hasty retreat; and when she did reappear at long last it was in a different dress, but in the excitement, this went largely unnoticed.

"A lovely little mover," said Norman Church enthusiastically, turning to Paddington as he presented the prize. "Very fleet. I wouldn't mind using you and your lovely lady in my Formation Team when we do our final demonstration."

Mrs Smith-Cholmley gave a shudder. "I don't think Mr Brown and I are open to engagements," she broke in hastily, as she caught a momentary gleam in Paddington's eye.

Paddington nodded his agreement. "I haven't brought any more marmalade sandwiches either, Mr Church," he said.

"Er... yes." Mr Church looked slightly taken aback. "Talking of marmalade sandwiches," he continued, recovering himself, "what are you going to do with all this food?"

Paddington contemplated the prize for a moment. It was a large hamper. An enormous one, in fact, and it was difficult to picture the many good things there must be inside it.

"I think," he announced, amid general applause, "I'd like to send my half to the Home for Retired Bears in Lima – if it can be got there in time for Christmas. I don't think they can always afford very much extra."

"It'll be done," said Mr Church. "Even if I have to fly it myself and divide it when I get there."

"There's no need to divide it," said Mrs Smith-Cholmley, amid renewed applause. "They can have my half as well. After all, there's no time to be lost, and it sounds a very good cause. Especially," she added with a wry smile at her partner, "if the Home is full of bears like Paddington. I wouldn't like to think of them going short of marmalade."

"I wonder what Mrs Smith-Cholmley meant by that last remark?" said Mr Brown, as they drove home later that night, tired but happy. He glanced across the front seat. "Have you any idea, Paddington?"

Paddington rubbed the steam from the window with his paw and peered out into the night. "I think it was to do with my chunks, Mr Brown," he replied vaguely.

Mrs Brown gave a sigh. Life with a bear was full of unsolved mysteries. "I know one thing," she said. "There may be a lot of deserving cases in the Home – and none more so than Aunt Lucy, I'm sure – but I very much doubt if they have any other bears quite like Paddington."

"Impossible!" agreed Mrs Bird firmly.

"Absolutely!" said Judy.

"With a capital I," added Jonathan.

But Paddington was oblivious to the conversation going on around him. The first snowflakes of winter were already falling and with the promise of more to come, not to mention the approach of Christmas itself, he was already looking forward to things in store.

"I think," he announced to the world in general, "I shall keep my bicycle clips on in bed tonight. I want to keep myself warm in case I have any more adventures!"

Paddington
on Top

Contents

Chapter One

PADDINGTON GOES TO SCHOOL

"PADDINGTON HAS TO go to school?" exclaimed Mrs Brown. She clutched at the front door of number thirty-two Windsor Gardens and gazed at the man standing on the step. "But there must be some mistake. Paddington isn't a..." She broke off as Mrs Bird gave her a nudge. "I mean, he's a..."

"May I ask *why* he has to go to school?" interrupted

the Browns' housekeeper.

The man consulted a pile of papers in his hand. "According to our information," he said, "he's been living here for a number of years and we've no record of a single attendance at St Luke's or anywhere else for that matter."

"But he was brought up in Darkest Peru," exclaimed Mrs Brown. "His Aunt Lucy taught him all she knew before he left. She had to go into a Home for Retired Bears in Lima, you see, and..." Her voice trailed away as she caught sight of the expression on the School Inspector's face.

"I'm very much afraid," he said, allowing himself a slight smile, "that neither the Home for Retired Bears in Lima nor Aunt Lucy happen to be on our list of approved establishments."

He snapped the file shut with an air of finality. "We shall expect to see him at school first thing tomorrow morning," he continued sternly, "otherwise certain steps will have to be taken."

Mrs Brown gazed after the Inspector as he disappeared down the road. "Tomorrow morning!" she repeated. "What *are* we going to do?"

"I think," said Mrs Bird wisely, "there's only one thing we *can* do. Make sure that bear arrives on time. After all," she added meaningly, "we do have his circumstances to think of. I daresay it's only a matter of the authorities setting their records to rights, but until they do, I think we'd better tread very carefully.

"And if Paddington *is* going to school tomorrow," she continued, "we'd better get busy as well. I must sew a name-tag on his duffle coat for a start. We shall never hear the last of it if that gets lost." Mrs Bird paused at the kitchen door. "Will you tell him or shall I?"

Mrs Brown gave a sigh. "I will," she said.

She knew exactly what Mrs Bird meant. Ever since Paddington first arrived on the scene, she'd had a nagging fear in the back of her mind that something like this would happen if only because they'd never actually reported his arrival to anyone, and the thought of breaking the news to him was not one she exactly relished.

But Paddington took the matter surprisingly well, and while the others busied themselves getting his things ready, he spent the afternoon going through some of Jonathan and Judy's old text books. The rest of the time he spent polishing his suitcase, and that evening he even had a bath without being asked, which was most unusual.

All in all, he looked so spick and span the following morning, even Mrs Bird's eagle eyes were unable to find fault.

"I still can't believe it," said Mrs Brown, as he set off down the road. "The house'll seem so quiet without him."

Mrs Bird gave a snort. "I should make the most of it," she said. "You mark my words, it'll be four o'clock and he'll be back home again before we've had time to turn round."

All the same, it was noticeable that the Browns' housekeeper spent an unusually long time cleaning the step that morning, and she didn't finish it until long after the small figure in a duffle coat and hat had disappeared around the corner.

But Paddington himself didn't have any time to dwell on the matter. The school was only a short distance away from Windsor Gardens and as he drew near, one of the teachers hurried forward to greet him.

"Good morning," he said. "I take it you're one Brown, P?"

"One *brown pea*?" repeated Paddington in surprise. He gave the man a hard stare. "No, I'm not. I'm Paddington Brown."

The man let go of Paddington's paw. "Er... that's really what I was asking," he said nervously. "I have instructions to check your arrival. If you hurry, you'll just be in time for the roll."

Paddington licked his lips. A roll sounded a very good way in which to start the day. "I think I shall enjoy that," he announced.

"Good," said the man, looking somewhat relieved. "We thought we'd put you in the Lower Fourth to start with. Mr Eustace's class. That's until we've had time to check your capabilities." He beckoned to a boy who was standing nearby. "Young Smith here will show you where to go."

"Gosh! Fancy putting you into old Eustace's class," said the boy sympathetically, as he led the way into the main building. "Hard luck! I should watch it. If he gets his knife into you, you'll be for it."

Paddington looked around nervously as he

followed the boy into the classroom. It was a large room with windows running the length of one side. There was a blackboard on an adjoining wall and a number of desks were dotted around facing it. But although there were several other pieces of equipment he couldn't see any actual cutlery, and he breathed a sigh of relief as he was ushered towards the front of the class.

There were about thirty other pupils already in the room and they all crowded around, anxious to make his acquaintance. Paddington was a popular figure in the neighbourhood and most of the class wanted him to sit near them.

There was soon an argument raging, and it was while the excitement was at its height that the door suddenly opened and an angular figure in a tweed suit entered the room.

"What's the meaning of this?" he bellowed. "Back to your desks at once!"

Standing on a platform in front of the blackboard, he glowered down at the class as they scurried to their places.

"Now," he called sarcastically, when order had been restored, "I assume I have your permission to take the roll?"

Anxious to make a good impression on his first day, Paddington busied himself behind his desk lid. "I shan't be a moment, Mr Eustace," he called. "I've nearly finished. I've got over thirty-three already!"

"Over thirty-three?" repeated the Form teacher in surprise.

"That's right," said Paddington. "That's one each and three spare."

"*One each and three spare?*" Mr Eustace stared at Paddington as if he'd suddenly lost the use of his hearing. "Three spare *what?*"

"Marmalade sandwiches," explained Paddington cheerfully. He lowered his desk lid. "I hope they'll do. I'm afraid I didn't bring any rolls. But I've got some sliced loaf and some of my special marmalade from the cut-price grocers."

"*Marmalade sandwiches!*" spluttered Mr Eustace. He

bounded from the platform, all thoughts of checking the list of those present driven from his mind as he peered inside Paddington's desk.

"I've a good mind to take these to the headmaster!" he cried.

It was Paddington's turn to look as if he could hardly believe his ears. "All thirty-three?" he exclaimed in amazement. "Even *I've* never managed that many."

"Silence!" shouted Mr Eustace as a titter ran around the room.

"I mean," he said, breathing heavily as he turned back to Paddington, "that I am confiscating them. Marmalade sandwiches indeed! I've never heard of such a thing."

Paddington slumped back into his seat. He'd never heard of anyone having their marmalade sandwiches confiscated either, and he looked most offended.

"You're not here to learn how to make sandwiches," said the teacher as he removed the pile and placed it on his own desk. "You're here to learn the three Rs."

"The three Rs?" repeated Paddington in surprise. Despite his feeling of indignation at the unexpected loss of his sandwiches, he couldn't help being interested at this sudden turn of events. "I didn't know there were *three* Rs."

"Ah," said Mr Eustace, with satisfaction. "We learn something new every day. The three Rs," he continued, "are Reading, Writing and Arithmetic, and today we happen to be starting with arithmetic."

He turned to the blackboard. "Now," he said, pointing to some figures, "I have written out a little problem, and I've made a deliberate mistake. Can anyone tell me what it is?"

In his haste to be first with the answer, Paddington nearly fell off his seat. "I can!" he exclaimed, raising his paw as high as he could.

"Ah, Brown," said the teacher, eyeing him slightly less disapprovingly. "I'm glad to see you're quick off the mark. What is your answer?"

"You don't spell arithmetic with an R, Mr Eustace," said Paddington excitedly.

Mr Eustace stared at him. "I know you don't spell it with an R," he said impatiently.

Paddington's jaw dropped. "But you just said you did," he cried hotly. "You said there were three Rs. Reading, Writing and Arithmetic."

"You did, sir," chorused the rest of the class.

Mr Eustace passed a trembling hand over his forehead. It suddenly seemed unusually warm in the classroom. "I may have *said* it," he began, "but I didn't mean it. That is... I..."

"I remember what it looks like," continued Paddington, pressing home his point. "My Aunt Lucy taught me, and she used to write it down. It begins with an A."

"I'm afraid," said the teacher wearily, "that I'm not familiar with your Aunt Lucy's curriculum."

Paddington opened his suitcase. "I'll show you a picture of her if you like, Mr Eustace," he announced.

"Then you'll be able to recognise it. She had it taken just before she went into the Home for Retired Bears..."

"I mean," said Mr Eustace testily, "that I don't know anything about her teaching capabilities – *if* she has any."

Paddington gave him a hard stare. It was one of his hardest ever. He was a polite bear at heart, but he was beginning to get upset by the way the conversation was going, especially when it had to do with his Aunt Lucy.

"She's very good at spelling, Mr Eustace," he said stoutly. "She's always sending me postcards..."

"Are you suggesting, bear," thundered Mr Eustace, "that I am not?"

"Oh, no, Mr Eustace," said Paddington earnestly. "I'm sure it's very good to get one out of three right."

Mr Eustace mopped his brow again as another titter ran round the room. He was normally very keen on discipline, but for some reason or other, he seemed to be losing his touch on this particular morning. It was definitely one of those days. For a moment or two he appeared to be taking advantage of his own arithmetic lesson by practising some counting, and then, as his eye alighted on the pile of marmalade sandwiches, a thought seemed to strike him.

"Since," he said, "you clearly have an interest in food, you may like to go out and do some shopping for me."

"Oh, yes, please," said Paddington eagerly. He felt as keen as Mr Eustace to bring the present topic of conversation to an end. "I often do Mrs Bird's shopping for her."

"Good," said Mr Eustace. "Perhaps we've found our true vocation at last."

Paddington's face fell. "Are you coming too, Mr Eustace?" he asked.

"No," said Mr Eustace, slowly and distinctly. "I shall not be coming too. But it so happens I need some fish..."

"Some fish?" echoed Paddington, nearly falling over backwards with astonishment. If Mr Eustace had asked for some chalk for the blackboard or even some rolls, he wouldn't have been surprised; but fish was the last thing he'd expected.

"Fish," repeated Mr Eustace, handing him some money. "Something in the nature of a herring or two would do admirably. You may," he added hopefully, "take as long as you like."

"Bears are good at shopping," said Paddington as he took the money and hurried towards the door, watched by thirty envious pairs of eyes. "I shan't be long."

Mr Eustace gazed after the retreating figure as if that was exactly what he feared, and sure enough, he'd hardly had time to bring the mathematics lesson to an end when the door burst open and Paddington hurried back into the room clutching a parcel wrapped in newspaper.

He looked rather apprehensive as he made his way towards the platform. Mr Eustace was clutching a knife in one hand and he appeared to be doing something to the contents of an old tin can.

"That was quick, bear," he said, trying to make the best of things as he looked up. "We're about to get under way with the next lesson."

Placing the knife on the table, Mr Eustace took the parcel and started to unwrap it. As he did so, the smile slowly disappeared from his face. Normally fairly red, his features began to resemble an overripe beetroot as he undid the last of the folds.

"And what is this, pray?" he demanded, holding a package up to the light.

"It's some fish fingers, Mr Eustace," said Paddington. "They were on special offer in the supermarket. The man said they would be all right so long as you eat them before next Tuesday."

"*Eat them!*" Mr Eustace glared at the package. "I don't want to *eat* them. I want to cut them up! They're for my biology lesson."

Reaching over, he grasped the knife on his desk and with one sweeping movement, pushed the tin can towards Paddington.

"Take this, bear," he thundered. "I shall call on you when it's time for practicals."

Paddington didn't need asking twice. He had no idea what Mr Eustace had in mind, but from the look on his face and the way he was brandishing the knife, he had no wish to stay and find out. Clutching the tin in his right paw, he backed towards the classroom door. When he reached it, he held his other paw up as high as it would go.

"If you please, Mr Eustace," he exclaimed, "I think I would like to be excused." And without waiting for an answer, he disappeared up the corridor as fast as his legs would carry him.

Paddington was the sort of bear who believed in going right to the top in times of trouble, and this definitely seemed to be one of those occasions.

On his way in that morning he'd noticed a door marked 'headmaster' and he didn't stop until he reached it.

The headmaster looked up in surprise as Paddington entered his study and collapsed into a chair in front of his desk. "I think Mr Eustace is going to put his knife into me!" he gasped. "He wants to call on me for his practicals!"

St Luke's was a large school, and like all large schools it had its fair share of problems. Even so, the headmaster began to look more and more unhappy as he listened to Paddington's tale of woe. He hadn't been best pleased when the Inspector had passed on the news of a new arrival halfway through the term, especially one who apparently hadn't been to school before, and it seemed as though his worst fears were being realised.

He stood up as a bell began to ring somewhere in the distance. "It does seem as though it's been one long misunderstanding," he said. "That's the midday bell. Perhaps we can talk about it over lunch. There's nothing like a spot of food for calming the nerves."

Ushering Paddington through the door, he led the way down the corridor. "You may eat at the teachers' table," he continued. "Just for today I'll make you food monitor. That means you'll be in charge of all the serving."

Paddington began to look more cheerful as he listened to the headmaster's words, and when he saw the pile of food laid out ready for them he grew more cheerful still, despite the fact that out of the corner of his eye he could see Mr Eustace glaring at him from the other end of the table.

After he'd finished serving out the soup, Paddington turned his attention to an enormous tureen full of stew.

"I think I shall like school after all," he announced, licking his lips as he passed the first plateful to the headmaster.

"I'm very pleased to hear it," said the Head. "After all," he added, "you'll be with us until you're sixteen, and that's a long time."

"Sixteen!" The ladle fell unheeded from Paddington's paw, and his eyes nearly popped out of their sockets as he gazed at the headmaster. "*Sixteen!* But I thought I was only here for the day!"

The headmaster gave a nervous chuckle. "I'm afraid it's the law now," he said, hurriedly turning to one of his colleagues. "And there's no getting away from it."

Paddington served the rest of the food as if in a dream. In fact he was so taken up with his thoughts that he quite forgot to give himself any, and several of the teachers were already passing their plates up for seconds.

When he came to again, Paddington began peering into the pot with a thoughtful expression on his face.

"Come along, bear," called Mr Eustace impatiently. "Don't let it get cold. There's nothing worse than cold stew."

The headmaster looked round. "Is anything the matter?" he asked. "You look as if you've lost something."

Paddington poked the contents of the pot with a spoon.

"I think I may have dropped Mr Eustace's tin in the stew by mistake," he announced.

All eyes turned towards the end of the table as a loud groan followed Paddington's remark.

The headmaster jumped to his feet in alarm. "Are you all right, Mr Eustace?" he asked. "You seem to have gone quite pale."

Looking at Mr Eustace, even his best friends would have had to admit that the headmaster's remarks about his complexion were the understatement of the year. He looked positively green as he sat clutching his stomach. "That tin," he moaned, "happens to belong to my biology class. It's the one I keep my worms in!"

Paddington looked up from the stewpot. "Would anyone else like any seconds?" he asked hopefully.

The headmaster removed an invisible speck of dust from his lapel as he gathered his thoughts. It had

taken him a long while to explain to the Browns
all that had happened to Paddington at St Luke's. It
hadn't been an easy task, particularly as he still wasn't
sure of all the facts himself.

"The long and short of it is," he said, "we... er...
that is, my colleagues and I, feel that until young Mr
Brown has a proper school uniform he'd be much
better off staying at home."

"A school uniform?" broke in Mrs Brown. She looked
at Paddington. "But we shall never get one to fit him."

The headmaster gave a cough as he rose to his feet.
"Er... exactly," he said. "I've had a word with the
Inspector and in the circumstances he's perfectly happy
to take my advice. All in all I think it will be much the
best thing."

He paused at the door and looked back at
Paddington with the suspicion of a twinkle in his eye.
"I'm sure you'll be pleased to know," he said, "that
your suspicions were ill-founded. Mr Eustace's tin
hadn't fallen in the stew after all. We found it under
the table. Both the worms and Mr Eustace are doing
very well.

"I have a feeling," he said, addressing Mrs Brown

as he made to leave, "that in any case, there's not much we at St Luke's can teach bears."

"I wonder what he meant by that last remark?" said Mrs Brown, when she came into the room after saying goodbye to the headmaster. "Have you any idea, Paddington?"

But Paddington had his eyes closed. One way and another it had been a tiring day at school and he wasn't at all sorry to put his paws up.

Mrs Brown sighed. She sometimes wished it wasn't quite so hard to tell what he was thinking.

"If you ask me," said Mrs Bird, reading her thoughts, "it's probably just as well. There's no knowing what we might find out – especially when it comes to school-bears!"

Chapter Two

PADDINGTON CLEANS UP

PADDINGTON PEERED THROUGH the letter box at number thirty-two Windsor Gardens with a look of surprise on his face.

In point of fact, he'd been watching out for the postman, but instead of the blue-grey uniform he'd hoped to see, Mr Curry, the Browns' next-door neighbour had loomed into view. Mr Curry looked as if he was in a bad temper. He was never at his best in the morning, but even through the half-open flap it was plain to see he was in an even worse mood than usual. He was shaking a rug over the pavement, and from the cloud of dust surrounding him it looked as though he had been cleaning out his grate and had just had a nasty accident with the ashes.

The expression on his face boded ill for anyone who happened to come within his range of vision, and it was unfortunate that his gaze alighted on the Browns' front door at the very moment when Paddington opened the letter box.

"Bear!" he bellowed. "How dare you spy on me like that? I've a very good mind to report you!"

Paddington let go of the flap as if it had been resting in hot coals, and gazed at the closed door with a very disappointed air indeed. Apart from an occasional catalogue, he didn't get many letters, but all the same, he always looked forward to seeing the postman arrive, and he felt most aggrieved at being deprived of his morning's treat, especially as he'd been half-expecting a postcard from his Aunt Lucy in Peru. Something she'd said when she'd last written had given him food for thought and he was anxiously awaiting the next instalment.

All the same, he knew better than to get on the wrong side of Mr Curry, so he decided to forget the matter and pay his daily visit to the nearby market in the Portobello Road instead.

A few minutes later, having taken his shopping basket on wheels from the cupboard under the stairs, he collected Mrs Bird's shopping list, made sure the coast was clear, and set out on his journey.

Over the years, Paddington's basket on wheels had become a familiar sight in the market, and it was often much admired by passers-by. Paddington took great care of it. He'd several times varnished the basketwork, and the wheels were kept so well oiled there was never a squeak. Earlier in the year, Mr Brown had bought him two new tyres, so all in all it still looked as good as new.

After he'd completed Mrs Bird's shopping, Paddington called in at the bakers for his morning supply of buns. Then he carried on down the Portobello Road in order to visit the antique shop belonging to his friend, Mr Gruber.

Paddington liked visiting Mr Gruber. Apart from selling antiques, Mr Gruber possessed a large number of books, and although no one knew if he'd actually read them all, it certainly seemed as though he must have, for he was a mine of information on almost every subject one could think of.

When he arrived he found Mr Gruber sitting on the horsehair sofa just inside his shop, clutching a particularly large volume.

"You'll never guess what today's book is about, Mr Brown," he said, holding it up for Paddington to see. "It's called 'Diseases of the Cocoa Bean', and there are over seven hundred and fifty pages."

Paddington's face grew longer and longer as he listened to Mr Gruber recite from the long list of things that could happen to a cocoa bean before it actually reached the shops. He always rounded off his morning excursions with a visit to his friend, and Mr Gruber's contribution to the meeting was a never-ending supply of cocoa, which he kept at the ready on a small stove at the back of the shop. It didn't seem possible that this could ever come to an end.

"Perhaps we'd better get some more stocks in, Mr Gruber," he exclaimed anxiously, when there was a gap in the conversation.

Mr Gruber smiled. "I don't think there's any risk of our going short yet awhile, Mr Brown," he replied, as he busied himself at the stove. "But I think it does go to show how we tend to take things for granted. We very rarely get something for nothing in this world."

Paddington looked slightly relieved at Mr Gruber's reassuring words. All the same, it was noticeable that he sipped his cocoa even more slowly than usual, and when he'd finished he carefully wiped round his mug with the remains of a bun in order to make sure he wasn't letting any go to waste.

Even after he'd said goodbye to Mr Gruber, he still had a very thoughtful expression on his face. In fact, his mind was so far away, it wasn't until he rounded a corner leading into Windsor Gardens that he suddenly came back to earth with a bump as he realised that while he'd been in the shop, someone had pinned a note to his shopping basket.

It was short and to the point. It said:

YOUR SHOPPING BASKET ON WHEELS IS IN SUCH GOOD CONDITION IT SHOWS YOU HAVE CHARACTER, DRIVE AND AMBITION. THIS MEANS YOU ARE JUST THE KIND OF PERSON WE ARE LOOKING FOR. YOU COULD EARN £200 PER WEEK WITH NO MORE EFFORT THAN IT TAKES TO VISIT THE GROCERS. I WILL BE IN TOUCH SOON WITH FURTHER DETAILS.

It was written in large capital letters and it was signed YOURS TRULY. A WELL-WISHER.

Paddington read the note several times. He could hardly believe his eyes. Only a moment before he'd been racking his brains to think up ways of earning some extra money so that he could buy Mr Gruber a tin or two of cocoa; and now, out of nowhere, came this strange offer. It couldn't have happened at a better moment, especially as he'd been tempted to break into the savings which he kept in the secret compartment of his suitcase, and which he held in reserve for important occasions, like birthdays and Christmas.

It was hard to believe he could earn so much money simply because he'd kept his shopping basket clean, but before he'd had a chance to consider the matter he saw a man in a fawn raincoat approaching. The man was carrying a large cardboard box which seemed to contain something heavy, for as he drew near he rested it on Paddington's basket while he paused in order to mop his brow.

He looked Paddington up and down for a moment and then held out his hand. "Just as I thought!" he exclaimed. "It's nice when you have a picture of someone in your mind and they turn out exactly as you expected. I'm glad you got my note. If you don't mind me saying so, sir, you should go far."

Paddington held out his paw in return. "Thank you, Mr Wisher," he replied. "But I don't think I shall go very far this morning. I'm on my way home." He gave the man a hard stare. Although he was much too polite to say so, he couldn't really return the man's compliments. From the tone of the letter, he'd expected someone rather superior, whereas his new acquaintance looked more than a trifle seedy.

Catching sight of Paddington's glance, the man hastily pulled his coat sleeves down over his cuffs. "I must apologise for my appearance," he said. "But I've got rid of... er, I've obtained so many new clients for my vacuum cleaners this morning I don't know whether I'm coming or going. I haven't even had time to go home and change."

"Your *vacuum cleaners!*" exclaimed Paddington in surprise.

The man nodded. "I must say, sir," he continued, "it's your lucky day. It just so happens that you've caught me with my very last one. Until I take delivery of a new batch later on, of course," he added hastily.

Taking a quick glance over his shoulder, he

produced a piece of pasteboard, which he held up in front of Paddington's eyes for a fleeting moment before returning it to an inside pocket.

"My card," he announced. "Just to show that all's above board and Sir Garnet like.

"You, too, could become a member of our happy band and make yourself a fortune. Every new member gets, free of charge, our latest model cleaner, *and*... for today only, a list of do's and don'ts for making your very first sale.

"Now." He slapped the box to emphasise his point. "I'm not asking forty pounds for this very rare privilege. I'm not asking thirty-five. I'm not even asking thirty. To you, because I like the look of your face, and because I think you're just the sort of bear we are looking for, *twenty-five* pounds!"

His voice took on a confidential tone. "If I was to tell you the names of some of the people I've sold cleaners to, you probably wouldn't believe me. But I won't bore you with details like that. You're probably asking yourself what you have to do in order to earn all this money, right? Well, I'll tell you.

"You sell this cleaner for thirty pounds, right?

You then buy two more cleaners for twenty-five pounds each and sell them for thirty, making fifteen pounds in all, right? Then you either keep the money or you buy six more cleaners and sell those. If you work hard, you'll make a fortune so fast you won't even have time to get to the bank.

"Another thing you may be asking yourself," he continued, before Paddington had time to say anything, "is why anyone who already has a vacuum cleaner should buy one of ours?"

He gave the box another slap. "Never fear, it's all in here. Ask no questions, tell no lies. With our new cleaner, you can suck up anything. Dirt, muck, ashes, soot... pile it all on, anything you like. A flick of the switch and whoosh, it'll disappear in a flash.

"But," he warned, "you'll have to hurry. I've a queue of customers waiting round the next corner."

Paddington needed no second bidding. It wasn't every day such an offer came his way, and he felt sure he would be able to buy an awful lot of cocoa for fifteen pounds. Hurrying behind a nearby car, he bent down and opened his suitcase.

"Thank you very much," said the man, as Paddington

counted out twenty-five shiny one pound coins. "Sorry I can't stop, guv, but work calls..."

Paddington had been about to enquire where he could pick up his next lot of cleaners, but before he had a chance to open his mouth, the man had disappeared.

For a moment, he didn't know what to do. He felt very tempted to take the cleaner straight indoors in order to test it in his bedroom, but he wasn't at all sure Mrs Bird would approve. In any case, number thirty-two Windsor Gardens was always kept so spotlessly clean, there didn't seem much point.

And then, as he reached the end of the road, the matter was suddenly decided for him. Mr Curry's front door shot open and the Browns' neighbour emerged once again carrying a dustpan and brush.

He glared at Paddington. "Are you still spying on me, bear?" he growled. "I've told you about it once before this morning."

"Oh, no, Mr Curry," said Paddington hastily. "I'm not spying on anyone. I've got a job. I'm selling a special new cleaner."

Mr Curry looked at Paddington uncertainly. "Is this true, bear?" he demanded.

"Oh, yes," said Paddington. "It gets rid of anything. I can give you a free demonstration if you like."

A sly gleam entered Mr Curry's eyes. "As a matter of fact," he said, "it does so happen that I'm having a spot of bother this morning. I'm not saying I'll buy anything, mind, but if you care to clear up the mess I *might* consider it."

Paddington consulted the handwritten list of instructions which was pinned to the box. He could see that Mr Curry was going to come under the heading of CUSTOMERS – VERY DIFFICULT.

"I think," he announced, as the Browns' neighbour helped him up the step with his basket on wheels, "you're going to need what we call the 'full treatment'."

Mr Curry gave a snort. "It had better be good, bear," he said. "Otherwise I shall hold you personally responsible."

He led the way into his dining-room and pointed to a large pile of black stuff in the grate. "I've had a bad fall of soot this morning. Probably to do with the noise that goes on next door," he said meaningly.

"My cleaner's very good with soot, Mr Curry," said Paddington eagerly. "Mr Wisher mentioned it specially."

"Good," said Mr Curry. "I'll just go and finish emptying my dustpan and then I'll be back to keep an eye on things."

As the Browns' neighbour disappeared from view, Paddington hurriedly set to work. Remembering the advice he'd been given a short while before, he decided to make certain he gave Mr Curry a very good demonstration indeed.

Grabbing hold of a broom which was standing nearby, he quickly brushed the soot into a large pile in the middle of the hearth. Then he poked the broom up the chimney and waved it around several times. His hopes were speedily realised. There was a rushing sound and a moment later an even bigger load of soot landed at his feet. Ignoring the black clouds which were beginning to fill the room, Paddington removed the cardboard box from his basket, and examined Mrs Bird's shopping. As he'd feared, some of it had suffered rather badly under the weight and he added the remains of some broken custard tarts, several squashed tomatoes, and a number of cracked eggs to the pile.

It was while he was stirring it all up with the handle of the broom that Mr Curry came back into the room. For a moment he stood as if transfixed.

"Bear!" he bellowed. "Bear! What on earth do you think you're doing?"

Paddington stood up and gazed at his handiwork. Now that he was viewing it from a distance he had to admit it was rather worse than he intended.

"It's all part of my demonstration, Mr Curry," he explained, with more confidence than he felt.

"Now," he said, putting on his best salesman's voice as he consulted the instructions again, "I'm sure you will agree that no ordinary cleaner would be any good with this mess."

For once in his life it seemed that Mr Curry was in complete and utter accord with Paddington. "Have you taken leave of your senses, bear?" he spluttered.

Paddington gave the cardboard box a slap. "No,

Mr Curry," he exclaimed. "Never fear, it's all in here. Ask no questions, I'll tell no lies."

Mr Curry looked as if there were a good many questions he was only too eager to ask, but instead he pointed a trembling finger at the box.

"Never fear, it's all in here!" he bellowed. "It had better all be in there! If it's not all in there within thirty seconds, I shall... I shall..."

Mr Curry paused for breath, suddenly at a loss for words.

Taking advantage of the moment, Paddington opened the lid of the box and withdrew a long piece of wire with a plug on the end.

He peered at the skirting board. "Can you tell me where your socket is, Mr Curry?" he enquired.

If Paddington had asked the Browns' neighbour for the loan of a million pounds he couldn't have had a more unfavourable reaction. Mr Curry's face, which had been growing redder and redder with rage, suddenly went a deep shade of purple as he gazed at the object in Paddington's paw.

"My socket?" he roared. "*My socket?* I haven't any sockets, bear! I don't even have any electricity. I use gas!"

Paddington's jaw dropped, and the plug slipped from his paw and fell unheeded to the floor as he gazed at the Browns' neighbour. If Mr Curry's face had gone a deep shade of purple, Paddington's – or the little that could be seen of it beneath his fur – was as white as a sheet.

He wasn't sure what happened next. He remembered Mr Curry picking up the cardboard box as if he was about to hurl it through the window, but he didn't wait to see any more. He dashed out through the front door and back into number thirty-two Windsor Gardens as if his very life depended on it.

To his surprise the door was already open, but it wasn't until he cannoned into Mr Gruber that he discovered the reason why. His friend was deep in conversation with the other members of his family.

For some reason they seemed even more pleased to see him than he was to see them.

"There you are!" exclaimed Mrs Bird.

"Thank goodness," said Mrs Brown thankfully.

"Are you all right?" chorused Jonathan and Judy.

"I think so," gasped Paddington, peering over his shoulder as he hastily closed the door behind him.

"No one's tried to sell you a vacuum cleaner?" asked Mrs Bird.

Paddington stared at the Browns' housekeeper in amazement. It really was uncanny the way Mrs Bird 'knew' about things.

"There have been some 'goings-on' down at the market this morning, Mr Brown," broke in Mr Gruber. "That's why I popped in. Someone's been selling dud vacuum cleaners and when I heard you'd been seen talking to him I began to get worried."

"When you were so late back we thought something might have happened to you," said Mrs Brown.

"Well," said Paddington vaguely, "I think it has!"

Paddington launched into his explanations. It was a bit difficult, partly because he wasn't too sure how to put some of it into words, but also because there was a good deal of noise going on outside. Shouts and bangs, and the sound of a loud argument, followed a moment or so later by the roar of a car drawing away.

"Fancy trying to take advantage of someone like that," said Mrs Bird grimly, when Paddington had finished.

"He seemed quite a nice man, Mrs Bird," said Paddington.

"I didn't mean the vacuum cleaner salesman," said Mrs Bird. "At least he gave you *something* for your money – even if it didn't work. I meant Mr Curry. He's always after something for nothing."

"He's too mean to get his chimney swept for a start," said Judy.

"And I bet he's still waiting to see if electricity catches on before he changes over," agreed Jonathan.

They broke off as the telephone started to ring and Mrs Bird hurried across the hall to answer it.

"Yes," she said after a moment. "Really? Yes, of course. Well, we'll do our best," she added after a while, "but it may not be for some time. Probably later on this morning."

The others grew more and more mystified as they

listened to their end of the conversation.

"What on earth was all that about?" asked Mrs Brown, as her housekeeper replaced the receiver.

"It seems," said Mrs Bird gravely, "that the police think they may have caught the man who's been selling the dud vacuum cleaners. They want someone to go down and identify him."

"Oh dear," said Mrs Brown. "I don't really like the idea of Paddington being involved in things like that."

"Who said anything about Paddington?" asked Mrs Bird innocently. "Anyway, I suggest we all have a nice hot drink before we do anything else. There's no point in rushing things."

The others exchanged glances as they followed Mrs Bird into the kitchen. She could be very infuriating at times. But the Browns' housekeeper refused to be drawn, and it wasn't until they were all settled round the kitchen table with their second lot of elevenses that she brought the matter up again.

"It seems," she mused, "that the man they arrested was caught right outside our house. He was carrying a cleaner at the time. He said his name was Murray, or Hurry or something like that... Anyway, he insists we know him."

"Crumbs!" exclaimed Jonathan as light began to dawn. "Don't say they picked on Mr Curry by mistake!"

"I bet that's what all the row was about just now," said Judy. "I bet he was coming round here to complain!"

"Which is why," said Mrs Bird, when all the excitement had died down, "I really think it might be better if Paddington doesn't go down to the Police Station. It might be rubbing salt into the wound."

"I quite agree," said Mr Gruber. "In fact while you're gone perhaps young Mr Brown and I can go next door and clear up some of the mess."

"Bags we help too," said Jonathan and Judy eagerly.

All eyes turned to Paddington, who was savouring his drink with even more relish than usual. What with Mr Gruber's book on diseases and the disastrous events in Mr Curry's house he'd almost begun to wonder if he would ever have any elevenses again.

"I think," he announced, as he clasped the mug firmly between his paws, "I shall never take my cocoa for granted again!"

Chapter Three

PADDINGTON GOES TO COURT

MR GRUBER WAS still laughing over Paddington's adventure with the vacuum cleaner when they met the next morning.

"Fancy all that coming about just because I happened to be reading a book on cocoa beans, Mr Brown," he said.

He gave another chuckle. "I wish I'd seen Mr

Curry being marched off to the Police Station. It must have been a sight for sore eyes."

Paddington nodded his agreement. His own eyes were feeling sore at that moment, but mostly through keeping them tightly shut in case he bumped into Mr Curry.

Apart from his eyes, his paws were also rather stiff. It had taken them quite a while to clear up the mess in Mr Curry's dining-room, but many hands make light work, and it was generally agreed that not even the Browns' neighbour could have complained about the way his room looked after they had finished.

"Anyway," said Mr Gruber, as he brought out the tray for their elevenses, "all's well that ends well. Although I must say it's a good job it didn't happen in some countries I could think of. In some countries, Mr Brown, you are thought to be guilty until you are proved innocent, whereas here it's the other way round. It's a very fine point, but it can make a great deal of difference sometimes."

Paddington listened carefully while Mr Gruber went on to explain about the workings of the Law.

"It sounds very interesting, Mr Gruber," he said at

last. "But it's a bit hard to understand if you've never been inside a court."

Mr Gruber slapped his knee. "Why didn't I think of it before?" he exclaimed. "If you could spare the time, Mr Brown, perhaps we could have one of our excursions. It's about time we had another outing. We could visit the Law Courts and then you could see what goes on. Would you like that?"

"Ooh, yes please, Mr Gruber," said Paddington eagerly. "I would like that very much indeed."

Paddington polished off the rest of his elevenses with all possible speed and then hurried back home to tell the others.

While he made some marmalade sandwiches, Mrs Bird prepared a flask of hot cocoa, and shortly afterwards he donned his duffle coat again and disappeared back up the road carrying his suitcase.

"I do hope they'll be all right," said Mrs Brown. "It's not that I don't trust Mr Gruber, but things do happen to Paddington and you know what some of these judges are like. I would hate to think of them both ending up in gaol."

"Knowing that bear," said Mrs Bird darkly, "I

think it's much more likely that any judge he meets will end up giving himself six months!"

Paddington would have been most offended had he been able to overhear Mrs Bird's last remark, but by then he was already heading towards the bus stop where he'd arranged to meet Mr Gruber.

Paddington liked bus journeys, especially when he was able to sit on the top deck and listen to his friend talking. Mr Gruber knew a great deal about London, and if Paddington had any complaint at all, it was that he always made the journey pass twice as quickly, so that it seemed no time at all before they drew up outside a group of imposing grey stone buildings and Mr Gruber announced that they had reached their destination.

He led the way through some tall iron gates and then up a flight of stone steps.

Paddington's eyes grew larger and larger as they passed through the entrance and he found himself in an enormous hall, almost as large as a cathedral. It was full of people bustling to and fro: some in ordinary clothes, others dressed in wigs and black gowns, and it was quite unlike anything he'd ever seen before.

Mr Gruber consulted his guidebook. "This is the main hall of the Royal Courts of Justice," he explained. "It's seventy-two metres long and twenty-four metres high."

He led the way up some more steps and suddenly they found themselves in a maze of corridors. "The courts themselves," he went on, "are dotted around the outside of the main hall, and you'll find that each one is hearing a different case.

"There are two sides to every disagreement, Mr Brown," he continued. "It's the job of the lawyers to argue the rights and wrongs and find out who is telling the truth."

"Can't they just ask them?" suggested Paddington.

Mr Gruber chuckled. "Unfortunately," he said, "the truth isn't always quite as simple as it looks, and even more unfortunately people aren't always as truthful as they like to make out. In the end it's the judge who has to make up his mind. That's why he's so important. It's like watching a television play – except, of course, it's much more serious if you happen to be playing one of the leading roles.

"Justice," said Mr Gruber, as he paused outside a door, "not only has to be done, but it has to be seen to be done as well. That's why they have a Public Gallery, and it's the right of every citizen to be present if he so wishes."

Mr Gruber's face fell as he tried the handle. "Oh dear," he said. "It seems to be locked. How very disappointing. I'm sure there must be some mistake. If you care to wait here a moment I'll see if I can find someone in authority."

Excusing himself, Mr Gruber hurried off down the corridor, leaving Paddington to wait outside the door. In point of fact he wasn't at all sorry to have a moment's rest so that he could take in all that Mr Gruber had told him, and there was so much activity all around he was only too happy to sit back and watch for a while.

Opening his suitcase, he took out a marmalade sandwich and then poured himself a cup of cocoa to while away the time. Mrs Bird's Thermos flask was a very good one indeed. It always kept things extremely hot, and the present contents were no exception. In fact, so much steam rose from the cup of cocoa, he had to wipe his eyes several times in order to see what was going on.

He put the top back on the flask and had only just finished closing his suitcase again when a man in uniform came up to him.

He stared at Paddington in surprise. "What do you think you're doing?" he asked. "This isn't a snack bar, you know."

"I'm waiting to go in," said Paddington. "I want to see justice done."

The man gave him an odd look. "What's your name?" he enquired.

"Brown," said Paddington. "Paddington Brown."

"Brown?" echoed the man. A change suddenly came over him. "Dear, oh dear," he said. "It's a good thing for you I came along. They're calling for you downstairs!"

"They're calling for me downstairs?" exclaimed Paddington. "Mr Gruber must have been quick!"

"I don't know about Mr Gruber," said the man, helping him to his feet, "but if you take my advice you'll get a move on."

Paddington didn't need asking twice. Grabbing hold of his suitcase he hurried down a flight of steps after the man and rounded a corner into another long corridor where, sure enough, he heard someone calling his name.

"Here he is," called his companion. "Found him upstairs having a tuck in."

"Well, you'd better look slippy," cried the second man, waving him on. "It's old Justice Eagle today and he doesn't like to be kept waiting."

Looking most alarmed, Paddington hurried through some doors and suddenly found himself in a room full of people.

The whole of one half was taken up by rows of seats on tiers, not unlike a small theatre, and facing them behind a bench on a raised platform was an imposing-looking man wearing a large wig.

He glared at Paddington over the top of his

glasses. "Where have you been?" he asked severely. "I suppose you realise you've been keeping the court waiting?"

Paddington raised his hat politely. "I'm very sorry, Mr Eagle," he announced, "but I'm afraid my eyes got steamed up."

"Your eyes got steamed up?" repeated the judge. "Upon my soul! In all my years I've never heard of that one before!"

"Mr Gruber and I were trying to get in," said Paddington, "but we were locked out."

"You were locked out!" exclaimed the judge. He gazed round the court in the hope of seeing who might be responsible. "This is an outrage. I will not have people prevented from appearing in this way."

"Mr Gruber wasn't very pleased either," agreed Paddington. "He's gone to see if he can find someone in authority."

"Er... quite so," said the judge, looking slightly more benevolent. He motioned to a man sitting in the well of the court. "Let us proceed. We've lost enough time already."

To Paddington's surprise, the man led him to a

box-like compartment at the side of the court and opened a small door for him.

Feeling very pleased that he was being given a seat with such a good view of all that was going on, Paddington climbed inside and was about to settle down when the man handed him a book.

"Do you swear...?" he began.

"Never," said Paddington firmly. "Mrs Bird wouldn't like that at all. And even if she did, I wouldn't."

The man looked around apprehensively at the judge and then decided to have another go. "Do you swear," he repeated, "to tell the truth, the whole truth, and nothing but the truth?"

"Oh, yes," said Paddington more cheerfully. "I was brought up by my Aunt Lucy, and she taught me never to tell lies."

"Silence in Court!" exclaimed the judge, as a titter ran round the assembly.

He consulted a sheaf of papers in front of him and then directed his gaze at a man in a wig and gown on the other side of the room.

"I see no mention of Aunt Lucy, Mr Cloudsworthy,"

he said. "Do I take it that the prosecution are not going to call her?"

"I don't think she would hear if you did, Mr Eagle," said Paddington. "She's in Peru."

"Aunt Lucy's in Peru?" repeated the judge. He adjusted his glasses and gazed at the prosecuting counsel. "I find this very hard to accept."

Mr Cloudsworthy looked as if he found Aunt Lucy's absence even harder to accept than the judge. Looking most confused, he shuffled through his own pile of papers and then had a hurried conversation with one of his assistants.

"Er, with respect, me lud," he said. "I don't think she's very important."

Paddington gave Mr Cloudsworthy a hard stare.

"Aunt Lucy's not important!" he exclaimed. "She brought me up!"

"I think," said the judge, after a long pause, "that you'd better start your questioning, Mr Cloudsworthy. We will deal with the matter of Aunt Lucy later."

"Yes, me lud," said Mr Cloudsworthy. He turned and directed his attention towards Paddington. "I take it," he said, "that you realise why you are here today?"

"Oh, yes," said Paddington. "I'm here because it's my right as a citizen."

Mr Cloudsworthy looked slightly taken aback. "Er, yes," he said. "Very commendable. Very commendable indeed. I take it, from your reply, that you have some knowledge of the law. May I ask if you've ever taken articles?"

"Never!" exclaimed Paddington hotly. "That's worse than telling lies."

"I didn't mean those sort of articles," said Mr Cloudsworthy crossly. "I mean the sort you have to take when you learn a profession. It's like an agreement to say you have to stay with someone until..." He broke off under Paddington's steady gaze and hurriedly changed the subject.

"I'll have you know," he continued, "that I have a very big case here."

Paddington peered at him with interest. "I've got a small one," he announced, holding up his suitcase. "I brought it with me all the way from Darkest Peru. It's got a secret compartment where I keep all my important papers."

"Really?" said Mr Cloudsworthy, trying to strike a jocular note as he caught sight of the expression on the judge's face. "I thought perhaps that was where you kept your briefs."

"My *briefs*?" echoed Paddington. "I'm only here for the day."

The judge took hold of his gavel and rapped the desk sharply. "Silence!" he bellowed. "This is no laughing matter.

"Briefs," he said, turning to Paddington, "are papers lawyers have to bring with them when they attend court."

"Oh, I don't have any of those," said Paddington, opening his case. "But I've got some marmalade sandwiches."

"May I see that?" asked the judge, as Paddington held one of them up for everyone to see.

Paddington handed the sandwich to one of the ushers, who in turn crossed and passed it up to the judge.

"Is this really part of the evidence you are submitting, Mr Cloudsworthy?" demanded the judge distastefully, as he took a closer look. "A bear's sandwich!"

Mr Cloudsworthy looked as if he was hardly sure of anything any more. Removing a handkerchief from inside his gown, he lifted up his wig and began mopping his brow. "Er... I... er, I'm not really sure, me lud," he stuttered.

"Mark this sandwich 'Exhibit A'," said the judge, handing it back to an official. "I will examine it more closely later."

"My sandwich is being marked 'Exhibit A'!" exclaimed Paddington excitedly. "That's some of Mrs Bird's special home-made marmalade. She will be pleased."

"We'd better call her then," said the judge. "Perhaps she'll be able to throw some more light on the matter."

"I've never even heard of Mrs Bird!" cried Mr Cloudsworthy.

The judge looked at him severely. "I really don't think, Mr Cloudsworthy," he said, "that you are conducting your case in the best possible fashion. You don't even appear to know your own witnesses. Call Mrs Bird!"

"Call Mrs Bird!" shouted someone at the back of the court.

"Call Mrs Bird!" echoed a voice outside.

"I don't think she's here either, Mr Eagle," said Paddington.

"Mrs Bird's not here?" repeated the judge. "But she's obviously a most important witness. Why isn't she here?"

"I expect she's out shopping with Mrs Brown," said Paddington. "She always goes out on Tuesday afternoons."

"Really!" barked the judge. "This is intolerable." He glared across the courtroom at the unfortunate counsel. "I've a very good mind to call a halt to the whole case."

Mr Cloudsworthy took a deep breath. "With the greatest respect, me lud," he said, "I would like to ask the witness one more question."

"Granted," said Mr Justice Eagle reluctantly. "But please do be brief."

Placing two trembling thumbs beneath his lapels, Mr Cloudsworthy fixed Paddington with his gaze as he made one last despairing effort.

"Where were you on the morning of the twenty-ninth?" he asked slowly and distinctly. "Think carefully before you answer."

Paddington did as he was told and considered the matter for a moment or two. "What time on the morning of the twenty-ninth, Mr Cloudsworthy?" he asked.

"At around eleven o'clock," said the counsel, looking slightly relieved that he was making some progress at last.

"I expect," said Paddington, "I was having my elevenses with Mr Gruber. We always have them around then. That's why we call them elevenses."

"Call Mr Gruber," said the judge wearily.

"Call Mr Gruber," said a voice at the back of the court.

"Call Mr Gruber," came an answering echo from outside.

By that time, everyone had become so used to the non-appearance of witnesses that a buzz of excitement went around the court as the door suddenly opened. Mr Gruber was accompanied by another man, and he looked more than pleased when he saw Paddington standing in the witness box.

"If you please, my lord," he said, addressing the judge. "I fear there has been a slight misunderstanding. As I'm sure your Lordship realises, there are a good many Browns in this world, and I have a feeling that two of them have become mixed up." He motioned to the man standing next to him. "I believe this is the Mr Brown you really wanted to see!"

The judge first gazed at Mr Gruber and then at Paddington, rather as if he not only agreed that there were a good many Browns in the world, but that there was even one too many for his liking. He appeared to be about to say something and then changed his mind and rose to his feet.

"It's been a very trying day," he said, wearily. "I think I shall hear the rest of this case in my private chambers!"

Paddington and Mr Gruber paused at the entrance to the Law Courts and gazed back at the great hall, still seething with life.

"What a good thing I heard my name being called when I did," said Mr Gruber, "otherwise there's no knowing what might have happened. It only goes to show how very careful you have to be in these matters, and that even a judge should never take things for granted."

Paddington looked as if he couldn't agree more. "Fancy Mr Eagle liking marmalade sandwiches," he said. "He told me he wished he could have some in his chambers every day."

"Judges are only human," said Mr Gruber. "They may look very grand when they're in court, but take away their wig and robes and they're just like anyone else. Except, of course, they need to be much wiser than most people. And often much more understanding.

"I don't suppose there are many bears who can say they've been inside a judge's private chambers," he continued, "let alone shared their sandwiches with one."

It had taken Mr Gruber some while to explain matters to the judge, but in the end even Mr Cloudsworthy had taken the matter in good part.

"Mr Cloudsworthy said that he wouldn't mind having me as a witness on his side another time," said Paddington. "Especially if my eyes were steamed up. I wonder what he meant by that?"

Mr Gruber coughed. "We shall probably never know, Mr Brown," he said tactfully, "but if you want my verdict, after all the goings-on we've been through I think we ought to have a nice cup of tea. There's a restaurant near here where they used to serve some delicious crumpets. If you still have any room left it might be worth investigating. What do you think?"

Paddington licked his lips. "I think, Mr Gruber," he said, as they made their way down the steps and into the world outside, "that you would make a very good judge too if you ever decided to be one."

Chapter Four

A BIRTHDAY TREAT

PADDINGTON PRESSED HIS nose against the door of
the Brightsea Imperial Theatre and peered at a notice
pinned to a board on the other side of the glass.

"I think we're in time, Mr Brown!" he exclaimed
excitedly. "It's called 'Bingo Tonight', and it's on for
two weeks."

Mr Brown joined Paddington at the door and

looked in at the darkened interior of the foyer. "That's not a play," he said. "It's a game."

"You know," said Jonathan. "All the sixes, clickety-click."

"All the sixes, clickety-click!" repeated Paddington. He had no idea what the others were talking about, but he didn't like the sound of it at all.

"It means they've closed the theatre down," exclaimed Judy. "It's been turned into a Bingo Hall."

The Browns gazed at each other in dismay. It was Paddington's summer birthday, and as a treat they had decided to take him to see a show. The day had dawned bright and sunny and on the spur of the moment they'd set off to visit Brightsea, a large town on the south coast, where plays were often tried out before being put on in London.

Paddington had talked of nothing else all the way down, and the news that he was to be done out of his treat was, to say the least, a bad start to the day.

"Perhaps you'd like to go and see the gnomes in Sunny Cove Gardens instead?" suggested Mrs Brown hopefully. "I did hear they've all been repainted this year..." Her voice trailed away as she caught sight of the expression on Paddington's face. Even the brightest of gnomes was hardly a substitute for a visit to the theatre, especially when it was a birthday treat.

"We could go down to the beach while we think about it," said Judy.

Mr Brown hesitated. "All right," he replied. "We'll get some ice creams on the way to be going on with."

Paddington brightened considerably at Mr Brown's remark, and after casting one more glance at the deserted theatre, he turned and followed the others as they made their way along the road leading to the promenade.

Although he was disappointed about the play, Paddington wasn't the sort of bear to stay down in the dumps for long, and when they came to a halt alongside a van and Mr Brown ordered six ice creams, including 'a special large cone for a young bear who's just suffered a disappointment', he felt even better.

Clutching the ice cream in one paw and his suitcase in the other, Paddington followed the rest of the family as they trooped on to the beach. His suitcase was full of birthday cards, a good many of which he hadn't really had time to read properly, and

he didn't want to let them out of his sight before he'd been able to go through them all again.

Mr Brown put some deck chairs near the water's edge, and while Jonathan and Judy changed into their costumes, Paddington made some holes in the wet sand with his paws and then let the incoming waves smooth them over again. It was all very pleasant, for the sea was warm, and calm enough to paddle in without getting the rest of his fur soggy.

It was while he was in the middle of making a particularly deep hole that he happened to glance up hopefully in order to see if there were any more waves on the way, and as he did so he suddenly caught sight of a speedboat. His eyes nearly popped out of their sockets as it shot past. In fact, if his paws hadn't been firmly embedded in the sand he might well have fallen over backwards with surprise.

It wasn't the boat itself that caused his astonishment,

for the sea was alive with craft of all shapes and sizes: it was the fact that just behind it there was a man skimming along the surface of the water on what seemed to be two large planks of wood. But before he had a chance to take it all in, both boat and man had disappeared from view behind the pier.

Paddington sat down on the beach in order to consider the matter. It looked just like the kind of thing for a birthday treat, and he wished he knew more about it. But Mr Brown had settled down behind his newspaper for a pre-lunch nap, and Jonathan and Judy were having a swimming race and had already gone too far to ask. For a moment or two he toyed with the idea of mentioning his idea to Mrs Brown, but she was busy helping Mrs Bird with a knitting problem. In any case, he had a feeling in the back of his mind that she might not entirely approve, so in the end he decided he would have to do his own investigations.

Mrs Brown eyed him nervously as he stood up and announced his intention of taking a stroll along the promenade.

"Don't be too long," she warned. "We'll be having

lunch soon. And I should take your duffle coat. It looks rather stormy."

Mrs Bird nodded her agreement. Since they'd arrived in Brightsea, a change had come over the weather, and the sky was now more than half-covered by clouds, some of which looked very dark indeed.

"You'd better have my umbrella as well," she said. "You don't want to be taken unawares."

Mrs Bird followed Paddington's progress up the beach. She was never very happy when he went off on his own, especially when he was wearing one of his faraway looks.

"Perhaps he wants to stretch his paws after the long car journey," said Mrs Brown, with more conviction than she actually felt.

The Browns' housekeeper gave a snort. "He's much more likely to be looking for the ice cream van again," she remarked.

All the same, Mrs Bird looked noticeably relieved when she turned and saw him peering at a row of posters on the promenade.

On the way down to the beach, Paddington had spotted quite a number of advertisements, and although he hadn't actually read any of them he felt sure there must be at least one which would provide an answer to his question.

As he made his way along the front, he stopped and examined several of them very carefully, but as far as he could make out, all they dealt with were things like Band Concerts and Mystery Coach Tours: none of them so much as mentioned boats let alone where he could buy any planks of wood.

Paddington had often noticed that whenever he went to the seaside, all the really good events were due to happen the following week, and it wasn't until he was well past the pier that he suddenly came across the one he had been looking for.

It showed a man standing on the crest of a wave behind a large red speedboat. With one hand he was hanging on to the stern of the boat, and with the other he was pointing to a sign which said QUEUE HERE FOR SIGNOR ALBERTO'S INTERNATIONAL SCHOOL OF WATER-SKIING.

There was some more writing underneath, most of which had to do with a special Crash Course for beginners, in which not only did Signor Alberto guarantee to get any of his pupils, regardless of age, out of the water and on to their skis in only one lesson, but he promised to present them with a special certificate afterwards to show their friends.

It all sounded very good value indeed, and Paddington was about to go down on the beach to where Signor Alberto's boat was moored, when he caught sight of yet another notice hanging from a nearby post. It said, quite simply: GONE TO LUNCH – BACK SOON. Feeling somewhat disappointed, Paddington turned to retrace his steps. As he did so, he saw some figures waiting on a bench a little way along the promenade. The bench seemed to belong to the skiing school as well, for as one of the occupants shifted his position, he caught a brief glimpse of Signor Alberto's name chiselled into the wooden back rest.

In his advertisement, Signor Alberto had said that he catered for anyone, no matter what their age, but as far as Paddington could make out, some of his clients looked as if they would be hard put to make it to the boat, let alone climb inside. As he hurried along the front to join them he began to get more and more excited. He felt sure that if they were able to water-ski he would have no trouble at all.

"May I join you?" he enquired, raising his hat politely.

The nearest man gave him an odd look. "I don't suppose it'll do any harm," he said grudgingly.

"The more the merrier," agreed the one sitting next to him as he shifted up to make room. "It'll help keep us all warm."

Paddington thanked them both very much and then squeezed in at the end. He waited for a moment

indigestion tablets, and from the look on his face as he caught sight of Paddington it seemed as though he was just about to have another bad attack of his complaint.

As he drew near he held out his hand. "Right," he said grumpily. "Where's your book?"

"My *book*?" repeated Paddington. "But I haven't got one."

"Hah!" said the man triumphantly. "I thought as much. I daresay that explains why you're here. You probably can't read either."

Paddington gave him a hard stare. "I do a lot of reading!" he exclaimed hotly. "I always read a story under the blankets at night before I go to sleep. Mrs Bird gave me a torch specially."

"I'm sorry," said the man sarcastically, "but we don't provide blankets here. I shall have to ask you to move on. Unless," he added, "you're over sixty-five?"

"Over *sixty-five*?" Paddington stared at the man as if he could hardly believe his ears. Although he had two birthdays a year he felt sure his latest one hadn't caused him to look that much older.

Already several passers-by had stopped to watch the proceedings and some of them started to join in.

"Fancy wanting blankets," said one. "Don't know what it'll come to next."

"Mollycoddling, I calls it," agreed another.

"Let him be," called a woman somewhere near the back. "We've all got to go that way sooner or later."

"Shame!" shouted someone else.

"That's all very well," said the man. "But I 'as my job to do. Suppose I let every Tom, Dick and Harry sit here, what then?"

"Tom, Dick and Harry?" repeated Paddington. He looked most upset. "I'm not one of those, Signor Alberto. I'm a Paddington."

"You're a Paddington?" echoed the man. Scratching his head, he turned to the crowd for sympathy. "What *is* he on about?"

The man who'd been sitting next to Paddington rose to his feet as light began to dawn. "I think I know," he said.

He pointed to a notice on the back of the bench and then turned back to Paddington. "This isn't a queue for Signor Alberto," he explained. "This is a special bench for *Senior Citizens*. This gentleman's Alf, the deck chair attendant."

"Alf, the deck chair attendant!" exclaimed Paddington, as if in a dream. He gazed at the newcomer indignantly. "Do you mean to say I've been waiting all this time for nothing?"

"Not for nothing," said the attendant, taking a ticket machine triumphantly from his inside pocket. "For ten pence. If you can't produce your old-age pension book on demand you 'as to pay ten pence an hour or else."

But he might just as well have saved his breath. Out of the corner of his eye Paddington had seen some activity around the ski boat, and taking advantage of the argument, he stuffed Mrs Bird's umbrella inside his duffle coat and crawled through a gap in the crowd while the going was good.

He felt sure that if ever there was a time to take to the water this was it, and, hurrying down the beach towards the boat, he approached a sweater-clad figure bending over the outboard motor.

"Excuse me, Signor Alberto," he announced, tapping him urgently on the shoulder. "I should like to take one of your crash courses in skiing, please. Starting now, if I may!"

The Browns gathered in a worried group on the promenade as they exchanged notes. There was so much noise going on – bursts of cheering alternating with loud groans – that it was difficult to make themselves heard; all the same it was obvious that in their search for Paddington they had drawn a blank.

"We've been to both ends of the promenade," said Jonathan.

"We've even tried the amusement arcade on the pier," added Judy. "There isn't a sign of him anywhere."

"I do hope he's not doing the undercliff walk," said Mrs Brown anxiously. "There isn't a way up for miles and he'll be most upset if he misses lunch – especially today of all days."

"Perhaps we could try asking the deckchair attendant?" suggested Judy. She pointed to a figure a little way along the front. "I bet he's good at remembering faces."

The deckchair attendant was hovering on the edge of a crowd who were leaning on the railings watching something that was taking place far out to sea, and he didn't look best pleased at being interrupted.

"A bear?" he said. "Wearing a duffle coat and carrying an umbrella. I expect that'll be the one I moved on about half an hour ago."

"You moved him on!" exclaimed Mrs Bird severely. "I'll have you know it's his birthday!"

"I daresay," said the man, wilting under her gaze, "but I never intended to move him on that far."

He pointed to a spot beyond the end of the pier, where a speedboat was bobbing up and down in the water. As the Browns turned to follow the direction of his arm, there was a roar from his engine and the boat moved off. Almost immediately a small, but familiar figure rose up out of the water a little way behind. It hovered on the surface for a moment or two and then, to a groan of disappointment from the crowd, slowly disappeared into the sea again.

It was only a fleeting glimpse, but brief though it was, the Browns gasped with astonishment.

"Good gracious!" cried Mrs Bird. "What on earth's that bear doing now?"

Mrs Bird's question wasn't unreasonable in the circumstances, but it was one which even Paddington himself would have been very hard put to answer. In fact, he'd been asking himself the very same thing a number of times over the last half hour. Although he had to admit that he'd enrolled for one of Signor Alberto's special 'crash' courses, he hadn't expected there to be quite so many crashes. As far as he could make out, every time he tried to do anything at all it ended in disaster.

But if Paddington was taking a gloomy view of the proceedings, Signor Alberto looked even more down in the mouth. The change in the weather had brought about a big enough drop in his takings as it was, but with what seemed like the whole of Brightsea watching his attempts to teach Paddington to water-ski he was beginning to think that trade might never pick up again. As he sat huddled in the back of the boat he looked as if he very much wished he was back on the sunny shores of his native Mediterranean again.

"Please," he called, making one last despairing effort, "we will try once more. For the very last time. Relax. You are toa da stiff. You ava to relax. You are like a stick in zee water."

Listening to Signor Alberto's instructions, Paddington suddenly realised that one of his problems was the fact that he still had Mrs Bird's umbrella under his duffle coat, so while the other's back was turned he hastily withdrew it, made some last minute adjustments to the tow rope and then lay back in the water again with the skis pointing upwards as he'd been shown.

Signor Alberto looked back over his shoulder, but if he felt any surprise at seeing Paddington's latest accessory, he showed no sign. In fact he looked as if nothing would surprise him ever again.

"Now," he called. "When I open zee throttle and we begin to move, you 'ave to pull on zee rope and push with your legs into zee water. Remember, whatever you do... watch zee 'eels."

Paddington looked most surprised at this latest

piece of advice. He'd never actually seen a real live eel before, and as the boat moved away from him and took up the slack, he peered into the water with interest.

Slowly and inexorably the boat gathered speed as Signor Alberto pushed home the throttle. Suddenly the rope tightened, and for a second or two it seemed as if he was about to be cut in two. Then gradually he felt himself begin to rise out of the water.

He'd never experienced anything quite like it before, and grasping Mrs Bird's umbrella, he began to wave it at Signor Alberto for all he was worth.

"Help!" he shouted. "Help! Help!"

"Bravo!" cried Signor Alberto. "Bravo!"

But there was worse to follow, for no sooner had Paddington become accustomed to one motion than there was a click and a sudden tug, and to his alarm Mrs Bird's umbrella suddenly shot open and he felt a completely new sensation as he rose higher and higher into the air.

The promenade loomed up and then disappeared as they turned at the very last moment and headed out to sea again. The cheers from the watching crowd

almost drowned the noise of the engine, but
Paddington hardly heard, for by that time there was
only one thing uppermost in his mind – and that was
to get safely back on to dry land again.

Mrs Bird had said that he might need her

umbrella in case he got taken unawares, but as far as Paddington was concerned, he'd never been taken quite so unawares in the whole of his life, for as he glanced down, he saw to his horror that the sea, which a moment before had been skimming past his knees, was now a very long way away indeed.

Mrs Bird opened and closed her umbrella several times. "They certainly knew how to make them in those days," she said with satisfaction.

"I bet they never thought it would be used for a bear's parachute skiing," said Judy.

"Perhaps Paddington could write a testimonial?" suggested Jonathan.

"I think we've had quite enough testimonials for one day," said Mrs Bird.

The Browns were enjoying a late lunch in a restaurant overlooking Signor Alberto's skiing school.

Paddington in particular was tucking in for all he was worth. Although he was looking none the worse for his adventure, there had been a moment when he'd thought he might never live to enjoy another meal, and he was more than making up for lost time.

He'd fully expected to be in trouble when he got back, but in the event the reverse had been true. The Browns had been so relieved to see him safe and sound they hadn't the heart to be cross, and Signor Alberto had been so pleased at the success of his lessons he'd not only refused any payment but he'd even presented him with a special certificate into the bargain. It was the first time anyone in Brightsea had seen parachute skiing, and if the size of the queue on the promenade was anything to go by there would be no lack of customers at his school for some time to come. Even a man who ran an umbrella shop nearby had come along to offer his congratulations. Despite the fact that the sun had come out again, he was doing a roaring trade.

"What beats me," said Mr Brown, "is how you managed to stand up on the skis at all. I didn't think you'd ever make it."

Paddington considered the matter for a moment. "I don't think I could really help myself, Mr Brown," he said truthfully.

In point of fact, he'd wrapped the rope around himself several times just to make sure, but he'd had such a lecture from Signor Alberto afterwards about the dangers of doing such a thing ever again he decided he'd better not say anything about it, and wisely the Browns didn't pursue the matter.

"Perhaps you'd like to round things off with a plate of jellied eels?" suggested Mr Brown, some while later as they took a final stroll along the promenade.

Paddington gave a shudder. What with the ice cream, the water skiing, and an extra large lunch into the bargain, he decided he'd had quite enough for one day, and eels were the last thing he wanted to be reminded of.

All in all, he felt he would much rather round off his birthday treat in as quiet a way as possible.

"I think," he announced, "I'd like to sit down for a while. Perhaps we could all go to Sunny Cove Gardens. Then you can watch the gnomes while I read my birthday cards."

Chapter Five

KEEPING FIT

CLENCHING HIS PAW as tightly as he could possibly manage, Paddington slowly raised his right arm until it was level with his shoulder. Then he bent it at the elbow until the paw itself was only a couple of centimetres or so away from the top of his head. Breathing heavily under the strain, he held the pose for several moments while he peered hopefully at his reflection in the bedroom mirror; but apart from a few slight trembles there wasn't really much to see, and as the glass began to steam up he let out his breath and relaxed again.

Mopping his brow with the end of the counterpane, he collapsed on to his bed and gazed disconsolately at a large pamphlet spread out in front of him.

It was full of brightly coloured pictures, most of which showed a day in the life of a gentleman called Grant Stalwart. Mr Stalwart, who seemed to spend most of his time dressed only in a pair of mauve tights, was shown in a variety of poses, a number of which were not unlike the one Paddington had just attempted.

However, looking at the pamphlet did nothing to dispel Paddington's feeling of gloom. In fact, the more he studied it, the more downcast he became.

If the picture was anything to go by, Grant Stalwart was able to do the most extraordinary things with his muscles. Bags of cement, iron bars; nothing was too heavy for him to lift, or too strong for him to bend in two. One picture even showed him standing alongside a gaily decorated Christmas tree, surrounded by a crowd of onlookers in paper hats who watched admiringly as he cracked some after-dinner nuts for them between his biceps.

Having fur didn't exactly help matters, but looking at his own arms, Paddington had to admit that he couldn't see any muscles large enough to dent a soft-boiled egg, let alone crack walnut shells.

It was all most disappointing and after one more glance at the pamphlet, he bent down and began to open a large cardboard box.

The box was labelled GRANT STALWART'S WORLD FAMOUS HOME BODY-BUILDING OUTFIT, and on the lid was yet another picture of Mr Stalwart himself.

Paddington's interest in the subject had begun soon after his visit to the seaside. While at Brightsea, he'd noticed some lifeguards doing their exercises on the beach, and at the time he'd been most impressed by the things they were able to do. Then, shortly afterwards, he'd come across an article in one of Mrs Brown's magazines about the dangers of taking oneself for granted, and his interest had been aroused again.

After reading Mrs Brown's article, he'd spent several

mornings doing press-ups on the bathroom floor, carefully testing himself on the scales both before and after. But either there was something very wrong with the scales at number thirty-two Windsor Gardens, or the marmalade sandwiches he'd eaten afterwards in order to restore his energy had more than made up for any lost weight, for if anything the needle had gone up slightly each day rather than down.

It was when he'd been glancing through the magazine again in the hope of seeing where he might have gone wrong that he'd come across Grant Stalwart's advertisement.

Not even his worst enemy could have accused Grant Stalwart of taking his body for granted, and the advertisement was ringed with pictures of cups and medals he'd won in nearly every country in the world. According to Mr Stalwart, the apparatus which had turned him into such a strong-man was worth thirty pounds of anybody's money, but notwithstanding that he seemed more than eager to share the secret of his success with anyone who cared to write in, provided they enclosed a five pound note. However, the thing which really clinched matters for Paddington was the solemn promise to any of his customers that if by the end of the first week they weren't filled to the brim with boundless energy he would refund their money without question.

There was a lot more in small print at the bottom of the advertisement, but Paddington didn't bother to read it; instead, he turned his attention to a section marked 'Testimonials from Satisfied Customers'. Although none of them seemed to be from bears, it still struck him as a very good bargain indeed, and he lost no time in completing his application form and sending it in.

But far from being filled with boundless energy, Paddington felt so worn out after his exercises it was as much as he could do to read through the instructions again, let alone ask for a refund.

The apparatus consisted of two tightly coiled springs which were attached at one end to a large metal plate. Each spring had a wooden handle at its opposite end, and the plate itself came ready-drilled with four holes and some special nonslip screws, so that it could be fixed to a convenient wall.

There were a lot of walls at number thirty-two Windsor Gardens, all of which looked only too convenient by Mr Stalwart's standards, but somehow Paddington couldn't picture the Brown family being very enthusiastic about having any springs screwed to them.

He tried jamming the plate between the bedrails, but after pulling the bed round the room several times without the springs giving so much as a creak let alone showing any signs of expanding, he gave up in disgust and decided to try his luck in the garden.

A few moments later he hurried outside armed with Mr Brown's bag of tools and was soon hard at work screwing the plate to a part of the fence that was safely hidden from the house by the garden shed.

After testing it several times in order to make sure it was firmly fixed, Paddington consulted his instructions again.

Mr Stalwart seemed to have no trouble at all with *his* apparatus. Muscles rippling, his tanned body gleaming, he scarcely batted an eyelid as he extended the springs to almost double their normal length; but however hard Paddington tried, he couldn't manage to pull his own springs apart by more than a centimetre or two, and when he did let go for a quick breather they shot back, catching his fur in the spirals and pinning him to the fence.

After a short rest, Paddington decided to have one more go. He freed himself from the springs and then gathered some spare stones from Mr Brown's rockery and placed them in a row along the ground so that he would have a good foothold.

This time he had much more success. After he'd got beyond a certain point it became easier, and he was just glancing round to see if there were any more stones when he nearly jumped out of his skin as a loud cry rang out.

"Bear! What are you doing to my fence, bear?"

Paddington wasn't at all sure what happened next, but in his fright he let go of the springs and as he toppled over he heard a loud crash from somewhere behind him.

When he picked himself up and looked round he saw to his horror that Mr Curry was dancing up and down on the other side of the fence clutching his nose.

Ever since the unfortunate incident with the vacuum cleaner, Paddington had managed to avoid meeting Mr Curry. In fact, had he been asked to produce a short list of the people he least wanted to see, Mr Curry's name would have occupied the first three places.

Anxious to make amends, Paddington hurried across the garden and peered over the top of the fence at the Browns' neighbour. "I'm sorry, Mr Curry," he exclaimed. "I didn't know you were poking your nose into my business."

Mrs Bird was always going on about Mr Curry, and the way he poked his nose into other people's affairs, but as soon as the words had left his mouth Paddington realised he had said the wrong thing.

He held up the springs. "I was only testing my new body-builder, Mr Curry," he exclaimed. "If I'd known you were there I would have waited until you had gone.

"Perhaps you would like to have a go?" he added hopefully, picking up Mr Stalwart's brochure and opening it at a page where a particularly skinny-looking man was shown struggling with a dumb-bell. "It's meant for seven-stone weaklings. There's a letter here from one just like you."

"What!" Mr Curry grew purple in the face. "Are you calling me a seven-stone weakling, bear?"

Paddington nodded, oblivious to the gathering storm clouds on Mr Curry's brow. "He's written a testimonial saying how good they are," he continued eagerly. "I expect if you had a go every day you could become an eight-stone weakling in no time at all. It's worth over thirty pounds and if it doesn't work you get your money back."

Mr Curry had been about to launch forth into a long tirade on the subject of bears in general and the one living next door to him in particular, but he suddenly seemed to change his mind.

"Thirty pounds?" he mused. "And you say there's a money-back guarantee?"

"Oh, yes, Mr Curry," said Paddington earnestly. "I wouldn't have got them otherwise."

"In that case," said Mr Curry briskly, "they certainly need a proper trial. I suggest you use the wall in my boxroom."

Paddington looked at Mr Curry rather doubtfully. "I think I would sooner use one of Mr Brown's walls, if you don't mind..." he began.

"Nonsense, bear!" snorted Mr Curry. And to avoid any further argument he reached over the fence in order to assist Paddington over.

"I shall test them myself," he announced grimly. "And if they don't work I shall lodge a complaint with the manufacturers. Don't you worry – I'll make sure we get our money back."

"*Our* money, Mr Curry?" repeated Paddington. "But..."

Mr Curry held up his hand. "Don't say another word, bear!" he exclaimed. "Fair's fair. I shall have to deduct the cost of making good the damage you did the other day in my dining-room, of course. But

I see no reason why you shouldn't receive a small percentage as well... if there's any left over."

Paddington began to look more and more unhappy as he carried his belongings into the house and followed Mr Curry up the stairs leading to his boxroom.

The Browns' neighbour had a way of twisting words so that even the most outrageous things sounded perfectly reasonable. All the same, he knew better than to argue for fear of making an already bad situation even worse, and he watched carefully while Mr Curry cleared a space and demonstrated exactly where he wanted the apparatus fixed.

"If you make a good job of it, bear," he growled, "I *may* not report our little upset just now. I shall be out for a while doing my shopping. I have to go to the chemist to get some ointment for my nose. You can have it ready for me to test when I get back."

Mr Curry took a deep breath and pounded his chest. "There's nothing like a spot of limbering up before the real thing."

Whatever else he might have said was lost in a burst of coughing, as he staggered out of the room and disappeared down the stairs. A moment later there was a loud bang from the direction of his front door and all was quiet again.

Heaving a deep sigh, Paddington turned his attention to the matter in hand. He wasn't at all keen on doing jobs for the Browns' neighbour, for they had a nasty habit of going wrong, and it was with a distinct lack of enthusiasm that he picked up Mr Brown's drill and set to work on the first hole.

Paddington had drilled holes in walls on several previous occasions and he'd always found it much harder than it looked when other people were doing it, but for once he had a pleasant surprise. Either Mr Curry's plaster was unusually soft, or Mr Brown's drill was extra sharp, for it went into the wall like a knife through butter and in no time at all, he had four neat, round holes ready to take the plugs for the screws.

However, if Paddington had learnt one lesson in life it was that there is a reason for everything, and it was when he pushed a plug into the first hole that he discovered why it had been so easy. Mr Curry's boxroom wall wasn't made of brick at all, but some kind of soft plasterboard. No matter how many plugs he pushed into the hole they simply disappeared from view, falling down behind as if into some bottomless pit. Mr Brown's box of plugs was a big one, but even so it was only a matter of moments before it was completely empty.

Paddington surveyed the scene with growing dismay. After Mr Curry's dire warnings there was only one thing he could picture which would be worse than making a poor job of fixing the springs to the wall, and that was leaving four unfilled holes instead.

As a last resort he tried using some extra-long screws in the hope that they would go right through into the other side, but as he contemplated the drunken way the apparatus was hanging he had to admit at long last that he was beaten.

Paddington took another look inside the box. Considering the number of different walls Mr Stalwart seemed to use for his equipment he felt sure he must have come up against the same problem at some time in his life; and sure enough, attached to the inside of the lid was a small packet he hadn't noticed before, and which had been there to deal with just such a situation.

When he opened the packet, four screws fell out, and each had spring-loaded side pieces, especially made to pop out behind hollow walls as soon as they reached the other side.

It needed only a few seconds' work with a screwdriver and the plate was safely in place. He was only just in the nick of time, for as he was putting the finishing touches to the last screw he heard the front door bang, and Mr Curry's footsteps began to draw near.

As he entered the room he eyed Paddington's handiwork approvingly. "Very good, bear!" he exclaimed, removing his coat. "Stand well back. I'll just show you how it should be done before I get in touch with the manufacturers."

Rubbing his hands together, Mr Curry picked up the handles, closed his eyes, and gave the springs a sharp tug.

If he didn't actually look like Grant Stalwart, it wasn't for want of trying. With his lips tightly compressed, he struggled to gain a foothold on the linoleum. Paddington did as he was told and stood well back, for he had no wish to be in the way if his screws did come out. But Mr Stalwart's special expanding screws were more than equal to the task. The plate was firmly fixed.

"I think, Mr Curry," he announced, "that the wall may come away before my springs do."

In the past, Paddington had often noticed that many a true word was spoken in jest, but even so, he was even less prepared than Mr Curry for what happened next.

The words had hardly left his mouth when there was a splintering noise and the Browns' neighbour suddenly shot past. Taking with him a sizeable part of the wall as well, he disappeared through the open doorway like a bullet from a gun.

In the silence that followed there was a sound not unlike dried peas raining down as Mr Brown's plugs fell through the gap in the wall and rolled across the floor. But Paddington was oblivious to them. He did the only thing possible under the circumstances. Hurrying across the room he hastily locked the door before Mr Curry had time to recover. Then he sat down on his box and gloomily contemplated the hole in the wall while he waited for the storm to break.

Mr Curry held out a sheet of typewritten paper. "Sign here, bear," he growled.

Paddington looked round at the Browns for guidance and then, at a nod from Mrs Bird, he picked up a pen and carefully wrote down his name, adding his special paw mark for good measure in order to show that it was genuine.

"Good," said Mr Curry. "I hope this will teach you a lesson, bear.

"This piece of paper," he reminded his audience, "makes over all rights in the apparatus to me.

"That means," he continued, "that any money due back under the guarantee will now come straight to me. I had intended," he said meaningly for the Browns' benefit, "to share the proceeds, but in the circumstances I feel quite within my rights to keep it all. Good day!"

Mr Brown looked from one to the other as Mr Curry left the house. He'd come back from his office rather late in the proceedings and so far he had only received a garbled version of all that had taken place.

"You're not letting him get away with it, are you?" he said. "If you ask me, seeing how he more or less browbeat Paddington into lending him the springs in the first place it would serve him right if he lost the thirty pounds and had to keep them."

"Thirty pounds?" echoed Mrs Bird, with a twinkle in her eyes. "Who said anything about thirty pounds?"

Mrs Brown held up a copy of her magazine and pointed to Grant Stalwart's advertisement. "They may be worth that much," she said, "*after* they've been paid for. But I'm afraid the five pounds Paddington sent in was only a deposit. There are another twenty-five to go."

Paddington nearly fell off his chair with surprise. "I've got another twenty-five pounds to go!" he exclaimed in alarm.

"No, dear," said Mrs Brown. "You haven't, but Mr Curry has."

As the full meaning of the situation sank in, Mr Brown began to chuckle. Then he felt in his wallet and took out a five pound note.

"I think," he said, "that Paddington ought to have his deposit back. It's worth every penny just to see right triumph over wrong for a change."

"Thank you very much, Mr Brown," said Paddington gratefully.

"I should be careful how you spend it this time," said Mrs Bird. "And always read the small print at the bottom of any advertisements."

Paddington locked the note away in his suitcase and then put the key inside his hat for safety. "Oh, I shall, Mrs Bird," he said earnestly.

"Perhaps," he added, as he considered the matter, "I could buy myself a magnifying glass just to make sure."

He reached out in order to help himself to some much needed toast and marmalade, and as he did so, he caught sight of his reflection on the side of the teapot.

"And if I have any change," he added thoughtfully, "I may buy some nutcrackers. I don't think my muscles will ever be big enough to manage your Christmas walnuts."

Chapter Six

PADDINGTON IN TOUCH

"GOOD HEAVENS!" EXCLAIMED Mr Brown, as he opened the post at breakfast one morning. "Fancy that!"

"Fancy what, Henry?" enquired Mrs Brown.

Mr Brown held up a short, handwritten note for everyone to see. "We've been invited to a rugby match," he replied.

Mr Brown's announcement had a mixed reception

from the rest of the family. Mrs Brown looked as if she didn't fancy the idea at all. Jonathan and Judy, who were enjoying the first day of their Christmas holiday, obviously fell in opposing camps. Mrs Bird passed no comment, and it was left to Paddington to sway the balance.

"A rugby match!" he exclaimed excitedly. "I don't think I've ever been to one of those before, Mr Brown."

"Well, it's really through you we've been asked at all," said Mr Brown, as he re-read the note. "It's from the headmaster of your old school. It seems they're having an end-of-term game in aid of charity. It's between the sixth form and a touring side from South America – the Peruvian Reserves. I expect that's why they thought of you."

"I didn't even know they played rugby in Peru," said Mrs Brown.

"Well, there must be at least twenty-six of them," said Mr Brown, "if they've managed to send over their reserves."

"You can borrow one of my old rattles if you like," said Jonathan.

"It had better be one that works both ways," broke in Judy. "Don't forget, Paddington's loyalties are going to be divided."

Paddington jumped up from the table clutching a half-eaten slice of toast and marmalade in his paw. "My loyalties are going to be divided!" he exclaimed in alarm.

"Well," said Judy, "you won't know which side to cheer. After all, it is your old school, and you do come from Darkest Peru."

Paddington sat down again. "Perhaps I'd better have two rattles," he said. "Just to be on the safe side."

"Don't you think a couple of flags might be better?" said Mrs Brown nervously.

"*Small* ones," agreed Mrs Bird. "We don't want any eyes poked out in the excitement. You know what rugby crowds are like, and there's no knowing what might happen once that young bear gets worked up."

With the memory of other sporting functions Paddington had attended still clear in her mind, the Browns' housekeeper was beginning to wish she'd taken a firmer stand at the start of the conversation.

But it was too late. Paddington was already

helping Mr Brown compose a letter of thanks to the headmaster, and as soon as breakfast was over he made preparations to go down to the market in order to see his friend, Mr Gruber.

Paddington had sometimes seen rugby being played on television, but it had always looked rather complicated and he'd lost interest after a moment or two. Going to see a real game, particularly one involving his country of birth and his old school, was quite a different matter and he decided he ought to know something more about the game. Paddington felt sure that among his many books Mr Gruber would have something on the subject, and as usual he wasn't disappointed.

After a few minutes' search his friend came up with one entitled "RUGBY – ALL YOU NEED TO KNOW FOR A POUND", which seemed very good value indeed.

But Mr Gruber waved aside both Paddington's money and his thanks. "I've had that book for more years than I care to remember, Mr Brown," he said, "and if it helps you out then I shall be more than pleased."

As Paddington got ready to leave, Mr Gruber announced that he would be closing his shop the following afternoon so that he, too, could go and watch the match. "I'll probably see you in the stand, Mr Brown," he said.

Paddington looked rather embarrassed. "I think we shall be sitting down, Mr Gruber," he said. "Mrs Bird told me I would have to wrap up well and to take a cushion because the seats are very hard."

Mr Gruber laughed. "When you go to a rugby match, Mr Brown," he said, "they call the places where you sit 'stands'. I'm afraid it's rather like the game itself – it's a bit difficult to explain."

As he took in this piece of news, Paddington felt more pleased than ever that he'd managed to get hold of a book on the subject and he hurried home to study it.

After a quick lunch time snack, he wasn't seen again for the rest of the afternoon, but if the sounds emerging from his bedroom were anything to go by it was obvious that he was getting a good deal of value out of Mr Gruber's book. Some of the bangs and thumps were very loud indeed, and they were punctuated every now and then by piercing blasts from a whistle and a noise which sounded not unlike that of crunching gears.

"Thank goodness the Peruvians haven't sent over a team of bears!" exclaimed Mrs Bird, voicing everyone's thoughts as Paddington's rattles rent the air for the umpteenth time. "If it sounds like that now, goodness only knows what it'll be like on the day."

When Paddington eventually came downstairs again his forehead looked suspiciously damp and there were several pillow feathers sticking to his fur. He had reached a particularly interesting section of his book called TACKLES – AND HOW TO DO THEM, and for the remainder of that day the Browns gave him a wide berth, especially as he kept casting thoughtful glances at their ankles whenever they went past.

Paddington slept well that night. In fact, after all his exertions he overslept and when he eventually came down, he was already dressed for the afternoon's match. Remembering Mrs Bird's warnings, he was wearing not only his duffle coat and hat, but two enormous scarves into the bargain; a blue one in

honour of the Peruvian side, and a red one in the school colours.

Apart from that, he was also carrying a large cushion, his suitcase, two rattles, a flag, a Thermos of hot cocoa, and a pile of marmalade sandwiches – several of which he ate in order to pass the time while he was waiting to go.

Because of the importance of the occasion, the school had taken over a small stadium next to their grounds, and when the Browns left the house a sizeable crowd was already beginning to make its way there.

Catching sight of some of his friends from the market, Paddington began to wave his flag, and by the time they joined Mr Gruber in the stand and the moment for kick off drew near, even Mrs Brown and Mrs Bird began to be infected by the general air of excitement.

Mindful of the nearness of Paddington's rattles, Mrs Bird handed round some pieces of cotton wool for their ears, and as the two teams trotted out on to the field they all settled back to enjoy themselves.

Paddington decided to keep one rattle in his right paw for St Luke's, who were at the far end of the field, and the other one in his left paw for the visiting team.

At first there was very little to choose between the two, but gradually the amount of noise issuing from his left paw grew less and less until eventually it petered out altogether.

It was clear from the start, that, good though they were, the visiting side were no match for Paddington's old school. The sixth form towered above their opponents and no matter how they tried, the Peruvian forwards couldn't penetrate their defences. In fact, the only good thing about it all was that for the most part, play took place at the end of the field where the Browns were sitting, so that Paddington had a good view of the game.

Despite reading Mr Gruber's book, he was hard put to follow what was going on. As far as he could make out, as soon as anyone picked up the ball, the referee blew the whistle and they had to put it down again, after which most of the players formed up in a circle with their heads together as if they were having some kind of discussion.

Paddington grew more and more upset as the game progressed, and when, towards the end of the first half, one of the Peruvian players was sent off the field for what seemed like no reason at all, he looked very unhappy indeed. Far from being divided, his loyalties were now almost completely on the side of the visitors.

"I'm afraid he's been sent off because he's got what they call a 'loose arm'," explained Mr Gruber, when he saw the look on Paddington's face.

Paddington gave the referee a hard stare. "I'm not surprised!" he exclaimed.

In his letter to the Browns the headmaster had said the match was to be a friendly one, but from where Paddington was sitting it looked as if the game was getting rougher with every passing moment. The way the Peruvians kept getting thrown to the ground, he wouldn't have been surprised if some of them had been sent off with loose legs as well.

During the interval Mr Gruber explained that having a loose arm simply meant the player in question hadn't been holding on to the man next to him in the scrum, and that he'd been sent off because he'd been guilty of the offence more than once.

"A scrum," said Mr Gruber, "is when the players form up into a group with their arms round each other in order to restart the game. It's very important to have it properly conducted."

Mr Gruber went on to list the various reasons for stopping and starting the game, but Paddington's mind was far away; and when, just after the middle of the second half, yet another of the Peruvian players retired hurt he could scarcely contain his indignation.

Mr Brown glanced at his programme. "That's hard luck," he said. "They're only allowed two substitutes and it seems they still have several players on the injured list from the last game. That means they'll be one short for the rest of the match!"

"Crikey!" said Jonathan. "They're eight points down already. They don't stand a chance."

He looked round in order to sympathise with Paddington, but to his surprise the space next to Mr Gruber was empty.

"I think young Mr Brown is taking things rather to heart," said Mr Gruber. "He's gone off somewhere."

"Oh dear," said Mrs Brown nervously. "I do hope he doesn't get lost in the crowd."

The words were hardly out of her mouth when Judy jumped up from her seat with excitement. "Look!" she cried, pointing towards the field. "There he is!"

Following the direction of her gaze, the Browns saw a familiar figure in a duffle coat and hat hurrying across the pitch.

"Oh gosh!" groaned Jonathan. "Trust Paddington."

The match being refereed by the St Luke's Games teacher and he'd been about to blow his whistle to restart it when something about the way the crowd was cheering made him pause. He turned and stared at the approaching figure in surprise.

"Excuse me," said Paddington, "but I've come to offer my services. I'd like to join the Peruvian Reserves, please."

The Games teacher looked at him uneasily. Although he hadn't actually met Paddington before, he knew all about him from the other teachers.

"I'm very sorry," he said, "but I don't think I can allow that. It really has to be someone from the country concerned."

"I come from Peru," said Paddington firmly. "*Darkest* Peru. And I'm very concerned."

"It's true, sir," broke in the school captain. "I'm sure the Head wouldn't mind."

The Games teacher ran his fingers round his collar. "It's all highly irregular," he said. "I'm really supposed to know the names of any substitutes *before* the match, but..." he looked round nervously as sounds of unrest came from the crowd, "it *is* in aid of charity, and... er... if no one objects..."

"We certainly don't," said the St Luke's captain sportingly.

"All right," said the Games teacher, turning to Paddington. "I'll hold up play for a moment while you get rid of your duffle coat."

"Get rid of my duffle coat!" exclaimed Paddington hotly. He gave the teacher a hard stare. "I'm afraid I can't do that. Mrs Bird said I had to wrap up well."

The Games teacher gave a sigh. He knew he was fighting a losing battle. "Perhaps," he said, as the other players gathered round, "you'd better meet the rest of your side."

"You are good at rugby, no?" asked the Peruvian captain as he shook Paddington's paw while he introduced the other members of his team.

"Well, no," agreed Paddington. "You see, I haven't actually *played* before. But I've read all about it in a book Mr Gruber lent me, and I practised some tackles in my bedroom yesterday with one of my pillows."

Fortunately the visiting team's command of English wasn't quite up to Paddington's explanations, otherwise they might not have greeted the arrival of their new team-mate with quite so much enthusiasm.

In any case, there was no time to dwell on the

matter, for with the crowd beginning to stamp and whistle at the long delay, the players quickly formed up again and waited for the referee to blow his whistle.

Paddington watched as they formed a scrum and one of the St Luke's team threw the ball into the tunnel formed by their legs.

There was a flurry of movement and almost immediately the ball came flying out again and as luck would have it, landed right at his feet.

Paddington raised his hat politely to thank the player who had thrown it, and then picked the ball up in order to examine it more closely. He'd never actually seen one close to before and he hadn't expected it to be quite so oval in shape. He was just wondering if he ought to tell the referee in case it had been squashed with all the rough play, when there was a pounding of feet from somewhere behind and what seemed like a tonne weight suddenly landed on top of him.

For a moment, Paddington lay where he had fallen, all the breath knocked from his body, and with a hard lump in the middle of his chest which, as he came to, he gradually realised came about because he was still clutching the ball.

"Very good," said the Peruvian captain as he helped Paddington to his feet. "We have gained two metres. Only eighty more to go. Now we have another scrum."

"*Another* one!" exclaimed Paddington in alarm. He began to move back in case the same thing happened again, but before he had time to get very far, let alone regain his second wind, the game was in full swing once more and one of the Peruvian forwards was already racing full pelt towards him.

"Catch!" he shouted, throwing the ball to Paddington.

"I don't want it, thank you very much," cried Paddington, and as the ball landed in his paws he threw it up the field as hard as he could.

Almost immediately, the referee blew his whistle.

"You're not supposed to throw it forwards," he said. "You're supposed to throw it back down the field."

Paddington stared at him in astonishment. If that was the sort of rule the Peruvians were up against, it was no wonder they were losing.

"Perhaps," said the captain, as the players formed up again, "you would like to be our 'hooker'?"

"That's the chap who has to try and get the ball when it's thrown into the scrum," explained one of the St Luke's side, catching sight of the puzzled look on Paddington's face.

Paddington eyed the other players doubtfully. He didn't like the way some of them were looking at him at all. All the same, he was a game bear at heart, and after a moment's hesitation he joined in the scrum and waited for the ball to arrive.

To his surprise it landed somewhere in the middle of the legs and then bounced straight back into his paws.

Hastily putting it inside his duffle coat for safety, he broke free of the scrum and hurried off down the field as fast as his legs would carry him. As he neared the far end he took a quick glance over his shoulder, but the rest of the players seemed to be having some sort of an argument with the referee and no one except the crowd was taking the slightest interest in his activities.

The roar which went up as Paddington placed the ball on the outer side of the touchline completely drowned the cries from the other players when they discovered what had happened. But, jumping with joy, the Peruvian side came running down the field in order to pat Paddington on the back.

"Is a very good try," said the captain. "Is a best try I never seen.

"Now," he added dramatically, "all you 'ave to do ees improve it and we are 'aving five points."

"I don't think I *could* improve it," gasped Paddington. "I don't think I could run any faster if I tried."

The Games teacher took a deep breath. He still couldn't understand how Paddington had managed to escape his and the other players' notice, but seeing was believing.

"He doesn't mean he wants you to do it all again," he said wearily. "He means you've scored three points for placing the ball over the line. Now, if you manage to kick the ball between the posts and over the cross bar you get two more points. That's what's known as 'improving' it."

Paddington gazed up at the goal posts while he considered the matter.

"I think I like it the way it is," he announced.

"In that case," said the captain, "I will call on Fernando."

Signalling to one of the other members of the

team he stood back with the rest of the players and waited expectantly.

"Hooray!" shouted Jonathan, as there was the sound of leather hitting leather and the ball sailed between the posts. "Five points to Peru!"

"*Darkest* Peru!" added Judy.

But their voices were lost amid the renewed cheers which rose from all around at the unexpected turn of events.

"Do you think they'll do it again?" asked Judy anxiously as the two teams ran back up the field amid a buzz of excitement.

Mr Brown glanced at his watch. "They'll have to look slippy," he said. "We're into extra time already."

Although none of the Peruvian side knew how Paddington had managed to fool their opponents, they knew better than to change their luck once it was running their way, and they made sure he was given possession of the ball as soon as it was in play.

Once again, with it safely tucked beneath his duffle coat, he hurried back down the field.

But this time the other side had him marked, and with one half of the team protesting to the referee as they realised what was happening, the rest set off in hot pursuit. Like hounds who had caught the scent of a fox, they gave chase, uttering whoops of revenge.

Paddington ran as fast as he could, but size for size his legs were no match for the sixth formers of St Luke's, and they were gaining on him rapidly.

To roars of encouragement from the crowd, he reached the line barely a whisker's length ahead, and with no time to look over his shoulder let alone stop to put the ball on the ground, he tore on for all he was worth.

He was dimly aware of a figure approaching him across the turf. Whoever it was had come from the crowd behind the goal area and was waving at his pursuers. He only just managed to pull up in time before they collided. As it was, they both fell to the ground and any remarks they might have exchanged were lost for all time.

At almost the same moment a long drawn-out blast from the referee's whistle brought both the St Luke's forwards and the game to a halt.

"What rotten luck!" exclaimed Jonathan. "Fancy getting in the way just as Paddington was about to save the game!"

"Rotten luck, nothing!" said Mr Brown, waving his programme in the air. "That's one of the rules of the game. You don't have to touch the ground. You can score a try by touching a spectator or an official provided they're not more than ten metres beyond the goal."

"That means they've drawn, then!" cried Judy excitedly. "Listen to everyone cheering."

"I'm not surprised," said Mr Brown. "Whatever the rights and wrongs of the matter, I think the crowd's had its money's worth. I doubt if they'll see a better game this season."

"Hear! Hear!" agreed Mr Gruber. "And I think a draw is a very fair result in the circumstances." He broke off as he suddenly caught sight of a strange expression on Mrs Bird's face. "Is anything the matter?" he asked with concern.

"I'm not sure," said the Browns' housekeeper faintly. "I'm really not sure at all. Will someone please tell me if I'm seeing things?"

As the others turned, they too caught their breath in surprise as they saw Paddington heading in their direction accompanied by his helper from the crowd.

She wore an odd-looking bowler hat and a poncho which was more than a little mud-stained and ruffled, but there was something very familiar about her nevertheless.

"Excuse me," said Paddington as they drew near, "but I'd like to introduce you to my Aunt Lucy!"

Chapter Seven

COMINGS AND GOINGS AT NUMBER THIRTY-TWO

TO SAY THAT the Browns could have been knocked down with a feather by Aunt Lucy's unexpected appearance at the rugby match wouldn't have been too much of an exaggeration.

They had all become so accustomed to the thought of her being a part and parcel of the Home for Retired Bears in Lima that never in their wildest dreams had they pictured her ever leaving its gates, let alone visiting England.

"Mind you," said Mrs Bird, when she came downstairs the next morning carrying Aunt Lucy's breakfast tray, "the more I think about it the less surprised I am. I can see now where Paddington gets his sense of adventure from."

"Don't tell us *she* stowed away in a lifeboat too!" exclaimed Mr Brown.

"No," said Mrs Bird. "She came by air – on a package tour. She's a founder member of the Peruvian Reserves Supporters Club, and she gets special privileges."

"Does that mean she won't be staying very long?" asked Mrs Brown.

"Ah, now that I can't answer," replied the Browns' housekeeper. "And I'm not sure if we ought to mention it at this stage. It might sound rather rude."

It was obvious that as far as Mrs Bird was concerned, Aunt Lucy could stay as long as she liked, and the Browns hastily changed the subject.

In any case, there were lots of things to talk about, and so many plans to be made that Jonathan, Judy and

Paddington filled up several pages of an old exercise book with a list that included everything from a visit to Paddington station to watching the Changing of the Guard.

When Aunt Lucy finally appeared she was dressed ready to go out. To the Browns' surprise she still had a label attached to her poncho. It was not unlike the one Paddington had first worn. On one side it said: PERUVIAN RESERVES SUPPORTERS CLUB, while on the other it had her name, AUNT LUCY, written in large capital letters, and her address: C/O THE HOME FOR RETIRED BEARS, LIMA, PERU.

"Never go out anywhere without a label," she said firmly, when she saw the others looking at it. "Especially in a foreign country. You never know what might happen."

"Very wise," agreed Mrs Bird. "It's a pity more people don't do it."

The next few days were hectic indeed. With Paddington and Aunt Lucy in tow, the Browns left home early each morning, seldom returning until late in the evening. And every night, over cups of cocoa, Aunt Lucy regaled them with stories of life in Peru,

and of the vast plains and mountains that lay beyond the city of Lima. At the end of it all, they were usually so tired they just tumbled into bed and fell asleep as soon as their heads touched the pillows.

All in all, they weren't sorry when, a few evenings later, she announced before retiring to bed that she would like to spend a quiet time the following day doing some shopping.

Mr Brown suddenly discovered he had some urgent business to attend to at his office, and it was agreed that Mrs Brown and Mrs Bird would take the rest of the family round the shops.

For some reason best known to herself, Aunt Lucy seemed rather pleased when she heard Mr Brown wouldn't be coming with them, but it wasn't until the next day that she revealed exactly why.

"I want to buy him a Christmas present," she announced.

"Oh, you don't have to do that," began Mrs Brown.

"But I do," said Aunt Lucy firmly. "It's been a great comfort to me over the years to know that Paddington has been in safe hands and I'd like to do something in return."

"Perhaps you could get him some pipe-cleaners," said Mrs Brown vaguely. "He's always running out."

"Pipe-cleaners!" repeated Aunt Lucy, looking most upset. "I'd like something more than that."

"How about something for his boat, Mrs Brown?" suggested Paddington.

Recently Mr Brown had begun taking an interest in boats and he'd even talked about buying an inflatable dinghy large enough to take the family on summer outings. With Christmas looming up the Browns had already started buying some accessories to go with it, in the hope that he wouldn't change his mind.

"We could go to the place where we bought them," said Judy.

"It's jolly good," agreed Jonathan. "They've even got a special machine where they teach you to sail. You put a coin in and it goes up and down just as if you were really at sea."

Aunt Lucy took all this information in. "I think I like the sound of that," she said, nodding her approval.

With the rest of the family wanting to do some Christmas shopping as well, it was quite late in the day before they finally reached their destination. As they entered the shop, a salesman detached himself from the counter and came forward to greet them. If he was surprised by the sudden arrival of so many unseasonable visitors, he managed to conceal it well.

"And what can I do for you?" he asked, rubbing his hands together in anticipation.

"We're really looking for something suitable for an inflatable dinghy," said Mrs Brown. "It's for a small Christmas present."

The man's face fell. "Perhaps," he said, "you'd like a pump... or a puncture outfit?"

"A puncture outfit!" exclaimed Paddington,

looking most upset. "Mr Brown hasn't even got his boat yet!"

He gazed round for Aunt Lucy to see if she had any ideas, but she was already clambering into a large boat which stood in a position of honour in the centre of the showroom.

"This is what I would like!" she said.

The salesman's face lit up. "Ah!" he exclaimed. "I can see I'm dealing with someone who knows about these things. That, madam, is our very *best* model. It's our luxury, self-inflating dinghy, as used by the navies and shipping lines all over the world." He pointed to a small canvas bag standing alongside. "You may find it hard to believe, but that's the bag it comes in. All you have to do is pull a string and in ten seconds it blows itself up, ready to use.

"It's practically unsinkable," he continued, "but should you ever find yourself in trouble, everything has been thought of. It comes complete with an automatic radio distress signal, sea-sickness tablets, electric torch, fishing-line and hook, iron rations, safety-pins, and a bag of suitable sweets. It isn't simply a boat – it's a way of life!"

Paddington and Aunt Lucy exchanged glances. "It sounds very good value," said Paddington.

"I'll take one," said Aunt Lucy, opening her purse.

Mrs Brown put her hand to her mouth. "But you can't..." she began.

Aunt Lucy fixed her with a stare. "I've made up my mind," she said.

"It's much too expensive," warned Mrs Bird.

"I have my savings," said Aunt Lucy. "*And* Paddington's allowance."

"Paddington's allowance?" echoed the Browns.

"He's always put some money by out of his bun

allowance," said Aunt Lucy. "He's often sent me a postal order, but I've never spent it."

The Browns looked at each other. They were learning something new with every passing moment.

"It all adds up," said Aunt Lucy. "Look after the centavos and the pounds will look after themselves," she added decidedly. "Besides, it will give me a great deal of pleasure."

The Browns stood back, powerless to intervene. In any case the salesman had already called over another assistant to help deal with his important new customer and they were both so busy washing their hands in invisible soap it was obvious there was no turning back. The Browns had no idea what the boat cost, for it didn't actually have a price written on it, and they didn't dare ask for fear of receiving another shock. But Aunt Lucy's purse was obviously more than able to withstand the strain, for the transaction was all over in a matter of seconds.

The salesman was so pleased he even let them have some free rides on the training machine, and Aunt Lucy in particular had such an enjoyable time pulling the lever which made it rock to and fro, it looked at one moment as if the boat might even capsize.

But much to everyone's relief she at last consented to climb out, and with their shopping finished, they made for the nearest bus stop.

The bus was crowded when it arrived, but Aunt Lucy and Paddington managed to find a vacant seat at the front of the top deck; Jonathan and Judy sat just behind them; and Mrs Brown and Mrs Bird made do with some seats near the back.

They hadn't travelled very far when Aunt Lucy suddenly looked round. "I feel sick!" she announced at the top of her voice.

"Oh dear," said Mrs Brown nervously. "Perhaps it was the boat? She did stay on rather a long time."

"And *hungry!*" added Aunt Lucy as an afterthought.

"But she can't..." began Mrs Brown, and then she broke off. She'd been about to say that no one could possibly feel both things at the same time, but she changed her mind. If anything, Aunt Lucy was able to look even more determined about matters when she had a mind to than Paddington.

"Perhaps I could get some sea-sickness tablets out of Mr Brown's dinghy bag," said Paddington eagerly.

"The man said there are some suitable sweets as well."

"I should get the tablets out first," called Mrs Brown. "But do it carefully," she warned. "It's so nicely packed. We don't want to get all the bits and pieces over the bus."

Paddington opened the flap of the canvas bag and felt inside. "It's all right, Mrs Brown," he called. "I think I can manage." He gave a tug at something inside. "I'll just get this piece of string out of the way first."

No one, least of all Paddington, knew quite what happened next. In any case, there was certainly no time to think about it. As he pulled the string, there was a loud hissing noise. The canvas bag started to bulge and as he staggered back, clouds of material began to billow forth like some gigantic flower, growing bigger and bigger with every passing moment. The other occupants of the bus watched in silent fascination as the boat began to take shape. It filled the gangway, pressed against the roof, and overflowed on to the seats, letting nothing stand in its way.

The man in the shop had said the operation was over in ten seconds but as Paddington clambered on to his seat for safety, it felt as if his whole lifetime was passing before him.

When the hissing finally came to an end, the hullabaloo that broke out as the passengers struggled to free themselves more than made up for the silence that had gone before.

The noise brought the conductor running up the stairs, and when he reached the top he nearly fell backwards down them again at the sight which met his eyes.

"'Ere!" he cried. "Who brought that up?"

"I didn't *bring* it up," gasped Paddington, as he peered over the stern. "It happened! I think I must have pulled the wrong piece of string by mistake."

The conductor reached up and rang the bell. "Well, you'd better pull the right one and get it off again, mate!" he exclaimed. "Toot suite! I'm not 'aving these sort of goings on on my bus!"

Paddington gazed at the dinghy and then at the narrow staircase behind the conductor. "I don't think I can," he said unhappily.

"We'll see what the Inspector 'as to say about *that*," said the conductor, making for the stairs. "'Ere, Reg," he called. "There's a young bear up 'ere with a boat!"

A pounding of feet heralded the arrival of the Inspector. Taking in the situation at a glance, he removed a penknife from an inside pocket and started to open it. "It's got a thing-a-me-jig for getting stones out of horses' hooves," he said, "but I don't know about getting boats out of buses. I'll have to use one of me blades."

Mrs Bird grasped her umbrella in no uncertain manner. "You're not sticking any blades in that dinghy," she said sternly. "It cost a lot of money."

The Inspector stared at her. "Are you with this bear?" he demanded.

"Yes," said Mrs Bird firmly. "I am."

"And so am I," said Mrs Brown, coming to the rescue.

"And we are too!" called out Jonathan and Judy.

The Inspector looked slightly taken aback at this rallying of forces, but before he had a chance to say anything else there was a loud groan from the front of the bus.

"Crikey!" said Jonathan. "That must be Aunt Lucy!"

"I'd forgotten about her in the excitement," broke in Judy.

The Inspector gazed in astonishment as Aunt Lucy suddenly appeared round the side of the dinghy. Her poncho was back to front; her hat was all askew; and altogether she looked very much the worse for wear.

"Are you all right, madam?" he asked, grateful for even the slightest kind of diversion he could actually understand and deal with.

"No," said Aunt Lucy sternly, "I am *not* all right. Why has the bus stopped? I want to go home!"

"She's come all the way from Peru," explained Mrs Brown, "and she's not really used to all this rushing about. I'm afraid she's feeling a trifle seedy."

The Inspector was still so taken up with Paddington and Aunt Lucy he really only half heard Mrs Brown's remark, but as he caught the tail end of it, his whole attitude suddenly changed.

"Why ever didn't you say so before?" he exclaimed.

He turned to Paddington. "If you'll kindly tell me

your destination, sir," he said respectfully, "I'll go down and direct the driver."

"Well, we *were* on our way to Windsor Gardens," said Paddington doubtfully. "Number thirty-two Windsor Gardens..."

"It's not on your route," broke in Mrs Brown.

"Think nothing of it," said the Inspector graciously. He gave the conductor a nudge. "We don't want any diplomatic incidents, do we?"

The Browns exchanged glances as he clattered back down the stairs.

"I wonder what on earth he meant by that?" exclaimed Mrs Brown.

"I don't know," said Mrs Bird. "And I certainly don't intend to ask." She cast a glance at Aunt Lucy, huddled on one of the seats with a very woebegone expression on her face indeed. "If you ask me, the sooner we get back home, the better."

The Inspector was as good as his word. Shortly after the bus started up it turned off the normal route and began threading its way through the maze of side streets leading to Windsor Gardens.

By the time they reached number thirty-two they

had been joined by several more vehicles: two police cars, an ambulance, and a red tender belonging to the fire brigade.

Mr Brown was already at home, and the noise as the procession drew up outside the house brought him to the door.

"Stand back, sir," said one of the policemen as he jumped from his vehicle. "We've an emergency here. This bus has been sending out a May Day signal all the way from the West End."

"A *May Day* signal!" exclaimed Paddington in surprise as he helped Aunt Lucy down the stairs. "But it's the middle of December."

The policeman took out his notebook as a babble of voices rose from all sides.

"A May Day signal," he said severely, "is an automatic radio signal for emergencies only. It's used by ships at sea and/or aircraft when they're in distress. But I don't know as I've ever heard it being used by a bus before."

Aunt Lucy fixed him with a hard stare. "*I'm* in distress!" she said firmly. "And I think I may have an emergency any moment now!"

The others stared after her as she hurried indoors closely followed by Paddington.

"I thought you said that bear was going to the Peruvian Embassy?" exclaimed the conductor.

"The Peruvian Embassy?" repeated Mrs Brown indignantly. "We certainly said no such thing."

"But you said she was C.D.," broke in the Inspector. "That stands for *Corps Diplomatique*, and people in the Diplomatic Corps are entitled to special treatment. That's why we brought her here."

"No," said Mrs Bird, as light began to dawn. "We didn't say C.D. We simply said she was feeling *seedy*. That's quite a different matter."

Mrs Brown turned to her husband. "Aunt Lucy bought you a Christmas present," she explained. "But I'm afraid it won't be a surprise any more. It's stuck on the top deck!"

The policeman snapped his notebook shut. It was becoming more and more difficult to catch up with all that had been going on, and he wasn't at all sure he wished to pursue the matter.

"I know one thing," he said. "I bet that's the only Christmas present this year that's arrived gift-wrapped in a number fifty-two London bus. Though how we're going to get it out without spoiling it is another matter."

"Perhaps," said Mrs Bird, "we could try pulling the plug out?"

"Try pulling the plug out?" repeated Mr Brown. "What is it? A bath?"

"You'll see, Henry," said Mrs Brown. "You'll see."

It was some time before order was finally restored, but when the Browns went back indoors carrying Mr Brown's boat they were pleased to find Aunt Lucy sitting at the dining-room table looking her normal self again.

Mr Brown could still hardly believe his good fortune, but she waved aside his thanks and pointed to a row of parcels neatly laid out in front of her.

"They're really meant for Christmas," she said. "But as Mr Brown's had his, I thought I'd like to see the rest of you open yours before I leave."

"Before you *leave*?" exclaimed Mr Brown. "Don't say you're not stopping for Christmas Day?"

"I'm only on an excursion," said Aunt Lucy. "Besides, I always have my dinner in the Home. We have special crackers with marmalade pudding to follow."

Mrs Bird opened her mouth. She was about to say that both these items would be readily available at number thirty-two Windsor Gardens if Aunt Lucy cared to stay, but she had obviously made up her mind, so instead she joined in the general excitement as everyone began opening their parcels.

Her own present was a paw-embroidered shawl, and there was a similar one for Mrs Brown.

"What a nice thought," she said. "It will be just the thing for the long winter evenings."

Jonathan and Judy each had an enormous jar of honey. "Made," said Aunt Lucy, "by bees who live in the gardens of the Home for Retired Bears. It's very sweet because they're always getting at the marmalade."

Last, but not least, Paddington opened his parcel. It contained a wrap-round dressing-gown, and a pair of Peruvian slippers.

Everyone applauded as he put them on, and a few moments later, after Aunt Lucy had shaken hands all round, he followed her out of the room in order to test them in his bedroom.

"You don't think," said Mrs Bird thoughtfully, as their footsteps died away, "that Paddington's planning to go back to Peru with her, do you?"

A sudden chill filled the air.

"It's really for him to decide," said Mrs Bird. "We can't stop him if he wants to."

"He'd have said something by now if he meant to," replied Mr Brown.

He was trying to strike a cheerful note, but he failed miserably as everyone sat lost in their own thoughts. A gloom descended on the gathering and it remained that way until a little later in the evening when the door opened again and Paddington reappeared. To their relief he was still wearing his dressing-gown.

"Isn't Aunt Lucy coming down too?" asked Mrs Brown.

Paddington shook his head. "I'm afraid she can't," he said rather sadly. "She's gone home."

"Gone home?" echoed the Browns.

"Aunt Lucy doesn't like goodbyes," explained Paddington, when he saw the look of consternation on everybody's face. "She asked me to say them for her."

He felt in his dressing-gown pocket and took out a sheet of paper. "And she gave me this for you to read."

Mr Brown took the note and held it up for all to see. It was written in large capital letters, and at the bottom there was a paw-mark to show it was genuine. It wasn't quite as neat as Paddington's, but there was an unmistakable likeness.

"THANK YOU VERY MUCH FOR HAVING ME AND FOR LOOKING AFTER PADDINGTON," he read. "NOW THAT

I'VE GOT USED TO IT, IT DOES SEEM A FUNNY NAME FOR A RAILWAY STATION. AUNT LUCY."

Mrs Brown gave a sigh as Paddington took back the note and disappeared upstairs again. "I suppose we ought to be thankful he isn't going," she said. "But I do wish Aunt Lucy had stopped a little longer. There are so many things I wanted to ask her. About Paddington's parents..."

"And his uncle," broke in Judy. "I've often wondered what happened to him."

"And how many bears there are in the Home," added Jonathan. "And what they do all day."

"Don't you think," said Mrs Bird wisely, "that in this world it's rather nice to have *some* things left unanswered?

"Anyway," she continued, as she stood up, "if we don't go upstairs quickly we shan't be able to say our goodnights to Paddington. After all the excitement he's had today I should think he'll be asleep in no time at all."

But for once Mrs Bird was wrong. When they entered his room he was still very wide awake. He was sitting up in his dressing-gown, and from the

bulge under his blankets it looked suspiciously as though he still had his new slippers on as well.

He was busily writing in his scrapbook. "I thought I would get everything down while I can still think of it," he said, dipping his pen absentmindedly into a nearby jar of marmalade. "So many things happen to me I have a job to remember them all sometimes, and it wouldn't do to miss any out. Aunt Lucy always likes to hear what I've been doing."

"We thought perhaps you were going back to Peru with her," said Mrs Brown, as she tucked him in extra tightly for the night.

"Go back to Peru!" exclaimed Paddington. He looked most upset for the moment. "I'm not old enough to *retire*! Besides, I don't think Aunt Lucy would like to think of me leaving home, even if I wanted to."

It was left to Mrs Bird to voice everyone's thoughts as they said goodnight, closed the door and crept back downstairs again.

"If anyone can think of a nicer Christmas present than that," she said, "I'd like to meet them!"

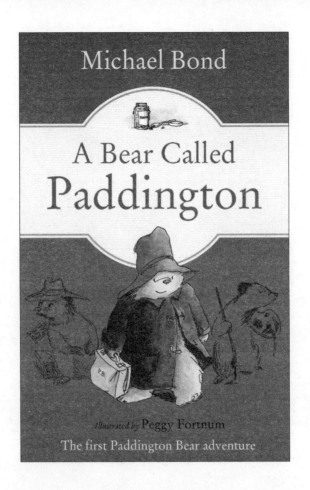

Michael Bond

A Bear Called
Paddington

Illustrated by Peggy Fortnum

The first Paddington Bear adventure

Paddington Bear had travelled all the way from
Darkest Peru when the Brown family first met
him on Paddington station. Since then their
lives have never been quite the same…

Michael Bond

More About
Paddington

Illustrated by Peggy Fortnum

The original adventures of Paddington Bear

When Paddington attempts home decorating,
detective work and photography, the Brown
family soon find that he causes his own
particular brand of chaos.

Michael Bond

Paddington
Helps Out

Illustrated by Peggy Fortnum

The original adventures of Paddington Bear

"Oh, dear!" said Paddington,
"I'm in trouble again."

Trouble always comes naturally to Paddington.
What other bear could catch a fish in his hat, or
cause havoc in the Browns' kitchen
just trying to be helpful?

Michael Bond

Paddington
Abroad

Illustrated by Peggy Fortnum

The original adventures of Paddington Bear

The Browns are going abroad and a certain bear
is planning the trip. But, as Mrs Brown worries,
with Paddington in charge, *"There's no knowing
where we might end up!"*

Michael Bond

Paddington
at Large

Illustrated by Peggy Fortnum

The original adventures of Paddington Bear

"*Even Paddington can't come to much harm in half an hour,*" said Mrs Brown.

But who else could hang Mr Curry's lawnmower from a treetop or set Father Christmas' beard on fire?

Michael Bond

Paddington
Marches On

Illustrated by Peggy Fortnum

The original adventures of Paddington Bear

"*I've never known such a bear for smelling things out,*" said Mrs Bird.

Paddington's fondness for marmalade earns him an invitation to an "important ceremony". It also leads him into a lot of trouble…

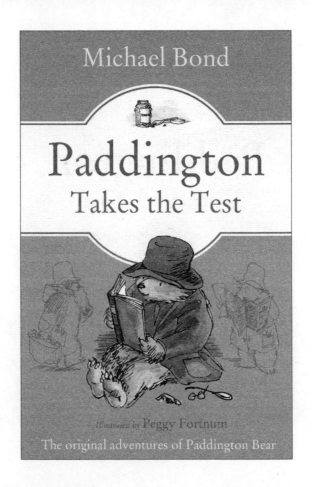

Michael Bond

Paddington
Takes the Test

Illustrated by Peggy Fortnum

The original adventures of Paddington Bear

"*Congratulations on passing your driving test!*"
said the examiner, grimly.

Who would have believed it possible, when he has
just sat on Paddington's marmalade sandwiches
and been driven into the car in front?

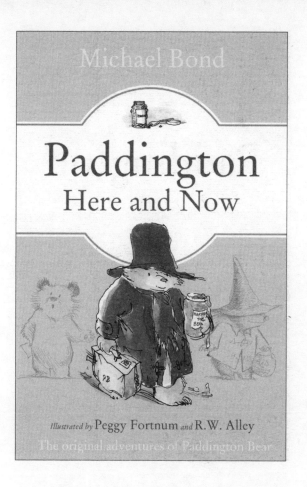

Michael Bond

Paddington
Here and Now

Illustrated by Peggy Fortnum *and* R.W. Alley

The original adventures of Paddington Bear

"I'm not a foreigner," exclaimed Paddington,
"I'm from Darkest Peru."

One day, a mysterious visitor arrives at number
thirty-two Windsor Gardens. Is it time for
Paddington to decide where 'home' really is?

Michael Bond

Paddington
Races Ahead

Illustrated by Peggy Fortnum and R.W. Alley

The original adventures of Paddington Bear

Find out what happens when Paddington causes
a London bus to be evacuated, and is mistaken
for a Peruvian hurdler!

Branch	Date
TS	4/14